I0823790

THE BOY IN THE WALL

Also by Jeffrey B. Burton

The Chicago K-9 Thrillers

THE DEAD YEARS *
THE SECOND GRAVE *

The Mace Reid K-9 Mysteries

THE FINDERS
THE KEEPERS
THE LOST

The Drew Cady Thrillers

THE CHESSMAN
THE LYNCHPIN
THE EULOGIST

* *available from Severn House*

THE BOY IN THE WALL

Jeffrey B. Burton

SEVERN
HOUSE

First world edition published in Great Britain and the USA in 2026
by Severn House, an imprint of Canongate Books Ltd,
14 High Street, Edinburgh EH1 1TE.

severnhouse.com

Cover and jacket design by Nick May at bluegecko22.com

British Library Cataloguing-in-Publication Data
A CIP catalogue record for this title is available from the British Library.

ISBN-13: 978-1-4483-1603-8 (cased)
ISBN-13: 978-1-4483-1903-9 (paper)
ISBN-13: 978-1-4483-1604-5 (e-book)

All Severn House titles are printed on acid-free paper.

Typeset by Palimpsest Book Production Ltd., Falkirk, Stirlingshire, Scotland.
Printed and bound in Great Britain by TJ Books, Padstow, Cornwall.

The manufacturer's authorised representative in the EU for product safety is Authorised Rep Compliance Ltd, 71 Lower Baggot Street, Dublin D02 P593 Ireland (arccompliance.com)

Praise for the Chicago K-9 Thrillers

"An unputdownable book filled with nonstop action, great characters, and a fantastic setting. This should be on every mystery fan's nightstand"
Andrew Gulli, Editor-in-Chief of *The Strand Magazine*, on *The Second Grave*

"It's likely *The Second Grave* will be on my Best of 2025 List. Very likely"
Kings River Life Magazine on *The Second Grave*

"The author [has] considerable talent"
Booklist on *The Second Grave*

"A gripping addition to the mystery genre . . . a standout and engaging read"
Book Junkie Reviews on *The Second Grave*

"The twists and turns will keep you reading"
Kings River Life Magazine on *The Dead Years*

"Another solid dog thriller . . . [with] twists you don't see coming. Fans of his previous books will enjoy this one"
Red Carpet Crash on *The Dead Years*

About the author

Novels in **Jeffrey B. Burton**'s critically acclaimed Mace Reid K-9 mystery series include *The Finders*, *The Keepers*, and *The Lost*. His Agent Drew Cady Thrillers include *The Chessman*, *The Lynchpin*, and *The Eulogist*. *The Boy in the Wall* is the third instalment in his Chicago K-9 thriller series, preceded by *The Second Grave* and *The Dead Years*.

Jeff lives in St. Paul, Minnesota, with his wife, Cindy, an irate Pomeranian named Lucy, and a happy galoot of a Beagle named Milo.

jeffreybburton.com

To Milo the Beagle—
Why'd you have to lift a hind leg and let stream onto the
box of children's clothing at the neighborhood garage sale?
You forced us to flee the scene as though we were shoplifters
and take a roundabout way home so not to pass by again.
And though I think we pulled it off . . . I was
truly mortified.

Acknowledgments

A standing O to the meticulous team of editors at Severn House—from Tina Pietron to Rachel Slatter to Leona Skene. Without their help, I'd make the Guinness World Records book for plot holes and typos. And I can't thank Nick May, designer extraordinaire, enough for bringing Alice and Rex to life with his ominous and eye-catching cover art. Also, thanks to my dear friend and college roommate, Dick Dentinger, a founding partner at B&D Associates, for all things masonry related. Last but not least, a heartfelt note of appreciation to my wife, Cindy, who moonlights as my editor, photographer, biggest fan, and part-time chauffeur as we cruise the highways and byways on our merry way to book signings, library chats, and book clubs.

Great men have great dogs.
—Otto von Bismarck

PART ONE

The Dogs in the Demo

Buy a pup and your money will buy
Love unflinching that cannot lie
—Rudyard Kipling

ONE

The little redhead in the front row was the iceberg to my *Titanic.*

I almost wept in delight when a stern-looking kindergarten or first-grade teacher with dark hair and flecks of gray—perhaps it was the principal herself—strode to the front of the auditorium as though she were Marshal Dillon, knelt down next to the curly-haired redheaded tyke, whispered something into his ear, and then took hold of his hand and escorted him to the back of the room, where he would be spending the rest of my presentation at her side. Red, who must have been all of five or six, had been sitting there—so close I could've reached out and strangled him—throwing me off my game. With an arm perpetually fluttering in the air, a box kite in the wind, what little train of thought I possessed was shattered by his endless babble over *what are the doggies' names again* and *how old are the doggies* and *can I give them a treat* and *do they bark* and *can I pet them.* If my K-9 show-and-tell had been held in the school's parking lot, I'd have had Alice and Rex make a break for the old Chevy Silverado while I jumped behind the wheel, and then we'd have burned rubber tearing ass out of Henry Horner Elementary School.

I'd answered a few of Red's questions, which only prompted additional stream-of-consciousness inquiries—fast-paced, rat-a-tat-tat—as well as snickers from some of the older students in the audience, who noted my demonstration circling the drain. At one point I brought a forefinger to my lips, thinking it might quiet the little fella, but it only served to prompt him to walk up to Rex and hold out his fingertips. A sappy smile was smeared across my face, as though I was in on the joke, as I spoke louder over Red's continuous chatter, and over the fifth graders' burgeoning mirth, until I began to turn red and the teacher or principal-slash-town-marshal came to salvage my early afternoon dog-and-pony show.

I could still see Red, in the back, his hand still fluttering in the breeze, his lips still moving, but—thank you, God!—he was too far away for me to hear.

This was exactly why I hadn't wanted to do this when Crystal cornered me into it a few weeks ago.

"Stop being so afraid of little kids," she'd said.

I shook my head in protest. "I'm not afraid of little kids."

I stared down at my sister, as I'm nearly a towering six feet in height to her not quite five eleven. It helped that Crystal had been shoeless at the time and I'd yet to take off my hiking boots. Not that Crystal would find any difference in height intimidating; my sister doesn't find much of anything intimidating. Plus, she's about a foot taller than me if you factor in IQ points. Crystal's built like an athlete, muscles like a gymnast, whereas I'm on the thin side, though I prefer the word *wiry*. Sadly, I'm more beanstalk than either Jack or the giant. My sibling and I share the same dark brown hair, with Crystal's being shoulder-length and subject to change as the seasons pass by, while mine is close-cropped and, yup, remains close-cropped.

"You call the kids on our block *Children of the Corn*," Crystal replied. "You bought lemonade from their stand all summer out of fear they'd egg our house if you didn't."

"Because that's what'll happen if you don't buy a glass from them little extortionists every time you drive past," I said. "Them neighbor kids know all our faces and which houses we belong to. Besides, Crys, you're never around to see what the main girl—you know, their ringleader—is up to. She doesn't smile, she doesn't laugh; she doesn't show any kind of emotion. I swear to God I've never seen her blink her eyes."

"She's just trying to sell lemonade."

"She gives me the creeps," I said. "I bet she levitates when no one's around."

Crystal rolled her eyes. "You'll be presenting at Henry Horner," she said. "None of our neighbor kids will be there."

Crystal and I live in Buffalo Grove, in a two-story we

inherited after our parents passed away. Henry Horner is in Arlington Heights. A close enough drive—if the lights were with me, I could be there in less than twenty minutes—but far enough away so the kids on our block wouldn't be in attendance.

"Cops do this all the time. It's called community outreach." My sister, Detective Crystal Pratt, is an investigator in the Violent Crimes Section inside the Area 3 Detective Division in the Chicago Police Department. "It helps CPD build positive relationships, so the kids perceive us as non-threatening. So they don't fear the police."

"OK, Officer Friendly—you go talk to the nose-pickers."

"I have," my sister insisted. "Several times already. All I'm asking is that you give a short talk about sniffer dogs and then demonstrate how Alice and Rex can follow some basic commands. It'll be easy-peasy."

I was going to do it, and Crystal knew I was going to do it, and I knew that Crystal knew I was going to do it . . . but that didn't mean I had to make it easy for her. "Hey—you want I should tell them about cadaver dogs? It is what I specialize in."

My name's Cory Pratt—call me Cor—and I am the part-time CEO, president, treasurer, and secretary at the COR Canine Training Academy. I run dog obedience classes throughout more than a few of the Windy City's suburbs. I say part-time because I'm currently a full-time student at Harper Community College, taking courses in computer science. I hate to boast but, when it comes to grades, I no doubt rank in the top 5 percent of the lower third of my class.

OK, that's probably nothing to brag about.

Please don't tell Crystal; she worries too much about me as it is.

"No, the little ones won't sleep for a year if you start in about dead bodies." My sister had nudged me into expanding my canine repertoire by working with sniffer dogs. More specifically, I began training human remains detection dogs, or, as they are more commonly called, cadaver dogs. Yup—Alice and Rex have been taught to hunt for the dead. We help law enforcement—CPD, other local PDs, various sheriff departments, now and again the FBI—when some poor soul's gone missing and is presumed dead.

Crystal continued. "Talk to them about service and therapy dogs. They'll love hearing about search and rescue dogs; they'll eat that up. Come on, Cor, you know this stuff inside out. It's a grade school, for crying out loud—they're going to love you; well, at least they'll love Alice and Rex." She then added, "Like I said, it'll be easy-peasy."

Clearly, easy-peasy had never bumped into the little redheaded tyke from the front row.

Which brings me to my current predicament, standing here—red-faced and microphoned up—in front of a few hundred students at Henry Horner Elementary School, trying to salvage what was left of my show-and-tell presentation.

I'm not positive but I may have talked about canines having three hundred million scent receptors while we mere mortals have only five million. How we're able to smell popcorn in a movie theater, and burning leaves, cooking smells, food gone bad and curdled milk, as well as a handful of other items, but dogs can decipher thousands of scents—they're supernatural; smelling is their world. I may have touched on how dogs can sniff out explosives and illicit drugs and narcotics, large amounts of currency, and certain kinds of cancer. I'm pretty sure I talked for a minute about how heroic search and rescue dogs were in finding people and saving lives.

I spoke from rote, robot-like, and believe I covered all the bullet points I'd jotted down on the three-by-five notecard in my back pocket; the talking points I'd rehearsed over the past few days. And I think the assembly enjoyed my speech, as the room quieted down; eyes were all on me and the pups and there was no more chuckling from the peanut gallery. But I couldn't be positive, as I'd spent the entirety of my presentation consciously avoiding eye contact with the curly-haired red devil in the back of the auditorium. I'm embarrassed to admit the kid had not only gotten under my skin, but inside my head; he lived there now, rent-free, sharing the square footage with the neighbor girl from the lemonade stand.

The two of them owned me.

Teachers don't get paid enough.

My canine duo, needless to say, went on to steal the show. Alice—her name lifted from my mother's middle name—is my seven-year-old bloodhound. She's a muscular eighty pounds, black and tan, and a sweetheart full of equal parts affection, protectiveness, and wrinkles. In fact, the loose skin and folds around Alice's face, jowls, and neck help her trap scent particles, and this allows her to hold onto smells as she tracks. When it comes to being an HRD dog, nothing gets past Alice.

My five-year-old springer spaniel's name is taken from my father's middle name. Rex is forty-five pounds of affection and goofiness. He's got floppy ears, of course, and a chocolate-and-white coat of moderate length. Rex is so full of energy—he'll run, run, run right on up until he curls into a ball and sleeps, sleeps, sleeps.

Springer spaniels were bred to chase birds into flight so hunters could then peg them off. Rex's forebears were often called "springing" spaniels due to their *springing* the game from cover. Rex and I have never hunted birds; however, should one happen to swoop down into the backyard, they'll face deportation in real time—no due process. The same holds true for any infringing squirrels or rabbits or cats. I imagine even if Godzilla set foot in our backyard—into Rex's backyard!—he'd be up in the giant reptile's grill faster than you could read the subtitles.

Don't get me wrong, though; Rex is a hunter . . . just for something other than birds.

And unlike me, Rex is a sucker for the limelight: a ham, a complete card, a showman down to his bone marrow. Alice enjoyed herself as well, as the two of them took turns demonstrating some basic commands. Rex would *sit* and *watch me* and then *come* to a round of applause. It went straight to his head, of course, and if his body would permit, he'd have taken a bow. Using a chew ring, Alice would *take it* or *drop it* to a chorus of praise. Rex would *speak* and then be *quiet* to a symphony of approval. Alice would *shake* my hand for the cheering horde. And, for the grand finale, I had the two of them *run* and then *walk* and then *sit* and then *speak* and finally *roll over*, all in unison.

It was Busby Berkeley. The kids loved it.

Though Alice and Rex did not receive a standing ovation—I doubted the grade schoolers were versed in standing Os—the two scored quite well on the handclapping front.

Turns out the person that saved me from the redhead was, in fact, Henry Horner's principal. "We cannot thank you enough for coming," she told me as I slipped my props and doggie treats into my backpack. "I hope you can stay awhile longer. We have treats set up in the cafeteria."

"I had a blast," I said as I zipped the bag shut. Several children hovered nearby, offering up fingers as well as petting Alice and Rex on their heads. The two were in hog heaven. "But I go to college and I've got a ton of homework I need to get done."

"Come on, Cory." She nudged at my arm. "I stopped by Sugar Moon on the way in this morning."

"Sugar Moon." I repeated the name of the bakery. I'd certainly heard of the place.

"Yes," she said and smiled. "Best chocolate chip cookies in Chicago."

"I can't say no to Sugar Moon," I said and pretended to glance at my watch. "Plus, more of the kids may want to meet Alice and Rex."

The principal—that's Principal Isaacson to you—and I stood near the end of the line of cookie trays set out along the cafeteria window that separated the kitchen from the dining area. I was working my way through a second chocolate chip cookie as we made small talk and, yup, if these weren't the best chocolate chip cookies in Chicago, they were definitely in the running.

"You should take one for the road," Principal Isaacson offered.

"You're too nice," I said. "You know my sister; the detective that helped set this up?"

She nodded. "I know Crystal."

"Would it be OK if I also brought one home for her?"

"Of course you can."

Chances of my sister ever knowing these cookies existed weighed in at slim to none.

That's when I heard Alice growl and I glanced her way. The dogs had been milling about close by, receiving all sorts of love and affection from their newfound groupies. I half expected to catch the redheaded tyke trying to slip a leg over Alice's back as though she were a ride at the rodeo. But her growl was more to alert me, to inform me of a discovery. A lump lodged in my throat as I spotted my bloodhound sitting twenty yards away and facing the cafeteria wall, her paw tapping at the floor beneath her. Rex sat at her side, peeking back my way.

"Oh, no," I said and set the remainder of my cookie down on a napkin.

"What?" Principal Isaacson asked as she followed my line of vision. "Did they piddle on the floor?"

"No," I replied as I realized I'd not be rattling off homework anytime soon. "I wish it were that."

TWO

"Why do you keep calling it murder, Detective? That implies a singular event. Truth is, you've stumbled across a double homicide, set in motion a quarter century ago."

"A double homicide?" Detective Mark Lahlum replied. "Wake me when you start making sense." Lahlum sat to Crystal's left, in the interviewer chair, while she perched in the observer seat. Across the table sat Daniel Styles; his chair, however, was bolted to the floor. They'd picked Styles up from a custom home in Glencoe and brought him back to the station. The man had graying hair and bifocals. He wore a green polo shirt and black jeans and looked every inch the chemical-engineer-on-a-day-off he claimed to be.

Lahlum led the interview as Crystal took notes. Though not officially game-planned, Lahlum shifted into bad-cop mode as Crystal became the empathetic officer; the understanding one. None of this Kabuki theater appeared necessary, as the man across the table had waived his right to an attorney and was in the process—albeit a lengthy one—of spilling his guts.

"I am making sense, Detective. I knew her back in the day, when we were practically kids. I imagine the two of you, and whoever's watching that video"—Styles glanced up at the camera in the corner of the interrogation room—"would like to hear about the first murder?"

"Only if we're not putting you out," Lahlum said. Crystal's partner had put on weight in the year she'd known him; his face thicker, his shoulders rounder, alongside an advancing waistline—portrait of a high school athlete settling into middle age.

Crystal's iPhone vibrated atop the table. She picked it up. Cory was calling; he'd likely just finished his service dog presentation at Henry Horner Elementary. She tapped the red button on the call screen and set it back down.

Styles leaned back in his chair. "I met her freshman year. She was heading back to the dorms and must have sensed me gawking, because she turned and looked my way. Those eyes of hers, they sparkled with mischief. And if they ever sparkled in your direction, detectives, you got to thinking maybe, just maybe, things were going to turn out all right." Styles then added, "That's exactly how it all began."

Lahlum sighed while Crystal prompted the man on with a quick nod of her head.

"Somehow I managed to introduce myself; somehow I managed to ask her out. We saw each other until summer break, until I . . . well, I shouldn't get ahead of myself." Styles plucked a tissue from the box of Kleenex in front of him. "One evening she smuggled me into the bathroom on her floor, dragged me to the mirror above the sink, and pointed at the full-length mirror on the opposite wall. 'Watch this,' she said as she stood between the two mirrors and brought her hands up and down. Her likeness reflected back and forth, mirrors within mirrors, and I watched as her hands fluttered across an infinity of duplicates. I pulled her toward me, stared into the mirrored millions, and saw images of us together for as far as the eye could see . . . as far as the eye could see, detectives."

Lahlum made a dramatic show of checking his watch and crossing his arms.

Styles looked hurt; the man looked genuinely saddened but continued his tale. "I kissed her right then and there, standing between the mirrors. I felt her breath in my mouth."

"Any way we can fast-forward the sappy shit," Lahlum said, "and cut to the chase?"

"If you insist, Detective, but the answers—all of them—lie in the past, so sit back and permit me a moment or two of my *sappy shit.*" He dabbed at the corners of his eyes with the tissue. "I'd spent a lifetime hidden away, my nose inside a book. I was unsure how to act, no idea how to conduct myself. I got all twisted up inside and I said things I didn't mean. And I meant things I could never find a way to put into words," he said. "It was the thinnest of ice." Styles dabbed again at his eyes. "I was a little lost boy, flailing the wrecking ball in the darkness." He stared back at the two officers. "I drove her away."

Crystal's phone buzzed a second time. Cory was calling again. She tapped the red button and then set the cell phone on her lap.

Styles ignored the minor disruption, cleared his throat, and continued. "After summer passed, I did my best to set it right. I apologized. I told her I thought the world of her. I told her about these *feelings* I had, how they terrified me because I suspected what they meant." Styles scratched at a cheek before adding, "She let it slip that she had a . . . *boyfriend*." His eyes glistened. "I felt carved up inside. I couldn't eat or sleep. I forced myself into the *boy meets girl, boy loses girl, boy gets girl back* manner of the old romantic comedies—you remember those old movies, don't you?—because if there was one certainty in my life . . . we were meant to be together, just like the images in the bathroom mirrors, the ones I told you about . . . together as far as the eye could see."

"You know what else goes on as far as the eye can see?" Lahlum said. "Your confession."

Styles held Crystal's gaze through moist eyes. "I spent the rest of the year in her periphery, calling now and again, pretending to be friends. Until one day, detectives, we sat on the steps of the campus auditorium, chatting in the afternoon sun. Eventually, she raised her hand, her left hand. The third finger from the thumb sported a diamond—an engagement ring. And she told me in the softest of voices she was getting married. I held it together long enough to feign happiness, all crooked smiles and dumbstruck congratulations. Then I mumbled goodbye and walked out of her life. I made it as far as the student union before the tears spilled down my face as the realization sunk in—*boy loses girl . . . and boy will never ever get girl back*." Styles dabbed again at his eyes. "You see, my own would be the first homicide. The one that went unreported those many years ago . . ."

"Oh, for Christ's sake." Lahlum looked as though he'd bitten into a lemon. "You had me going with the double homicide bullshit, you really did."

Styles shook his head at Lahlum's profanity. "The main part of me ceased to exist that afternoon on the auditorium steps, Detective. It's the perfect definition of murder." Styles set the spent tissue on the tabletop. "Do either of you believe the old adage—that time heals all wounds?"

Crystal nodded and Lahlum joined her.

"Then I guess I'm a romantic, because love doesn't carry an expiration date as though it were a carton of milk. Time passed; the ache never did—a silent river running deep. Her cards and letters—I've kept them all—have yellowed with age. And whenever I stare in the mirror, detectives—a little lost boy stares back."

Crystal's iPhone buzzed again. She glanced down. Cory had now left a voicemail. Probably bellyaching about his presentation; wanting to dance her into picking up Taco Bell for dinner.

She leveled her eyes on Styles and asked her first question of the interview. "How did you know where she lived?"

"The Internet—it did all the heavy lifting. Everything was there. And try as I might, I couldn't let it lie. Phone numbers, their current address, a history of addresses. They'd seen a bit of the country, they had, before coming home. I brought up a satellite image of their house, even got a description based on their property ownership. It was as though I knew where to roam, to see what might have been, detectives—once her husband and I finished with our tête-à-tête."

Crystal's phone buzzed a fourth time. Still Cory; this time he was texting. Call ASAP!, his message read. She cursed silently. Her brother knew better than to keep pestering her at work. There would be a discussion about this tonight.

"Speaking of her husband, he owns his own consulting firm, software this or that, and offices out of their home. The GPS app on my phone led me straight to their doorstep. Her husband even answered the door, barefoot in sweats and a T-shirt. I have to admit he was quite pleasant," Styles said. "At first, anyway. He even let me in when I told him I was an old friend of his wife's, from our college days. But as I explained how I came to be there, much like I'm doing with you right now, detectives, in a calm and friendly manner—wouldn't you say I'm being calm and friendly?"

"Yes," Crystal replied before Lahlum said anything acidic that might send Styles spinning off in a different direction when they were so close to bringing his confession home. She texted Cory, Give me an hour, and then shut down her smartphone so there'd be no further interruptions.

"Thank you, Detective. I thought as much," Styles said, his attention focused on Crystal. "Anyway, he became quite anxious. Agitated, actually. Not what you'd expect in a consultant; perhaps it was best he worked at home. I began to question what she saw in the man. And he kept getting louder, and louder still, insistent I leave at once . . . until I couldn't think or talk and I . . . I had to make him quiet. Please understand. I never meant to hurt him, never, but how could I face her after all these years and compete with that kind of commotion?"

"Jesus," Lahlum whispered, no longer frustrated at the sluggish pace of Style's disclosure.

"But when I was through, I carried him downstairs and placed him, gently, on the recliner in the family room, right in front of his flat-screen TV. It was as though he were taking a much-needed nap. You both were there—you saw how peaceful he looked."

Crystal paused a second and then prodded. "What happened next?"

"Well, she and I met, of course. My car blocked her from entering her spot in the garage. I watched from the window as she turned into the driveway and parked beside it. She must've been used to his having clients over for meetings or the like. I watched as she came up the steps and, let me tell you, detectives, the years have been kind to her. Even with two kids of her own away at college, just a couple of age lines. Smile lines, actually." Styles took a deep breath and continued. "I opened the door and let her in. She didn't recognize me, not off the bat anyway. I wear glasses now and my hair's gone gray. We said hello and she asked if he was getting what I needed. I nodded politely. She asked if I wanted a glass of lemonade. How terribly kind. 'Sure,' I replied. 'I love lemonade.' She headed past me toward the fridge. I inhaled deeply, the smell of her hair, her perfume, her every little thing—and in that instant, that moment in eternity, I was young again."

"Then what?" Crystal said.

"She handed me a glass and headed down the hallway. I called after her. I guess it was my voice, the intimate nature in which I spoke her name—as though from a lifetime ago. She stopped in her tracks, turned, and stared back at me, a perplexed look in those blue eyes. And then I watched as the past and present blurred, as the years melted away, as the realization sank in. I said hello again and, after all of these years, these unforgiving years, she came toward me, a half-smile across her face. So many things I wanted to tell her; so many things I needed to say."

"Then what?" Crystal repeated.

"The moment passed, and all of a sudden she wanted to know what I was doing there and where her husband was. I explained how he was napping in the basement and how nice it would be if we could do some catching up . . . but she couldn't find it in herself to relax. She backed away from me and went looking for him. I slowly finished the lemonade. I wouldn't want to be rude now, would I? Then I walked down the steps to the family room. And there she sat, detectives, the love of my life—cupping one of his hands to her heart—smartphone cradled in her lap." Styles finished his confession. "Together, we sat and waited . . ."

Silence washed over the interrogation room as both detectives digested what they'd just heard. Crystal watched as Styles hung his head. No longer using a tissue; a tear splashed onto the interrogation table, followed by another.

Suddenly, there was a rap on the door as it swung inward. Sergeant Harris loomed in the frame. He stared at Crystal. "Your brother just called. He says it's an emergency."

THREE

"It was hectic," Principal Isaacson said. "The Board of Education and Capital Planning decided that the school would get a facelift instead of being demolished. We spent all summer with electricians and plumbers, HVAC technicians, contractors, subcontractors, and a parade of carpenters, plus we got all-new appliances for the kitchen."

"So instead of vacation," I said, "you had to be here every day to let the remodelers in?"

"No, thank God. Several of us drew straws and round-robined a schedule, so my husband and I got in our two weeks at the cabin. My VP was a godsend, a handful of teachers were kind enough to volunteer, the head janitor and his assistance took some turns; even the school counselor filled in for several days."

"Elementary schools have counselors?"

"They realized they needed them after you came down the pike," Crystal said before Isaacson could reply.

"Good one," I replied.

The principal chuckled and then pointed at an older woman in a black pantsuit, who was heading in our direction. "And this angel not only rose to the challenge; she also made sure the trains ran on time."

The aforementioned angel was named Suzanne Nickless, who I took to be the grade school's office administrator or office manager. She carried a manila folder and, after a quick round of introductions, said, "I can call the masonry contractor that put in the partition." She glanced down at her binder, which I figured held an assortment of invoices and work orders. "They could remove a few of the blocks to grant you access. They might even do it for free since the police are involved."

"Thanks, but that won't be necessary," Crystal said. "We've got a contractor we use and he'll be here any minute." My sister added, "We don't want to make a big deal out of this, as it may turn out to be nothing."

I read between Crystal's lines. The last thing she'd want to do would be to tip off the masonry contractor that had spent a chunk of the summer doing block work at Henry Horner, as well as constructing the cafeteria wall, in case Alice and Rex had indeed discovered something nefarious hidden within the partition. If my dogs alerted me accordingly, which I knew they had—then the masonry workers on the grade school remodel would rise to the top of Crystal's list of suspects.

Suzanne nodded, turned, and, before exiting the cafeteria, edged up to the remaining box of cookies and picked one out as though she were selecting a winning scratch-off card. She glanced our way before taking a bite, caught me gawking, and gave a sheepish smile. I wasn't one to talk, having chomped three additional cookies while waiting for Crystal to arrive, so I shot back a thumbs-up. Then both Principal Isaacson and Suzanne headed back to their offices to do whatever principals and office administrators do at the end of their workday.

I turned to my sister. "So the guy dated the wife a hundred years ago and then he shows up out of the blue to kill her husband?" Besides eating a cookie herself, Crystal told me about her latest case as we waited for the brick guy to show up.

"More like twenty-five years than a hundred," Crystal replied. "By all appearances, the guy lived a normal life: he worked as an engineer, had never been arrested for anything, yet he had this one obsession."

"She's the one that got away, only not really—that's a hell of an obsession."

Alice and Rex swiveled about our feet, periodically reaffirming the presence of something not quite right inside the cafeteria wall. While waiting for Crystal, I'd taken the two of them out to the side of the elementary school so they could do their business with a modicum of privacy, sans audience, as the children boarded their yellow buses for their ride home. I'd given the pups treats to eat and water to lap, but they were getting antsy. Normally, they'd be at home scarfing dinner by now. If one of the janitors had an extra sledgehammer lying about in a broom closet, no doubt Alice and Rex would've smashed in an opening by now.

"Well, the guy will have nothing but time to ponder his obsession for the next couple of decades."

We heard a noise, turned toward the cafeteria doors, and spotted a man with a thick beard shoving a wheelbarrow our way. It was Jay Dentinger, the master mason Crystal and CPD had utilized in the past. As Dentinger approached, I recognized a few tools of his trade—a brick hammer, a couple of different-looking trowels, a masonry saw, and a half dozen other devices I wouldn't have a clue which end to hold.

"Sorry I'm late; it's rush hour out there." Dentinger parked the wheelbarrow where we stood, but his gaze fixed on the cooks' buffet window. "Are those cookies from Sugar Moon?"

"When you're done, Jay," Crystal replied. "When you're done."

Half an hour later, three blocks had been removed from the wall. There was now a gap big enough for someone to scrunch down and sneak a peek inside. All eyes swiveled my way. I glanced behind me but spotted no one standing there. Then I realized the gist of their stares.

"But I dressed up today," I protested. "These are my chinos, and I just bought this shirt for the presentation."

"Don't worry, Cor. I'll take care of them," Crystal said. "You don't know how to wash dress clothes anyway."

She did have a point.

My sister is six years older than I am. She moved back home after Mom and Dad passed away, right after the funeral. Our parents died in a car wreck when I was halfway through junior year in high school. The two went out on a date night—a movie and a meal—and never came home. A winter storm swept off Lake Michigan and turned the city into an ice cube.

Dad was pronounced dead at the scene; Mom died in the ambulance on the way to the hospital.

It was a dark time for me; a very dark time.

Crystal thought it best for me to finish high school in Buffalo Grove, to maintain some semblance of normality as opposed to getting shipped off to one set of grandparents or the other. We've shared Casa de Pratt ever since. Crystal scored the second floor whereas the dogs and I frolic in my basement man cave. My sister and I share the first floor for any meals, or streaming our TV shows, or sharing of war stories from work or school.

"You're thin; you ought to be able to squeeze in there and shine a light around." Dentinger had chiseled out two of the lower concrete blocks near where Alice and Rex had alerted me, as well as a separate block above one of the lower ones. The wall stretched from the hallway down the entire length of the cafeteria and onward into the kitchen. I imagined it was where the line formed for lunch. The blocks Dentinger removed were both eight inches in height and width, and another sixteen in length. "If I cut more out," he said, "it'll be a bigger job to set right."

I glanced from Crystal to the master bricklayer.

"I ain't squeezing in there," Dentinger replied to my gaze. "This is the cafeteria, so it's going to be a pile of dead rats." He patted his stomach and added, "Squeezing in is above my pay grade."

Pay grade, I thought as I fished my iPhone from my pocket. I knew what I made for a living and I pondered: in what conceivable universe was I above Dentinger's pay grade? I got down on my knees and tapped the Flashlight icon. Then I scrunched down on my stomach, glanced again at Crystal and Dentinger, and wormed my way forward. I stuck my head under the two-block-high gap in the wall. It was like looking inside someone's mouth. There was a small opening in the darkness, perhaps all of two inches, between the concrete blocks and what appeared to be a rigid sheet of Styrofoam insulation. I brought the flashlight up by my cheek and squinted into the shadows but could see nothing in the opening between the block and the Styrofoam.

I twisted about, adjusted my stance, and pressed a couple of fingers into the insulation behind the wall of concrete. It had no give; I assumed it pressed tightly against the partition on the opposite side of the cafeteria. I thought for a second about electricians, how they had to set up electrical outlets before the stonework was complete, so a janitor could plug in a vacuum or whatever kind of electric doohickey he's got for mopping or polishing all of this cafeteria floor space. But that was a moot point, as the space needed to run electricity wasn't nearly wide enough to hide human remains.

"Any rats?" Dentinger asked.

"I don't see any." I slid away from the hole in the wall and glanced at Alice. She sat a couple of feet to my left, staring straight ahead. "OK, girl," I said and sat up. I pressed my palm again against the Styrofoam and received the same results as earlier. What was my bloodhound telling me? I slipped my arm back into the gap, sliding it behind the barricade of concrete, into the narrow opening, and slithered it a foot inward and then pressed against the insulation.

Same results.

I slid my arm out, shook it, and glanced up at Crystal.

"False alarm?" she said.

"Let me see how far I can reach in," I replied and returned my arm behind the partition. I lay back down and shuffled forward until my shoulder was inside the three-block cavity. My arm reached the point where Alice was facing, and I pressed again against the insulation . . . only this time there was no Styrofoam to press against and my fingers fumbled around some sort of crevice.

I slipped my arm back out, stood, and noticed Principal Isaacson had returned to the mix. She was glancing down at her watch, likely wondering when we'd be getting the hell out of her school so she could go home for the evening.

"Do you see where Alice is staring?" I said. "There's no Styrofoam insulation in that area; instead, there's some kind of a nook or cubbyhole."

"On the other side of the wall," Isaacson said, "is where the faculty lounge used to be, prior to the remodel." The principal pointed above my bloodhound's head. "I'm pretty sure the sink was in that spot."

"Oh, OK," Dentinger said. "You hit a pipe chase, Cory?"

"A what?"

"That's the space where the plumbing to the faculty lounge was housed."

Crystal turned to the mason. "Could you fit a body in a place like that, Jay?"

Dentinger shrugged. "It's pretty narrow, but I imagine so. You want me to pop out a few more blocks?"

I sat back down, noticed how wide Principal Isaacson's eyes had become at the talk of hidden bodies, and said, "Let me give it one last shot."

I got my shoulder as far into the gap in the wall as possible. At this point my arm felt as though it'd fallen asleep, but I stretched it into the two-inch opening, my fingers prodding further, passing over dried-up chunks of mortar, passing the point where the Styrofoam ended and the nook began. I stretched further, as far as I could, and worked my fingers around a corner, sliding them upward, and—Dentinger was correct—my fingertips brushed against a pipe. I slid my hand down, back to the floor, and felt something foreign. It was plastic or a tarp; a sheeting of some kind. Could it be a vapor barrier? But that made no sense, especially since it was draped about the floor.

Crystal must have spotted the confusion on my face. "What, Cor?"

"Just a second." I let my fingers inch forward, beneath the sheeting, until they bumped up against a ripple of protrusions. "What the hell?" As my fingers danced over the lumps—chalky nubs—it dawned on me . . . and I scraped my forearm yanking it from the gap in the wall and spider-crawled backward as though I'd seen a ghost.

I knew what I'd just touched . . . toes.

FOUR

"Did you catch the news?"

"What?" Wade spoke into his cell phone. "There's no 'hello,' no 'how are you?'"

"If you'd caught the news, I'd know how you are."

"Why?" he asked, now somber. "What happened?"

"They found the body."

"That's not possible." Wade left his office and stepped past the break room, where his colleagues were stuffing Tupperware lunches into a refrigerator and picking out desired pods for the coffee maker. He headed into the staircase for added privacy.

"Finding a body inside a wall at an elementary school tends to make a big splash," the voice on the phone replied. "It's even made the national news."

"How could this happen?"

"It's insane. They brought a canine handler in to speak to the students," the voice informed him. "Turns out the dogs he brought along were trained in human remains detection, you know—cadaver dogs."

Wade rubbed his chin. "Oh shit."

"Oh shit is right. The school had treats set out in the cafeteria and the dogs went straight to the section in the wall and worked their magic."

Wade took the steps down until he was in between floors. "Doesn't matter; they'll get nothing."

"Maybe so, but instead of it being a missing person case, it's now a murder investigation."

"What do you suggest we do?"

"Absolutely nothing. It's over—we sit tight and pray to God we survive this," the voice replied with more than a hint of exasperation. "I don't know how many times I have to keep saying that."

Wade kept quiet, his mind spinning.

"Are you still there?" the voice asked after a beat.

"Yes," Wade replied.

"OK, then." Followed by: "Tell your twin."

FIVE

"Is Brielle coming over tonight?" Crystal asked. My sister sat at the kitchen table, going over case files she'd brought home; something she did most evenings.

At the sound of Brielle's name, Rex shot down the basement steps, returning an instant later with his favorite toy—a knotted sock with which to play tug-of-war. *Play* isn't quite the right word, though. Rex is far more than passable as a human remains detection dog, but my springer spaniel's true love, what he lives and breathes for, is tug-of-war. If it were an Olympic event, he'd sport a gold medal around his neck in lieu of a dog collar. Brielle has yet to weary of Rex's knotted sock and the tournament begins as soon as she steps through the front door.

Like me, Brielle is a full-time student at Harper Community College. We started hanging out—OK, we studied together; no funny business—during summer school and the tradition continued as Harper's fall semester kicked into play last month, during the second half of August. Brielle loves the pooches, she likes my sister and, I think, finds me mildly entertaining.

"No," I answered. I sat on the living room couch with Alice warming my feet. Though my bloodhound kept both eyes on Rex, she'd not moved a muscle since he came galloping up the stairs. She'd learned long ago, with the rest of us, not to mess with Rex's sock unless you were fully committed and ready to throw down. I took a sip of beer and added, "She's out with him tonight."

Him was Brielle's boyfriend, a guy named Adam who worked at some downtown ad agency, where he spent his days ferreting out the best publications or programs or places in which his agency's print or radio or TV or Internet or whatever advertisements should appear. I know this because a Harper's classmate threw an end-of-summer party a few weeks back which

Brielle, of course, had been invited to and, in return, had invited me to. I got all excited to go, but when Brielle arrived on the night of the party, Adam came along with her. In fact, Adam chauffeured us to the gathering in his new Toyota Prius, which, by the way, had plenty of legroom for a third wheel like me in the back seat. And, at the get-together, as Brielle worked the room, I learned everything there was to know about Adam's budding career as a media buyer.

I forget if he asked me anything about my life.

"Oh," Crystal said in response, and left it at that.

My sister likes Brielle, but she doesn't want me to get hurt. Crystal's got it in her noggin that my being the ashtray in a romantic triangle might have some kind of detrimental effect on my mental health and well-being. Yes, I like Brielle. I'll be the first to admit it. My wee little heart goes a bit pitter-pat whenever she shows up on the scene. But I knew exactly where I stood and, heck, it sure was nice to have a female classmate as a friend—it hearkened back to high school in the days before my parents died. And even though I didn't consider Brielle and Adam the greatest of matches, certainly not in Romeo and Juliet's weight class, he seemed like a good enough guy.

Sure, once or twice, as I lay in bed at night, waiting on sleep, I may have pondered how much fun it'd be to have some kind of superpower. I'd love the ability to take over someone's body for a few minutes without them knowing. Perhaps have Adam dry swallow a handful of Ex-Lax Maximum Strength tablets right as he and Brielle are heading into a fancy five-star eatery for a multi-course meal. Then, after the pills have been swallowed, I'd relinquish control. Better yet, if Brielle's parents ever invited Adam over for dinner, as soon as he pulls into their driveway, get him to pound ten shots of Jack Daniel's, and dribble an eleventh one over his shirt, before having him rap his knuckles hard as hell on the front door . . . and then relinquish control.

As you can tell, I've not given it much thought; however, the possibilities are endless.

Crystal then said, "You should take Alice and Rex to dog parks."

"Why?" I asked. "The two goofballs already get a ton of exercise."

"You'd be able to meet people; you know, other dog lovers."

I stared at Crystal. "You mean *meet girls*?"

My sister shrugged. "Well, right off the bat you'd have something in common with them."

I got a little irritated. "How's your love life going?"

"You know me; I work all the time," she replied. "But I recently browsed some online dating sites."

My irritation morphed into curiosity. "You did?"

"A billion couples have met that way and I wanted to see how they're set up. It turns out you can filter by age, likes and dislikes, and a bunch of other settings." She peered up from her case files and added, "I bet they've even got a place to list all that weird stuff you've got going."

"Good one," I commented as it dawned on me my sister hadn't been browsing dating sites for her own use. "Did I tell you Brielle wants to fix me up with a friend of hers?"

"Oh," Crystal said again. "What do you think of that?"

"You know I hate blind dates, Crys, but Brielle said her friend's really nice. She even sent me a picture of her so I know she doesn't look like Sasquatch."

"And?"

"She's good-looking," I admitted, "but I told Brielle I'd have to think about it."

"Think about it?" Crystal raised her eyebrows. "Just go for it."

It was my turn to shrug. "But if we don't hit it off or if we date and it goes bad, I'd hate for Brielle to get pissed off at me."

"You're overthinking this," she said, her work now forgotten. "I know you have feelings for Brielle—everyone in Buffalo Grove knows you have feelings for Brielle—but you've got to get on with your life and not just hang around hoping she breaks up with her boyfriend."

"I'm not waiting for her to break up with Adam," I said, hoping my detective sister didn't have a spare polygraph hidden about the house. "Besides"—I glanced at my springer spaniel as he lay on the living room carpet, facing the entryway, licking at his knotted sock and hoping for Brielle to make an appearance—"I think I'd have to arm wrestle Rex for her."

She chuckled and then her iPhone must have buzzed as she glanced down at the table. She picked it up and said, "Crystal Pratt." As she listened, she stood and headed for the sliding glass door, to slip onto the deck for additional privacy. Alice must have sensed something was up as she rose, shook herself off, and trailed in Crystal's wake.

I grabbed a second can of Rolling Rock from the fridge, popped it open, took a sip, and was toying with tossing a bag of popcorn in the microwave when my sister stepped back inside. The phone call had been short, but clearly long enough for a look of concern to spread across her features.

"What?" I asked.

"The body was in too bad a shape to have a family member view the remains, so the medical examiner went the DNA route," Crystal said. "Turns out it is the missing boy."

SIX

KENILWORTH TEEN STILL MISSING
Chicago Tribune

No new developments have arisen in the case of Patrick "Ricky" Shortridge, the Kenilworth teenager who was last seen when he departed his friend's house in the early evening of June 24th in order to ride his bike home in time for dinner. Although Shortridge's hybrid bike (road and mountain) was found abandoned in a nearby park, no witnesses have come forward, the authorities have been unable to track the adolescent's movements via park or residential security cameras, and no ransom demands have been made, suggesting kidnapping was not a motive in the youth's disappearance. Residents of Kenilworth, an affluent village along Chicago's North Shore, have voiced a great deal of concern over the missing teen as Kenilworth has long been considered one of the safest places to live not only in Chicago, but in the United States.

This article includes Patrick Shortridge's photograph from his eighth grade yearbook as well as a more recent picture of Shortridge taken from his fourteenth birthday party in April of this year. Kenilworth PD asks that you contact them if you have any information regarding the teenager's whereabouts. An attorney for the Shortridge family has mentioned how "overwhelmed" they are "by public support," and that the family is offering a $50,000 reward for any tip leading to their son's safe return. Local Kenilworth shops have offered an additional $50,000 for Shortridge's safe return.

After her phone call, Crystal jumped behind the wheel of her Honda HR-V and zipped back to the precinct while I googled

Patrick Shortridge to refresh my memory on the poor kid's case. Unless you'd just awakened from a lengthy coma, most Chicagoans were aware of Shortridge's disappearance. It led the news for days on end. And though I'd followed the story per the occasional top-of-the-hour news blip earlier in the summer, I was fuzzy as to any specific ins and outs. The *Tribune* article from late July served as a good summation but, quite frankly, there weren't enough details for me to sink my teeth into.

Unfortunately, being privy to what I knew now—I'd never forget what my fingers brushed against inside that cavity in the cafeteria wall—there wasn't going to be a happy ending or *safe return* for the missing Kenilworth teen.

I had several questions for Crystal, but doubted I'd still be up by the time she got home.

SEVEN

"Was he burned to death?"

"The pathologist is running tests on whatever tissue remains, but he said no," Crystal replied. We huddled over the coffee maker as though that would make our aging Braun BrewSense drip faster. "Shortridge was dead before being set on fire." My sister shook her head and sighed. "Thank God for small favors."

It was quarter past six in the morning. I'd not been awake when my sister returned home last night, but heard her tiptoeing about the kitchen in a failed attempt to keep soundless, so I came upstairs to greet her before she headed out for the day. I fed the beasts as she prepped the coffee maker, making this morning's pot particularly strong.

"But why burn the poor kid?"

"Maybe to scorch off the flesh to conceal what had been done to him, or maybe the killer knew he'd be hiding the remains inside the school's wall and didn't want the stench to give it away." Crystal added, "Remember the baby rabbit that got stuck inside the garage and died?"

"Yeah—we didn't need Alice or Rex to tell us something had perished in there." I'd not hung around the elementary school after I'd verified what my dogs had alerted me to: that there were, in fact, human remains hidden behind the cafeteria wall. That had been enough for me; I didn't need to see anymore. I left after Crystal called for reinforcements and master mason Dentinger began prying out additional blocks. I remained confused on one point, though. "If the remains were burnt to a crisp, what was left to wrap in the tarp?"

"It wasn't a full cremation, Cor. I could have dealt with that," she replied. "This was as bad as anything I've ever seen. It wreaked havoc on the skin layers; cells and soft tissue—destroyed. What remained looked like white leather on bone. Jesus—it looked like something out of *The Walking Dead*."

I stepped back from the coffee maker. "But if you go to all the effort of burning the body, why not just toss whatever remains in the woods or into a lake?"

"Good question. Maybe the burn was done in some secluded place, away from prying eyes, but you still don't want to leave any evidence behind," she said. "Say good old Uncle Waldo lets you enjoy his cabin whenever he's not there. You don't want Uncle Waldo or any of his neighbors tripping over a femur bone on their morning nature walk"—she glanced at Alice and Rex, snoozing in the living room—"or a dog digging up a skull, and suddenly your favorite uncle's telling the authorities you're always at his place when he's away."

"So the Shortridge boy is abducted in June, after school's out for the summer—which kicks off cabin season," I said. "The lakes are crowded with fishermen and boaters and waterskiers who might report something suspicious, or maybe there's a sunbather with a pair of binoculars who might wonder what the stranger in Uncle Waldo's rowboat has just dumped into the water."

Crystal nodded. "No matter who owns the property—you, your uncle, a rental company—the last thing you'd want is for someone to stumble across a burial ground or splatters of DNA. You don't want anything pointing back at you."

"The poor kid was taken on June twenty-fourth," I said, recalling the date from the newspaper article. "When did the masons put up the wall?"

"About a week or two later, during the first half of July," Crystal said. "According to the paperwork, the masons were there twelve days, but they did more than just the cafeteria wall—restrooms and other areas."

I watched as the coffee maker finished brewing and said, "But serial killers wouldn't give a damn, would they? I mean they'd just dump the body out in the middle of nowhere and let some farmer or hikers or kids find it." As you can tell, I'm well-versed when it comes to mass murderers—hey, I stream a ton of TV shows, not to mention Crystal and I came face-to-face with the Dead Night Killer last fall and lived to fight another day. "Then they'd get all jazzed up when their kills are found and make the news."

"We've not made the leap to this being the work of a serial killer."

I changed tack. "Could it be a pedophile covering his tracks?"

"We're not thinking pedophilia, either." Crystal poured two cups of coffee, took her cup to the kitchen table, sat, and took a sip while I fumbled around with the carton of cream. She went on to explain, "Shortridge was fourteen; he was going to be a freshman in high school. He was skinny but tall for his age; not a prepubescent child."

I understood my sister's point. "Full-grown men would be terrified by some of the ninth graders I went to school with."

Crystal shrugged. "Mainly, Cor, my thoughts keep going back to Henry Horner and all that construction work."

I sat down across from her. "What do you mean?"

"Well, unless you're a gang member performing some kind of initiation ritual, or gunning after a rival gang, murder is more of an individual endeavor. Killers tend to work alone. It's not like you call Uncle Waldo and say, 'Hey, I caught my wife cheating. Are you available Friday to help with the strangulation?' No, because Waldo would turn around and call the police." Crystal took another sip of her coffee. "But this whole school remodel thing, hiding Shortridge inside the cafeteria wall during the summer renovation—it just screams of a two-person job."

"But if I'm screwy enough to kill someone, and I want to avoid prison, I'd do whatever it takes to hide the body," I said. "Even if it put me at risk because, hey, I'm already at risk."

Crystal shrugged again. "The security cameras were turned off. It was summer, so no threat of a school shooting or anything like that. Principal Isaacson informed us all materials and school property were locked away in classrooms not undergoing renovation, that teachers were instructed to take anything of value home with them for the summer months, and that the construction workers were responsible for the security of their own tools and equipment. That's why the masonry contractor fenced off part of the school's parking lot, to keep their stuff from being stolen."

I followed up on Crystal's train of thought. "Construction workers came and went throughout the day, at their own convenience, with just Isaacson or some other staff member opening the doors in the morning and locking them up in the evening after everyone had left. I imagine Isaacson or whatever staff person spent their day in the office playing *Angry Birds* or reading a book."

My sister nodded. "You or I could have walked in wearing a T-shirt that had *City Inspector* or *Electrician* printed on it and no questions would have been asked."

"Why would it take two people to hide the body?" My sister once informed me she appreciated my bouncing questions or ideas off her. She said it helped her focus on an investigation or even view the case in a different light. It made me feel like I was Watson to her Sherlock Holmes—well, at least Jude Law's version of Dr. Watson. He was cool. Perhaps Crystal was just being kind, humoring me; either way, I continued, "You watch the school until the masons head out to Wendy's or Arby's or wherever they go for lunch, then you pull your truck up to the front entrance—you know, where the kids are dropped off. You unload a cart that'll transport the remains, which are tucked inside a box, maybe a huge toolbox or a cooler, to the cafeteria, and ten minutes later you're back inside your truck and heading down the highway."

"So many things could go wrong with that scenario if you're doing it all by yourself," Crystal said. "But if you pull up and get the cart and box ready while your partner in the *City Inspector* shirt slips inside to make sure no one's in the cafeteria. Then, he flashes you a thumbs-up—the all-clear sign—for you to hustle over with the cart and the box. Then he acts as a hall monitor as you wrestle the plastic tarp shrouding Shortridge's body, his charred remains, under the pipes in the pipe chase opening. That alone could take several minutes to make it all look right, but if a carpenter or plumber happens by and spots you wrestling some kind of rigid tarp behind a half-built partition, well, red flags go up and your goose is cooked," she said. "A two-person team would make it a hell of a lot easier and not leave so much to chance."

"If that's the case, then two of the trade workers at the school were involved," I said. "Otherwise, how would anyone else even know about a wall or a pipe chase or the best day to sneak a body in?"

"That's what Lahlum and I were discussing last night. But this is where it gets a little dicey, Cor—flyers about the school's remodel, what was being done, went out to all the parents last spring. Principal Isaacson was even giving tours in April and May to anyone interested in what areas were being modernized." Crystal checked her watch and pushed her half-empty cup of coffee off to one side. "Arlington Heights has a free newspaper that comes out once a week. It's got an online presence, too. And the paper needs all sorts of filler articles to sell ads, so the Henry Horner renovation was a recurring feature that included a ton of photographs of the work in progress. Also, with all the traffic and equipment coming and going, any of the hundred nearby homes would certainly be aware of the construction." Crystal stood. "And like I said, anyone could walk in wearing a *City Inspector* shirt or a carpenter's belt and no one would say 'boo.'"

"I don't know," I said after a second. The whole thing bugged me. "It seems like so much work, Crys. Why not just dump the body in a pond somewhere and be done with it?"

"I don't think the killer—*or killers*—wanted Shortridge to be discovered anytime soon, if ever." Crystal then added, "But you were a fluke, Cory; the monkey wrench tossed in the gears. You screwed up their plan."

PART TWO

The Girl in the Car

The most affectionate creature in the world is a wet dog.
—Ambrose Bierce

EIGHT

Past Days

Olive Cripps was happy today.

Elated, actually.

And it had been a long time since she'd felt this way.

You'd have to rewind the clock seven years, back before the evening her furniture-mover father came home after a lengthy day of hoisting sofas and cabinets, mattresses and box springs, tables and chairs, bookshelves and overflowing boxes in the scorching heat of a mid-July day, patted his eight-year-old daughter on the top of her head, drank a large glass of iced tea, sat down in the rocking chair that took up the bulk of their tiny porch, closed his eyes, and died.

He was only twenty-nine.

When the table was set for dinner, Olive was sent to fetch her father. And there she found him . . . motionless . . . slumped forward in the rocking chair.

Her mom came running when she heard Olive's screams.

She adored her father. He was a good man and Olive worshipped the ground he walked on. Now and again, the two of them would sneak off to the nearby movie theater; an activity her mother found frivolous. Olive loved musicals. Her favorite, of course, was *The Wizard of Oz*, which the two had seen three times in the year before he passed away. And though they both enjoyed *The Little Rascals* shorts that played before the feature films, the two of them couldn't get enough of the Marx Brothers. In fact, Olive remembered how her father would scrunch up his face as he goofed around with her in order to look amazingly like her favorite Marx brother of all—the silent one, Harpo.

It broke Olive's heart that, as time passed by, her father's image grew fuzzy and faded from her mind. Her mother had only one photograph—their wedding picture—from before Olive was born. And her father looked so young in that picture; he was practically a baby himself. Outside of school and her chores at the hotel, Olive had little free time, but every once in a great while, she'd sneak away whenever one of the musicals or comedies came to the local theater and pretend she was sitting there in the dark with her father, holding onto his hand.

And whenever she saw Harpo Marx, her eyes grew moist.

Her father had also been the one to nickname her Olive, short for Olivia.

Two months after his death, Olive and her mother were forced to vacate the one-room bungalow the family had been renting. Several of her father's close friends, mostly fellow movers, came by one evening and helped them migrate across town to an entirely different quarter of Joliet—a place called Emerald Lawns—and into an efficiency apartment in the basement of a complex a half-mile hike from the Wexford Hotel. The Wexford was where Olive's mother straightaway began cleaning rooms in the morning, as well as cooking in the kitchen for both the hotel's lunch and dinner crowd. Before and after school, Olive chipped in, too. Like her mother, and father before her, Olive was a hard worker—vacuuming hallways on the various floors, scrubbing dishes, emptying ashtrays, polishing the silverware, helping to shovel the walkway in winter, and, on the day she turned fourteen, Olive began waitressing in the hotel's main dining room.

Which was where she first met Lansing.

He'd been seated in her section, where he ordered a steak—medium rare—with a baked potato and steamed broccoli, a mug of Meister Bräu and, for dessert, a slice of homemade blueberry pie. And each time Olive checked on Lansing or brought him his meal, he peppered her with questions about herself. How long had she been waitressing? Did she enjoy her job? Did she meet any interesting people? Was she originally from Joliet?

He listened and nodded along as she answered. And when

Lansing eventually asked about her family, he got a little misty-eyed when she told him about her father's premature death.

She stood near the kitchen entrance that first evening and watched as Lansing prepared to depart the restaurant. She took in his black hair, slicked back both on the top and sides, his muscular build, thick wrists and broad shoulders—how he filled out that gray suit of his, how he was several inches taller than she was; perhaps five ten if you tossed in his dress shoes. Lansing must have sensed her gaze as he glanced back her way and smiled as he exited the dining room.

He was a sight to behold.

That was when Olive felt something in the pit of her stomach; something she'd never felt before. Quite frankly, she was petrified, and stood there motionless as though glued to the floor. A minute passed before she let out a breath. And when she went to clear Lansing's table, she saw he'd left her an entire dollar bill as a tip; much more than the nickels and dimes she'd been used to collecting.

Lansing came back to the hotel's dining room a second time, not quite a week later, and requested he be seated in Olive's section, where again he asked her questions and, when queried in return, even coughed up a little bit about himself. Lansing was from Western Springs, a "nice enough" suburb of Chicago. He was about to begin his third year at the University of Chicago, where he was following in his father's accounting footsteps. Yet before the school year kicked in, he was helping himself to the family's new Chevrolet Stylemaster and taking short little day trips to some of the cities surrounding Chicago, which was what brought Lansing to Joliet and the Wexford Hotel for dinner in the first place.

And today, two weeks later—right as Olive began thinking she'd never see her *new friend* again, a thought that made her melancholy—he showed up in the dining room, smiling as though he'd seen her only yesterday as he took it upon himself to sit in her section.

And when she set his customary mug of Meister Bräu atop one of the hotel's coasters, Lansing looked up at her and asked, "Would you like to go for a ride in the Stylemaster?"

Olive felt herself blush at the question but quickly nodded her assent. "That would be fun," she said. "If you could wait until my shift is over."

"Of course," he replied.

The next part was tricky, though. The last thing she needed would be for anyone working at the hotel to inform her mother they'd spotted Olive stepping into a customer's car—a man's car, no less—no matter if it were with the best of intentions. "Perhaps I could meet you at the post office?" she said and glanced toward the street out front. "It's a few blocks down and one street over."

Lansing stared at her a long second. "Sure," he said finally. "I'll find it."

An hour later, Olive's shift came to an end. She washed both her hands and face in the women's restroom off the hotel's lobby.

And then she left for the post office.

NINE

"The family is destroyed."

Crystal was at her desk, speaking on the phone to a detective named Lynne Claypool. Claypool worked the CPD's Special Victims Unit, which had been investigating Patrick Shortridge's disappearance. SVUs handle missing persons cases; they also investigate domestic violence incidents, as well as youth who commit felonies. Claypool had been involved in the Shortridge case since the morning of June 25th, when Kenilworth PD discovered the teenager's bike abandoned in a nearby park. Without his bike, it looked less like fourteen-year-old Patrick had run away from home; rather that an abduction had occurred.

"Losing a child is heartbreaking enough," Crystal replied, "but in such a horrendous manner—how do you pick up the pieces?"

"I'm not sure the pieces ever get picked up."

Crystal had CPD's Victim Information Notice form displayed on her laptop screen. It was not of much help, though, as it only provided the incident—Missing Persons— and Shortridge's first and last name, as well as the date and time of the occurrence. The form had been completed by Patrick's parents and Kenilworth PD when they went to the police station to report their son's disappearance on the evening of June 24th. Crystal knew the form by heart and wasn't expecting to find additional details but brought it up in case there were any additional notes in the margins.

There weren't.

Since Patrick was only fourteen, as per standard procedure the National Center for Missing & Exploited Children, as well as the National Runaway Safeline, were notified.

"First, we checked hospitals and urgent care clinics, thinking Patrick had been involved in a car or biking accident, that he was unconscious, and, at his age, carried no ID. Our efforts there, of course, did not pan out," Claypool said. "Then we dusted Patrick's bike for fingerprints but only found matches from his little sister and his best friend, in addition to his prints. There were no unidentified fingerprints; nothing for us to run through AFIS." AFIS was the Automated Fingerprint Identification System, a national database maintained by the FBI. The detective continued bringing Crystal up to speed on SVU's investigation into the missing teen. "No witnesses came forward. Not one. No security cameras cover the sidewalk next to that stretch of the park, the sidewalk Patrick would have taken to ride his bike home—near where his bike was found. I believe the perp was aware of the blind spot." Claypool's voice was gravelly and Crystal laid odds the detective was a heavy smoker. "I also believe the perp had been waiting there for Patrick, waiting in ambush. Maybe an SUV or van sat there with a door open, and he just grabbed the kid off his bike and tossed him inside." She added, "Real quick, toot sweet."

"If it was an ambush," Crystal said, "that means the perp had been following Patrick; the perp knew his route home."

"Yes."

"But no ransom demands or note; not a kidnapping?"

"No," Claypool replied. "His parents have money—not Bill Gates rich, but comfortable."

"No hits off the reward money."

"Just a few phone calls from people having seen a kid here or there in the general vicinity. All very hazy and vague, nothing we could run with. Plus, it was summertime in Kenilworth; kids were everywhere."

As Claypool spoke, Crystal tapped at her keyboard and brought up Patrick's entry, which still remained on CPD's Missing Persons website. It referenced the teen's juvenile status, provided a case number and a recent photograph of Patrick as well as his age, gender, race, height—five seven, weight—one hundred and twenty pounds, eyes—brown, hair—brown, and last contact, which listed the area where Patrick's bike had been discovered. It also mentioned Patrick's clothing. He'd been wearing a white T-shirt, a pair of black Nike running shorts, and black Air Jordan sneakers. The NCIC number from the missing person record entered into the National Crime Information Center's Missing Person File was also included.

Claypool filled Crystal in on what Patrick's parents had done the evening of his disappearance. When their son hadn't returned home in time for dinner and wasn't answering his cell phone or responding to text messages, they contacted the friend their son had spent the afternoon with, who informed them Patrick had left in plenty of time for him to have arrived home by then. As his son's bike was not in the garage, Mr. Shortridge drove the route Patrick would have likely taken to get home and, with no luck, he then navigated a couple of the less-likely routes his son may have taken. Meanwhile, Mrs. Shortridge stayed at home in case Patrick arrived and worked the phone lines, calling the homes of her son's other friends, talking to both them and their parents. After Mr. Shortridge returned home empty-handed, the two waited another half hour before they went to the Kenilworth police station to report their son as missing.

There is no waiting period when filling out a missing person report. Since adults can get into car accidents or wind up in the ER in a million different ways, or sneak off to happy hours with friends or colleagues, Crystal knew common sense was ultimately the guide in reporting someone as missing; however, when it came to juveniles, these reports held more of a sense of urgency as their absences could not so easily be explained away. CPD defines a missing juvenile as a person under the age of seventeen whose whereabouts are unknown by the person having responsibility for their welfare, chiefly a parent or guardian.

"I interviewed Patrick's circle of friends, his best friends. A lot of tears—they weren't hiding anything," the SVU detective said. "We kept Patrick's disappearance alive in the media, hoping someone in the community would have some information, any information, but that didn't pan out either. I've never felt so useless." Claypool added, "To be honest, I was hoping you were calling to tell me you found the killer."

"I wish I was," Crystal said. She then asked, "You were with the family when they were notified Patrick's remains had been found, right?"

"Yes—it's the worst part of my job, and it's the main reason I'm taking early retirement next year," the detective replied. Crystal now heard street noise over her cell phone and figured Claypool had stepped outside to sneak a smoke. "I was also the one that walked the Shortridges through your list of construction firms and contractors and the names of the tradespeople that worked on the school remodel."

"I heard they didn't recognize any of the names or organizations."

"Well, Mr. Shortridge had heard of some of the construction firms, but only because they're well-known, not because he's done any business with them or had them work on his house. The Shortridges have absolutely no ties to Henry Horner Elementary School, nor have they ever lived in Arlington Heights." Crystal listened to a few seconds of traffic noise before Claypool continued. "My instinct tells me it's random. The killer spotted Patrick somewhere in Kenilworth—at the mall, at an arcade, hanging out at a burger shop with his friends, or riding around on his bike. Then he stalked the poor kid until an opportunity presented itself. This wouldn't be the first time something like that has occurred. I don't know—maybe sexual, maybe not."

Similar scenarios had crossed Crystal's mind. "Could you do me one more favor, Lynne, and set up a meeting with me and the Shortridges?" she asked, getting to the meat of the matter, why she'd really contacted the SVU detective. "I'm hoping to visit them at their home, ask a couple of questions, non-intrusive questions, and check out Patrick's room, you know—get a feel for the case."

There was a pause before Claypool responded. "Patrick's disappearance broke the family in half . . . and now this, finding their son in such a manner, burned and hidden inside a wall. That doesn't provide closure, Detective Pratt. Far from it. Mrs. Shortridge—Jennifer—is under sedation. Heavy sedation. That's her life now. And Mr. Shortridge hasn't slept in forever; he's just going through the motions."

"I can't begin to understand what they're going through."

"And that poor little girl of theirs," Claypool said and sighed. "I've been in this job too long. I figured my heart was callused, completely scabbed over by now. But when I think of that poor little girl . . . I get choked up and want to cry."

"I'm hoping you could be there for the introductions. You've been interacting with them since June, Lynne—they know and trust you." Crystal then thought of little girls and broken hearts. "I know it's not a cure-all, but I happen to have two of the best therapy dogs in the world that would love to meet her."

A second passed before the SVU detective replied. "Bring them."

TEN

Past Days

"What's the matter, Olive?" Lansing asked gently. "You don't seem to be yourself today."

The couple sat on a thick wool blanket, drinking Coca-Cola, a few feet from his Chevrolet Stylemaster. Neither the car nor the two of them could be spotted from the road. Lansing had let her drive the Stylemaster today, a first, and she brought them to the special place where they'd been parking, two or three times a week, for the past couple of months. Originally, Lansing had found the spot by driving them several miles outside of Joliet, where the two tripped over a seldom-used gravel road from which he was able to angle the Stylemaster down the embankment in order to disappear into a patch of woods. Once in the woodlands, he was able to navigate between enough trees until the car was completely out of sight of any passersby.

That first evening they chatted with the windows down, making small talk about nothing in particular, and then, after a long moment of awkward silence, they leaned into each other and kissed. Olive had never been kissed on the lips before, certainly not like this. Long, hard, wet. Something ignited inside her, like fireworks across the sky. They kissed some more and Olive got frightened. She told Lansing she needed to get home, as soon as possible. It was imperative she be there before her mother returned home from work.

Lansing nodded, the perfect gentleman. He did as he was told.

Several days later found the two of them in the same secluded spot among the trees. This time the passion got the better of Olive and they did more than kiss.

Several days after that, again in their special place, all caution was thrown to the wind. The two made love . . . and Olive's life was forever changed.

But today, Olive was not herself; she was not herself at all. Olive hadn't slept much in the past week. She was frightened again; this time terrified. And she couldn't keep the news to herself any longer. "We need to talk," she finally said.

Lansing had slipped out of his dress shirt and set it down on his lap. A look of concern spread across his features. "OK."

A tear slid down Olive's cheek. "I'm two weeks beyond . . . beyond that time of month." Her voice trembled. "And I was sick this morning."

Lansing stared at Olive a long moment. "You're pregnant?"

"I don't know," she said slowly, but then she nodded. "I think I am."

Lansing glanced toward the gravel road, then to the Stylemaster, and then to the blanket they sat on before his gaze returned to Olive. "It's OK, sweetheart," he said and brushed away a lock of sandy hair that had fallen over her eye. "It's going to be OK."

Olive wiped at moist eyes with a forearm and returned his gaze. "Is it?"

"Of course it is," Lansing said. He cupped her cheek in the palm of his hand. "In fact, it's going to be better than OK, sweetheart." He smiled and stood. "In fact, let me get the Kodak. I'm going to immortalize this moment."

"Oh, no," Olive said and reflexively ran fingers through her hair.

"Oh, yes," he replied as he rooted about a camera bag in the back seat of the car. "I'm excited, I really am. And you want to know something else? I hope the baby has your eyes." He glanced her way and added, "Don't give it another thought, Olive. I'm going to take care of you."

ELEVEN

"She's going to be pissed off," Garrick said in a whisper.

"She's always pissed off."

The two sat on barstools at the deserted end of the tavern. The Old Timer's Tap—a dive bar in Hegewisch his brother had heard about, far south side of Chicago—hadn't been open fifteen minutes, on a weekday no less, and the joint was a quarter full with what Wade took to be regulars, like Norm and Cliff on *Cheers*; perhaps here to partake in a liquid lunch and then a stick of gum on the way back to the office. The place was perfect. They'd pay their bar bill in cash and no one at the tavern had ever seen Wade or his brother before, a major plus on the off chance one of the barflies overheard a sentence or two of what the siblings had been chatting about.

The vodka cranberries weren't bad, either.

"But this time she'll be major-league pissed off at us. She's been adamant nothing happens to the girl."

"Well—how terribly *sexist* of her."

Garrick frowned and set down his cocktail. "She's not going to find it jokie-joke, Wade," he said. "Not one bit."

Wade looked at his brother. They were identical twins and, even a couple years from the big three-o, could still confuse folks from telling which of them was which. Though Wade sported his longer, they had the same black hair, the same hazel eyes, the same lofty height and thick, muscular builds. For today's meeting, Garrick wore a Bears cap down over his brow so no one in the tavern would remember it was a pair of twins who sat in the corner and conspired.

"I know she won't, but we didn't get into this for half measures, did we?" he said. "It was all or nothing."

His brother shrugged. "So what's the plan?" he asked. "They pulled her out of school."

"Yeah, but we know from scouting about where she'll go if

she goes anywhere. She likes that little playground with the swings and slide and monkey bars and shit." He finished what remained of his drink. "If she's not going to school, I'm sure she'll be there a couple times a day."

"But she won't be alone. They'll have a babysitter or someone watching her."

"Don't hit the babysitter too hard," Wade said and raised a hand to flag the bartender in order to settle their bill. "Unless it's a family member. Then you can hit them a little harder."

TWELVE

Past Days

"Hey, Olive Oyl," Donny at the reception desk called across the hotel lobby. "You've got a message."

Olive walked over, curious. This was a first. She'd never received a message before and suspected Donny, always the kidder, was putting her on. "Really?"

"Yes sirree Bob," he replied. "A *gentleman* called not more than five minutes ago and wanted me to let you know that"—Donny glanced down at a piece of scratch paper before handing it to her—"*the Stylemaster will arrive at precisely four o'clock.*"

She felt herself begin to blush. Donny had put added emphasis on the word *gentleman*. Olive read the note and, sure enough, it was word for word what the hotel receptionist had just broadcast to the mercifully empty lobby.

"You buying a new car, Oyl?" he asked. Donny had nicknames for everyone at the hotel and once he realized she went by Olive, he tacked on *Oyl* after the cartoon character from the *Popeye* comic strip. More often than not, Donny just called her Oyl.

Donny was in his midtwenties. After the war—he'd served in the 702nd Tank Battalion in the United States Third Army, one of Patton's boys—Donny had married his high school sweetheart. The couple had a rosy-cheeked toddler that Olive or her mother watched whenever the two found time to sneak away for dinner or catch a movie. As soon as Donny's shift at the Wexford ended for the day, he took two different buses in order to make it across town to Joliet Junior College in time for night school to begin. The G.I. Bill funded his studies; business administration classes, he'd once told Olive.

Donny was a busy man; happy, but busy.

Olive shook her head. "Not today." Then she did an

about-face, to head back to the dining room before Donny could quiz her more on the note's meaning.

"Because if you are," he called after her, "I'm going to start waiting tables."

She shot him an over-the-shoulder smile and said, "That would be a lot of tables, Donny."

He chuckled and returned to work.

Olive entered the nearly empty dining room. It was half past three in the afternoon and the lunch crowd had long since dispersed. The dinner rush wouldn't kick in for another hour, so meeting Lansing at four would work out fine. Ruth—the other waitress working the Saturday evening shift—had just arrived. Ruth could cover for Olive for a few minutes while she went out to meet with him. This was the first time Lansing had called for her at the hotel. This was the first time he was bringing the Stylemaster to the Wexford's front entrance to pick her up instead of all the cloak-and-dagger at the post office.

It was a day of firsts.

Her heart beat faster. She'd not seen Lansing since she told him she was pregnant. That had been last week. She'd begun to fret over the past several days, but if Lansing was coming to the hotel, that meant the time for hiding was over.

It was going to be OK after all, Olive thought.

Or, as Lansing had promised her—*Don't give it another thought, Olive. I'm going to take care of you.*

His coming here would make it authentic; it would make it official. They'd get a chance to talk, and then Lansing would have dinner as he waited out her shift, and then the two of them would sit down with her mother. Olive's heart beat even faster as she considered the implications. People at the hotel and her school would find out.

Olive would become the center of gossip.

But none of that mattered as long as Lansing was by her side.

Don't give it another thought, Olive. I'm going to take care of you.

Sure enough, the Stylemaster appeared at the hotel's entrance at four o'clock sharp. Olive slipped through the revolving glass doors and smiled. A thick and solemn-faced man in a suit held the back door open for her. She knew Lansing came from money, but she didn't know he came from chauffeur-level money. Olive slipped quickly into the back seat, her smile dissolving as she realized Lansing wasn't waiting for her in the back of the car.

Instead, a thin man in a white suit and gray fedora sat in the front passenger seat. He didn't bother turning his head to greet her.

"I'm Lansing's father," he said. "Unfortunately, he won't be joining us today."

The back door shut and a second later the chauffeur was behind the wheel. As they pulled away from the curb, Olive spotted Donny stepping out from the hotel's lobby, staring her way, a look of concern across his face.

THIRTEEN

"I'm not good at this," I said for the fifth or sixth time. My sister and I were in the Silverado, Alice and Rex were in the back seat staring out windows as we headed toward the Paul-and-Jennifer-Shortridge residence in one of the more exclusive sections of Kenilworth, a suburb about fifteen or so miles north of downtown Chicago. After the pups and I find human remains, we're fortunate enough to fade into the background of the investigation. Our job is done. Rarely, if ever, do I deal with members of the victim's family. I had a nightmare of a time dealing with the grief and pain and horror involved in my parents' deaths. As a result I'm an awkward stumblebum, unsure of how to behave whenever others are suffering through similar despair. I find it difficult enough to mumble "Sorry for your loss" at a funeral even though I know I'll be in my truck a minute later, peeling out of the parking lot and picking up a slice of pizza on the drive home. "I'm not sure about this at all, Crys."

"You'll do fine," she replied. "Just introduce Alice and Rex to Charlotte and let them do the rest."

"You hear that, guys." I spoke to the back seat. "This is all on you."

We pulled into a broad two-story Victorian with a four-car garage on what seemed at least an acre lot. The lawn was thick and green and likely maintained by a landscaping service. There were a handful of front-yard trees and I spotted a wooden privacy fence that stretched off from the side of the house as we approached, likely indicating a backyard pool.

Nice digs.

I parked on the far side of the driveway, behind a silver Subaru Outback which Crystal mentioned belonged to the detective who would be meeting us. In fact, by the time I had the hounds leap from the back seat to the driveway,

I had turned to see a fifty-something woman in a dark green pantsuit on the front walk, chatting with Crystal.

"You won't be seeing Jen today," the woman informed my sister as I approached. "Let's just say she's *indisposed*. But Paul's parents have flown in to stay with them for a while, for support." The woman nodded my way and slipped a cigarette between her lips. "You the guy with the dogs, huh?" she asked as she brought a lighter up to her mouth.

"Yes."

"This is my brother, Cory," Crystal introduced me as I held out my hand. "Cory and his dogs are the ones that found Patrick's remains at Henry Horner."

"Oh," she said and shook my hand, her lighter inadvertently cupped between our palms. "I'm Lynne Claypool; I'm with the Special Victims Unit."

"Nice to meet you," I replied. Crystal mentioned the SVU detective was taking early retirement in a year or two. Hers was one of a thousand jobs I could never do. "I wish it were under different circumstances."

Claypool nodded a second time. "Nothing personal, but I think we'll limit today's activity to only bringing Detective Pratt inside to meet with Paul and Paul's father," she said. "But it'll work out, because Charlotte and her grandmother just left for the playground. It's a short walk from here and they're expecting you." The detective added, "Let me tell you how to get there."

FOURTEEN

Past Days

"Just to clarify, you are not Lansing's first—far from it," the man in the passenger seat announced to the car, not bothering to look back at Olive, not giving her the time of day. "Clearly, my son enjoys his little road trips?"

They were sailing along, hitting the outskirts of Joliet; a different route than the one she and Lansing had been taking over the past couple of months. She doubted the thick-faced driver or the man in the white suit had any knowledge of her and Lansing's special spot among the trees. Olive regretted having gotten into the Stylemaster with these men. She had yet to say a word, her heart an ice cube in her throat, and she glanced from Thick-face to White-suit to the door handle next to her wrist.

"Don't even think about it," White-suit said as if in response to a query. "At this speed you'd get horribly mangled. Horribly."

White-suit had tilted his head in a manner to take her in with one eye, like something a bird might do, and Olive studied his profile. He was fiftyish, clean and freshly shaved; he had the appearance of a man who lived his life freshly shaved. Quite frankly, he had an air of importance about him, of high status—to the manner born—not unlike the men who stayed in the more-expensive suites at the Wexford; the men hotel management required the older and more experienced staff to attend.

And then Olive spotted the resemblance—White-suit's square chin, his hawkish nose—and she knew he had told her the truth.

The man in the white suit was indeed Lansing's father.

Olive felt the color drain from her face and she felt her heart beat faster—only this time in dread.

"What's going on?" she asked. Olive clung to the hope this

was all some sort of misunderstanding, some kind of harmless miscommunication. "Where's Lansing?"

"Calm down, dear girl—I told you he wouldn't be joining us. But there's no need to fear; after all, today is your lucky day."

Olive eyed him suspiciously but kept quiet. What was there to say?

After a long moment, he spoke to the thick-faced man, the driver. "I don't think the girl trusts us, Alvin."

"It's like I told you this morning, boss."

"What was it you said, Alvin?"

"That whorelets grow like weeds in Joliet," Thick-face replied.

White-suit turned to Olive, this time she could see his entire face. "Is that true?" he inquired. "Do whorelets grow like weeds in Joliet?"

Olive's eyes stung and blurred as tears began to form. She looked down and spoke in a muted whisper.

"What did you say?"

"I'm only fifteen." Olive's voice trembled; tears trickled onto her lap.

White-suit stared at her for what seemed an eternity before replying, "I hate to be blunt, dear child, but do you believe anyone cares? In my life, we've been through two world wars and a depression." He then added, "Do you honestly believe anybody will care whether you're fifteen or not?"

Thick-face commented, "Squaws were popping 'em out at age twelve."

Olive caught her breath, stunned at what was unfolding inside the sedan.

The Stylemaster had once been the most welcoming place in the world—full of hope, full of possibility, and the sense that she might not suffocate after all, which, let's face it, Olive thought, is what she'd been doing since her father sat down in his favorite rocking chair on a hot summer night and passed away. But now the Stylemaster seemed smaller than the tiny closet she and her mother shared.

The Stylemaster was no longer a place of hope or possibility.

Now it was a dark and dank place.

It was foreboding.

It was a place of suffocation.

"Do you know what this is?" As though a magician performing a parlor trick, a twenty-dollar bill appeared between White-suit's index and middle fingers. "See how nice and crisp it is—brand new—I picked it up at the bank yesterday, right before they closed for the week."

Olive said nothing.

"Remember how I told you it was your lucky day," he said and flicked the bill in her direction. Olive didn't move as the twenty-dollar bill floated to the floor of the back seat. White-suit sighed. "What an ungrateful little bitch," he said. "I have no idea what my son saw in you."

Olive wiped wet eyes with a forearm.

"Enough with the waterworks," White-suit said. "That's a lot of money for—what was the word you used, Alvin?—a *whorelet*. And you can use it"—he peeked down at her abdomen—"to have it taken care of . . . if you know what I mean."

Thick-face added, "She knows what you mean."

White-suit nodded in response and continued. "Or you can give it to your mother, to shut her up when you tell her what you've been up to lately. Or you can use it to grease the wheels with a replacement daddy." White-suit thought a moment before adding, "Better yet, find some dunce cap and spread those pretty legs of yours—you'd want to do it sooner than later—and the dunce cap will never know the kid's not his."

"Won't be the first time a thing like that's happened," Thick-face said. "Just bat those eyes of yours next time you serve a guy his chipped beef. He'll have you up in his room and bent over the sink in no time."

"You have such a charming way with words, Alvin. Has anyone told you that? A dyed-in-the-wool romantic, you are," White-suit said before turning his attention back to Olive. "The sooner you spread your legs for the next schmuck, the harder it'll be for him to do the math. Just tell him *it came early*. And then you can spend that twenty-dollar bill on yourself."

FIFTEEN

Paul Shortridge waited for Crystal in the front entryway.

"My deepest sympathy for your loss, Mr. Shortridge," she said and shook his hand after Detective Claypool made introductions. Crystal added, "And I apologize for disturbing you today."

Shortridge nodded and contorted his lips into what might broadly be deemed a smile. The man possessed that thousand-yard stare Crystal had seen before. If she turned around and left the premises immediately, Crystal doubted if he'd be able to describe what she looked like or confirm if she'd even been there at all.

"Shall we go to the kitchen?" Claypool asked, the SVU detective now acting as tour guide.

Shortridge nodded again and the three of them trekked through a spacious living room, past a hardwood dining table that could seat a fighter squadron, and into a kitchen the size of a houseboat. The center of the cooking area was taken up by a massive island, its countertop made of marble with a dozen or so padded stools tucked beneath it. Crystal imagined this is where most dinners, certainly the informal ones, took place. On one stool sat an older gentleman—thinning gray hair, thin face, rimless designer glasses—who glanced up from the newspaper he'd been reading. Crystal took him to be Patrick's paternal grandfather.

Her hunch was validated when Paul said, "This is my father, James. He and my mother are visiting from Scottsdale."

The elder Shortridge rose to greet Crystal. She shook his hand and again expressed her condolences.

Claypool then took control of the reins. "Would anyone like some coffee?"

"No, thank you," Crystal said. The two men stayed silent, a tacit no.

"OK, then," Claypool said. "Let's take a seat and Detective Pratt has a couple of questions to ask."

Both Crystal and Claypool took seats at the island, Grandpa Shortridge returned to his perch and, after another moment, Paul pulled out a stool.

Crystal began. "First off, I want to thank the two of you for taking the time to talk with me today."

"Of course," Grandpa Shortridge replied. "We want to help in any way we can."

"My hope is to ask you a few questions about your son and grandson"—Crystal looked from Paul to his father—"but I'd also like to take a peek in Patrick's room, so I can get a feel for his personality; what Patrick liked or maybe even what he didn't like."

Grandpa Shortridge nodded and a moment later Paul followed suit.

Crystal set her pocket notebook down on the countertop and took out a pen. "I know Detective Claypool and other SVU detectives have asked many questions since June, and Lynne has been kind enough to share that information with me. It's all been very helpful." Crystal then glanced down at her notes and said, "I realize teenage boys aren't big into diaries, but did Patrick keep one?"

Grandpa Shortridge shrugged and looked at his son.

After a moment, Paul said, "No."

"Do you know if Patrick had any journal writing assignments from English or other classes?"

Paul shook his head, his thousand-yard stare gazing right through her.

"I went through Patrick's room with both Paul and Jen and we didn't find a diary or any type of journaling activity," Claypool confirmed. "Of course, you know how boys are—those types of assignments might be the first things tossed in the bin at the end of the quarter."

Crystal thought about the Journal app on her iPhone and said, "They never did find Patrick's cell phone, did they?"

"No. And we were never able to track it." Claypool frowned. "We believe Patrick's cell phone was destroyed around the time he was abducted."

Crystal scribbled in her notepad and continued. “Did Patrick have a calendar he could add events to? Parties or gatherings, or any get-togethers he didn’t want to miss out on?” She thought for a second. “Perhaps the calendar in Outlook or Gmail on his PC?”

Claypool said, “We checked his laptop and he didn’t use the calendar function.”

Then Paul Shortridge spoke. “Jen gave the kids calendars at Christmastime. Ricky kept it on his desk, but”—he glanced at the SVU detective—“we paged through each month and my son only used it to jot down Cubs games he wanted to catch on TV.” Crystal was surprised at the extent of Shortridge’s answer; his longest yet. Perhaps it was a pleasant memory. Paul then added, “Ricky loved the Cubs.”

“Did you take your son to some of the games?”

Paul nodded and said, “I’d bring my son and one or two of his friends to a game or he’d catch a game with a friend’s family.” Paul repeated, “Ricky loved the Cubs.”

Crystal shot Claypool a discreet glance. Per the SVU detective’s theory, Wrigley Field could have been a location where Patrick’s killer might have spotted him. Although it’d be damned difficult for a stalker to follow the family from the stadium to where their car was parked and then get back to his vehicle in time to follow them to Kenilworth.

But you never know.

Crystal was reminded of Daniel Styles’s recent confession; the troubled man who, decades after they’d dated, had killed the husband of his college girlfriend. There’d also been an item in the headlines about a family that had taken a long weekend in Florida, staying at a motel in Orlando. Their sixteen-year-old daughter would go to a nearby coffee shop to pick up cups of joe in order to get her parents up and at ’em, so they could get to Disney World when the park opened. She’d say hi to the morning barista and laugh at his jokes, and a month later he turned up at the family’s Chicago home, after the bus dropped her off from school. He doused her with Mace and was dragging her to his car when a neighbor spotted the tussle, ran over, and wrestled the guy to the ground. The police found flex cuffs, blankets, and camping gear stuffed in the trunk of his car.

Yup . . . you just never knew.

"Where did Ricky hang out with his friends during the summer months?"

The elder Shortridge took a stab at this one. "They'd ride their bikes to the mall to grab a pop, or play some games or people watch—that is, check out girls."

Paul nodded along with his father; it was familiar terrain. "Ricky and his friends would go to Pee-Wee Field if they wanted to hit some balls. Or they'd play soccer at Townley Field," he said. "You know how boys are—always on the go."

Detective Claypool said, "We've got an extensive list of Ricky's favorite locations."

"Good." Crystal nodded, flipped shut her notebook, and slipped it back into her breast pocket. These were really icebreaker questions, so she'd get to know the Shortridge family as the investigation evolved from that of a missing person case to homicide.

"Can I see Ricky's room?"

SIXTEEN

Past Days

"Where's Lansing?" Olive said from the back seat, startling herself, amazed she could even speak.

"Oh, don't you worry about my son, he'll be just fine. He got a serious tongue-lashing when he brought this *situation* to my attention. And believe you me, he won't be taking the Stylemaster out on any road trips for a good, long while."

For the first time Olive held the man in white's gaze. "I will be speaking to Lansing."

White-suit focused on her as though she were a rare bird. "Is that steel I see in your eyes? My God, Alvin—the whorelet's got some steel in her eyes," he said. "Who would have thought it possible? Well, here's a quick lesson for you. Stare into my eyes, girly-girl, and you'll see nothing but steel." White-suit then stressed: "And it's the steel in my eyes that makes it fuck sure I'll do whatever needs doing to protect my family."

Olive felt dizzy; she felt herself teetering on the edge of a cliff, an abyss, as a fresh wave of dread washed over her, soaking her to the bone. Olive wasn't sure she'd be able to keep down the sandwich she'd eaten for lunch.

"Perhaps Lansing mentioned I'm an accountant. If that came up, my boy did not lie to you—I am a tax accountant—but I doubt Lansing told you about some *very special* clients of mine. In fact, Lansing does not know about these clients. And the last thing anyone with a functioning brain would ever want to know is who my clients are," he said. "Isn't that right, Alvin?"

Olive watched from the back seat as the thick-faced man slowly nodded his agreement.

"I need to talk to Lansing." Olive swallowed hard. "He owes me that much."

"My son owes you nothing . . . and you will never talk to

Lansing again. Do you understand me?" He glared at her and said, "The steel is still in your eyes." He turned to Thick-face. "I'm afraid, Alvin, I'm just not getting through to her."

"I warned you about that," Thick-face said.

"Don't rub it in." White-suit settled back into his seat and stared at the road ahead. "If I remember correctly, we'll be passing a strip of woodland called Stump Acres. Interesting name, don't you think? We passed it on our way into town," he said. "When we hit the junction, Alvin, please take the turnoff."

"Happy to."

White-suit half-turned, his profile back on display. "I bet they sell Christmas trees there after Thanksgiving, but I'm not from Joliet, so take it with a grain of salt," he said. "Once we get there, Alvin will march you into the pine trees, perhaps a hundred yards or so." The man in white shrugged. "And that will be that—there'll be no more tears, no more threats to ruin my son's life . . . and no more steel in your eyes, for that matter." He added, "It'll all be over."

"What?" Olive's eyes grew wide. She pressed herself backward into the seat cushion, as though that would offer escape. "You can't be serious."

White-suit raised an eyebrow. "But we're almost there," he said. "In fact, I'm positive it's the turnoff up ahead."

"That would be—" Her voice stammered and she stopped mid-sentence. Olive's shoulders began to quiver. "That's . . . murder."

"Only if you get caught." Thick-face spoke from the driver's seat.

Olive exhaled, a rush of air escaping her body. Thick-face kept his left hand on the steering wheel but in his right was a black revolver. He held it sideways for her to see, its barrel pointed at the roof of the vehicle.

"Do you know the damage a snub nose can do to a person's face?" the man in white asked. "Oh, don't worry; he's not going to do anything in my car. All that blood and tissue on the upholstery—we'd never be able to scrub that off. No, Alvin will walk you into the pines first." White-suit sighed. "I'll feel awful about this—I truly will." Then his voice turned cold.

"But only for a night or two. And if anyone finds what's left of your body—after the coyotes have eaten their share—well, it's just another trailer-trash slut fucked and killed by a drifter before he hopped aboard a passing train."

The Stylemaster began to slow as it approached the crossroad that led into Stump Acres.

"No," Olive whispered. She realized White-suit was dead serious and the monster driving the sedan would do whatever was requested of him. They were not fooling around. Olive spoke quickly, "Please, God—no."

"You will never talk to my son again?"

Olive shook her head. "I won't," she said, her heart pounding, her face devoid of color; tears flowing, glaciers melting down her cheeks.

"Is that a promise?"

"Yes," Olive said and she meant it. "I promise." She didn't want to die. Not here, not today.

"On your life?"

"Yes," she repeated.

White-suit skipped a beat before he added, "On your mother's life?"

Olive gasped. She felt sick to the core of her being; like cancer, everything spiraling out of control. "I will never talk to him again," she said, adamantly. A string of saliva hung from her upper lip. "I promise you."

White-suit stared at her for another eternity. "I'd like to believe you. I really would, but you need to comprehend a fact of life—a simple fact of life—as we move onward from today," he said. "Are you ready?"

Olive nodded.

"If Lansing so much as notices you following him around campus or spots you across the bookstore or cafeteria, or if his name shows up on a birth certificate, it won't be my face you're going to see. In fact, you're never going to see me again after today." White-suit scratched at his cheek and continued. "Alvin's will be the last face you ever see as he drags both you and your mother into the pine trees at Stump Acres."

Olive Cripps wept quietly as they drove her back to town.

SEVENTEEN

Unbelievable.

Not that I'm complaining about skipping out on my afternoon database management course, but I sit next to Brielle in that class; it's the bright spot of my day. She and I hang together at Harpers, a clique of two—studying or grabbing a bite to eat or pretending to laugh at one of my lame jokes. I think fellow classmates assume we're an item. I know I'm weird, but I kind of like the notion that fellow students imagine Brielle and I are an item.

At least in some alternate universe or dimension we're a couple.

But instead of whiling away the afternoon with Brielle, I was traipsing about the side streets of Kenilworth, in search of an asphalt pathway that departs the thoroughfare and snakes down into some kind of fancy-schmancy playground for the neighborhood rug rats. Thank God I had Alice and Rex along with me. They kept me from looking as though I'm some kind of pervert out on the prowl. I glanced at my watch. It wasn't yet mid-afternoon and today was a school day, which meant the play area would likely be deserted.

In a certain manner I was pleased not to be stuck hovering about the Shortridge residence. I'm not good at interacting with grief-stricken or traumatized adults. Out here I'd be able to avoid the verbal bumbling and fumbling that would ensue if I encountered either of the parents of the poor kid the dogs had discovered tucked inside the wall at Henry Horner Elementary School. There was nothing I could say, no words in the dictionary to hasten along the healing process.

There were no words at all.

I hoped I was better equipped to deal with their child, the little Shortridge girl, to—as Crystal phrased it—"just introduce Alice and Rex to Charlotte and let them do the rest."

Damn. It occurred to me I'd forgotten the name of Charlotte's grandmother. My early-onset Alzheimer's must be kicking in. The SVU cop at the house had not only provided directions to the playground but also told me the grandmother's name, yet now I was drawing a blank. No worry; she was the paternal grandmother, so I could get away with calling her Mrs. Shortridge, which would be the respectable thing to do in the first place. There was no getting around the grandmother—who would be mourning the death of her grandson—but perhaps the mother of some preschoolers would be there, sharing a bench, consoling her.

Crystal would be coughing up more than the usual Taco Bell for my doing her this solid. We were rapidly approaching Applebee's territory.

My bloodhound and springer spaniel were having the time of their lives. If the two had smartphones, they'd be snapping pictures and shooting videos. The streets of Kenilworth were a new place for them to explore and conquer; an undiscovered country in which to carve out their turf with the sporadic tinkle.

I glanced ahead, where the boulevard reached its crest. This was the spot where the SVU cop informed me I'd find the asphalt footpath that wounded its way down into the play area. A wave of trepidation washed over me. It was showtime. I readied my somber face for meeting Charlotte and her grandmother. Then, I would introduce the two of them to Alice and Rex, step back, and let the pups take over.

Dear Lord, please let it be as easy as that.

As soon as I stepped onto the pathway, I spotted the little girl. The trail serpentined another fifty yards before dead-ending at several park benches in the shade of a few towering elm and maple trees. I imagined bored-to-death parents loved the benches and the shade provided.

Charlotte was coasting down a plastic slide that appeared as though it'd been made by Fisher-Price. She caught sight of me and smiled. Actually, I think Charlotte's smile was reserved for Alice and Rex as the three of us cut across the field of grass. The seven-year-old was slim, had a thin face and wavy brown hair down past her shoulders. She wore pink leggings and a light blue V-neck T-shirt with long sleeves. I watched as she jogged across the sand—the slides and swings and crawl tubes and ramps and monkey bars were in a sea of sand; safety, you know—to an older woman in jeans and a red cardigan sweater. I took this older woman to be Charlotte's grandmother. There were no astonishing powers of deduction at play here—no insight worthy of Hercule Poirot—as Charlotte and her grandmother were the only two at the playground.

Until suddenly they weren't.

EIGHTEEN

There wasn't a speck of dust on Patrick's desk or shelves or windowsills or atop the bed's headboard. Other than keeping their son's room tidy, Crystal figured it looked exactly as it did when Patrick left the house that ill-fated June day to spend the afternoon with his best friend. Sure enough, there was a bat and baseball glove in one corner of his bedroom. Sure enough, there was a laptop on Patrick's desk with headphones, earbuds, and even a virtual reality headset sitting near the keyboard. Sure enough, a small bookshelf on the wall above his desk contained biographies on famed athletes—mostly baseball and football stars, one on an Olympic swimmer. The books were written at a middle schooler level, meaning G-rated, no shenanigans. Sure enough, a full-length mirror hung on Patrick's closet door—after all, what's a teenager without a nearby mirror? Sure enough, Patrick's walk-in closet was filled with button-down shirts and hoodies, a couple of trendy sweaters, jeans and cargo pants; tennis shoes, sneakers, and a pair of sport sandals littered the hardwood floor; and old board games and comic books were stacked on a half shelf.

And, sure enough, a pinboard containing pictures of Patrick and his family and friends was hung on the wall next to the room's only window.

Crystal leaned in close to examine the pictures.

"You the detective they said was stopping by?"

Startled, Crystal spun around. There, in the doorway, was Jennifer Shortridge. The woman was shrouded in baggy sweats; both her shirt and pants were gray. Her hair was a bird's nest of ash brown. Her eyes were puffy, her skin pale. She stood shoeless in ankle socks and looked as though she'd clawed her way out from a laundry bin.

"Yes," Crystal said and quickly introduced herself.

Mrs. Shortridge remained in the doorway. "You the one working Ricky's case?"

"Yes," Crystal said again. "I am one of many detectives working on Ricky's case."

The two locked eyes. Crystal chose not to walk over and force a handshake, thinking it better to give the grief-stricken woman her space. However, it wasn't lost on Crystal that Mrs. Shortridge had yet to enter her son's room. Crystal guessed it might be Mr. Shortridge who'd been keeping Patrick's room dust-free.

"Find my son's killer," the woman said finally, and with that she was gone; disappearing silently into the hallway, perhaps back to her room . . . perhaps back to her bed.

Crystal let out a breath and resumed looking at the images on Patrick's pinboard. The picture at the top of the board included his older brother. In fact, all three Shortridge siblings were in the photograph, wearing swimsuits and smiling at the camera. The photo was likely taken at the pool in their own backyard. Ricky looked younger than the image used for his missing person listing; perhaps it was taken the summer before he began junior high. And the youngest, Charlotte, looked all of four or possibly five, in her Little Mermaid bathing suit. The older son appeared to be in his late teens; perhaps it was the summer he'd graduated from high school.

The kids looked happy.

None of them had a clue what was heading their way.

Detective Claypool had filled Crystal in on what became of the older Shortridge boy. She shook her head and stepped away from the pinboard . . . so much sorrow for one family to overcome.

Suddenly, her phone buzzed. Crystal fished it out from her pocket. Cory? Not that much time had passed since their arrival and her brother understood the sensitive nature of what she was doing at the Shortridge residence.

Why would he be calling?

It wasn't like him.

NINETEEN

Past Days

"She's been fed." Olive's mother handed her Darlene as soon as Olive arrived at the apartment. Mrs. Cripps slipped on her jacket, as Tuesday was grocery night and she had a bus to catch. But before heading out she gave the toddler a light tap on the tip of her nose with a forefinger. "Who's my darling, huh? Who's my little darling?" she said. "Yes, you're my little darling, Darlene."

As soon as her mother departed, Olive set her daughter down in her playpen and went into the bathroom to wash the perspiration from a lengthy shift off her face. She glanced in the mirror and wondered—not for the first time—who it was that stared back at her. It certainly couldn't be Olive, as she was only seventeen years old.

The woman in the mirror looked thirty.

Or older.

When she was born, Darlene had been the spitting image of Lansing—the absolute spitting image. Olive's mother explained how it was natural for newborns to initially resemble their fathers; evidently, it kept cavemen from realizing the babies weren't theirs and tossing them off the cliff. Olive nodded along at her mother's explanation but reckoned it was an old wives' tale. Darlene's likeness toward her father did dissipate over time; however, Lansing's eyes stayed put.

And whenever Olive looked at her child, Lansing stared back at her.

Olive dropped out of school as soon as her pregnancy began to show. Then she worked as many hours as the Wexford Hotel would allow—only, management requested Olive clean rooms and mop floors, vacuum carpets and dust. The hotel did not want her on display in their dining room.

Too many questions may have arisen; too many tongues might wag.

Soon after Darlene was born Olive went back to the Wexford full time, doing whatever tasks were requested of her, but—praise the Lord—the hotel eventually allowed her to return to the dining room, back to waiting tables. Olive needed the tip money. Her mother now worked in the Wexford's kitchen from the break of dawn to the end of the lunch rush. Depending on their schedules, Olive would drop Darlene off with either the housewife in 302 or the one in 412 at nine thirty sharp so she could be at the Wexford by ten. Olive worked until seven most evenings, occasionally later if the hotel was holding an event. Her mother would return home after her shift and retrieve her *little darling* from the women in 302 or 412; however, as soon as Olive came through the door, all parental responsibilities fell on her shoulders until Darlene went down for the night.

And so it went—day after day, month after month.

With the additional money coming in, the trio was able to migrate from the efficiency apartment in the basement to a one-bedroom on the second floor. And though the apartment was next to the staircase, and though the walls were paper thin, it served as home.

Darlene cooed and babbled the day away but had yet to utter her first words. Olive suspected that when she did, it would be to address her grandmother as "Mama." And Olive couldn't blame her one bit. In fact, she was more than grateful her mother had stepped into the role. Lord knows one of them had to. Olive was cast more as the doting older sister or, if she were being completely honest—older sister would suffice.

Olive's mother spent her evenings smoking Lucky Strikes and reading the daily paper whereas Olive avoided cigarettes and stuck mainly to the entertainment section—movie or theater reviews, gossip columns, Hollywood news. On most days Olive was able to get her hands on a newspaper a hotel guest had read and discarded. Tonight was no exception. Tonight, she brought home a copy of the *Chicago Sun-Times* that a diner had abandoned at their table.

Olive wasn't sure how the story caught her eye. She never

thumbed through the announcement section; and, unless it was a movie star, Olive had zero interest regarding who in high society was marrying whom. However, this particular announcement was at the top of the page. In fact, it was the first one listed, and Olive imagined the surname leapt out at her.

Lansing was getting married.

> Mr. and Mrs. Victor Evans, the bride's parents, along with Lansing's mother and father, have the pleasure of announcing the marriage of their children, Patricia Anne and Lansing Thomas, on June 25th, 1949 at Holy Trinity Lutheran Church in Chicago, IL. Lansing graduated from the University of Chicago, where he met Patricia—the love of his life—and has recently begun work as a staff accountant at the accounting firm that bears his father's name.

The announcement went on to name his father's firm and concluded with "the couple looks forward to spending their honeymoon in Hawaii."

Olive read the wedding announcement and, though Darlene had begun to cry—a diaper change, no doubt—she ignored the clamor and read through the announcement three more times before setting the paper down. Olive wasn't sure how she felt or, quite frankly, if she felt anything at all. She'd not been torn asunder; there was no anger or resentment . . . and there was no heartbreak. Olive doubted there was anything left inside of her to break, much less her heart.

It was just more suffocation in a world of suffocation; such was Olive's lot in life. There was nothing else for her. Olive had accepted this *simple fact of life* after a particularly harrowing car ride she'd once been taken on to the outer limits of Joliet.

Yes . . . this was her lot in life.

But, in the back of Olive's mind, in the middle of the night when she couldn't find sleep, the thought would come to her in the darkness.

Perhaps it might have been best for all concerned, including her, had Olive opted for a stroll into the pine trees at Stump Acres.

TWENTY

Out of nowhere a man stepped onto the sand of the play area, heading straight toward Charlotte. He had to have emerged from behind one of the elms or maples. Grandma Shortridge caught sight of him first, looked perplexed, and then frightened. His attention lay on Charlotte, though, and I watched as she glanced his way, sensed something wicked, and shriveled against her grandmother's thigh in fear. The man picked up speed as he closed on their proximity.

What the hell?

As Grandma Shortridge's mouth dropped, I realized I'd stumbled onto an attack.

"Go," I said to Alice and Rex. The two dashed forward, ahead of me, toward the figures in the sand of the playground. *Go* wasn't *Sic*; my dogs wouldn't attack, but I needed them there ASAP to stop whatever this man had in mind. Then I shouted, "Charlotte!" and three heads swiveled my way.

I sprinted the remaining yards, coming to a halt in front of the Shortridges, blocking them from the mystery man. My dogs don't speak English but they're fluent in body language, especially when it comes to threatening behavior, and they sandwiched between me and this stranger who'd materialized out of a clear blue sky. I was glad they were between us, as mystery man had several inches on me. And he was brick-shithouse big. Though it was a hot day in late September, the man sported a dark hoodie, its hood up, cinched tightly. A Bears cap was pulled low over his brow. All I could see was a slice of lips and nose and eyes, none of which appeared friendly. He wore thin black gloves and his fists were clenched; his wrists thrust out from the sleeves of his sweatshirt as though two-by-fours from a lumber yard.

And his eyes burned with rage as he glared my way.

The man was not a happy camper.

"Who the fuck are you?" he said, low and guttural.

Thank God Alice and Rex were making their presence known, up close and personal, growling and glaring back at the man—the call of the wild with a jungle gym in the background. Without them, I figured I'd be on the sand, laid prone, nose shattered and wondering what had become of my teeth.

"I'm with the cops, pal," I said, wanting to be Bruce Willis, probably sounding more like Pee-wee Herman.

He flipped a glance at the asphalt trail and then back my way. "Bullshit you are."

I heard a scream. Charlotte. My head darted back. Another man, same Bears cap and dark hoodie, had snuck up from behind. He was three feet from the little girl, his hand stuck inside a pocket.

"Alice," I shouted. My bloodhound spun and leapt, landing between Charlotte and this second mystery man who'd appeared from nowhere. He jolted backward as Alice snarled and barked. Yes, she knew threats and body language and was ready to rip into him.

Rex growled and I faced forward. The first mystery man was a foot closer, his hand also inside a pocket, but Rex was putting on a hell of a show. Dogs look heavier than they are. Rex was forty-five pounds, looked ten heavier, and was set to throw down. The dirty little secret, though—Rex is more bark than bite. Alice was the one to do real damage. I knew she'd handle the second guy. But if my guy pulled whatever it was he had hidden in his hoodie pocket, Rex would tear after the guy's sleeve or pant leg. I'd throw myself into the mix and try to knock brick-shithouse to the ground.

I prayed to God the big man wouldn't call Rex's bluff.

He spoke again, still low, still guttural. "Take the dogs and walk away."

"Ain't happening," I said, still channeling Bruce Willis. "These are K-9s," I added. "Police dogs."

He glared at me. I glared at the hand he had stuck inside his hoodie.

"What's the plan?" Mystery man number two spoke for the first time, causing Alice to snarl louder.

"Don't bleed out," I said, stretching the truth. Alice and Rex weren't pit bulls bred to fight; they weren't even police dogs—neither of them would be going for throats.

Yes, Alice would do serious damage to mystery man number two. No matter what occurred, his day would be ruined. But I wasn't so sure how things would play out with me and Rex against mystery man number one.

There was further growling and glaring before the man facing me spoke a final time. "I'll be seeing you."

I said nothing. I was Bruce Willised out.

Then he turned and headed toward the asphalt trail leading up to the street. A second later his partner joined him.

"Get to the trees," I told Charlotte and her grandmother. Then I dodged toward the park benches, behind one of the larger elm trees, the dogs at my heels. My fear was the mystery men had firearms inside their coat pockets; that the two of them would regroup, turn back, and start shooting.

A minute passed as I caught my breath, my heart a lump in my throat. Finally, I peeked out from behind the tree. The two men were gone.

I'm sure everyone in the neighborhood heard me sigh with relief.

I looked toward the opposite end of the playing field, where Charlotte and her grandmother had fled. They remained concealed in the small patch of woods there. Good. Then it dawned on me—that had to be where mystery man number two was lying in wait.

None of this made any sense.

What the hell had I just walked into?

My iPhone was in my hand a second later. I brought up Crystal's phone number and stabbed at it with my forefinger.

After what I'd just been through at this Kenilworth playground, Applebee's was off the table.

I'd be holding out for The Cheesecake Factory.

TWENTY-ONE

"It was like out of a prison movie, Crys, where they're in the main yard and an inmate marches over to shiv another prisoner." I shook my head and continued. "It wasn't any kind of child-molester thing."

My sister's face was white; it had remained that hue since her arrival at the park a minute after I'd sent out my SOS. "I know—pedophiles don't work in tag teams. They don't grab kids while adults are standing right there in front of them. And they're not going to carry a kicking, screaming child back to wherever the hell they've parked their car and risk a dozen neighbors getting involved."

We had yet to leave the playground. A squad car was parked where the walking path curved up to the avenue's sidewalk. SVU Detective Claypool and a Kenilworth cop were at the park benches, in the shade, talking to Charlotte, who was seated next to her grandmother. Someone had provided the two of them with water bottles. Another Kenilworth officer was in the play area, looking at footprints in the sand. Paul Shortridge and his father hovered near the bench, eavesdropping on the discussion, hearing what had transpired. Alice and Rex fluttered about the small park, jogging to the tree line, then off to check on Charlotte and her grandmother, before zipping back to see what Crystal and I were up to.

"You can rule out any misunderstanding as well, Crys. There was no confusion; no wires were crossed." I swallowed hard. "They came here to kill Charlotte."

"But why kill a little girl?"

"I have no idea," I said. "Maybe someone paid them to." I felt like an idiot saying that out loud. Who on planet Earth was going to take out a hit on a second grader?

"So, Charlotte and her grandmother got here about ten minutes before you did." I nodded as Crystal pieced together the timeline. "These two men had to have knowledge of this playground, they had to know Charlotte came here, and they had to know she wasn't in school today."

"That's a scary thought."

"Yes, and it means they've been casing her house or following her around." Crystal glanced up to where the squad car was parked. "The men could have driven past, glanced down and, sure enough, Charlotte was here. They park their vehicle up the street and"—my sister looked around the play area—"one of them takes the pathway coming down from the opposite side of the park, from the opposite street, and he hides in the trees by the benches." Crystal then looked toward the patch of woods on the far side of the playground equipment. "The other one threads his way through those trees, works his way near where Charlotte is playing, and waits for a signal or hand gesture or text message from his partner."

I squinted against the afternoon sun. The woods where the second man had come from—where Charlotte and her grandmother had fled to in case of ensuing gunfire—weren't exactly a national forest or anything. The trees and undergrowth slanted up a slight ridge that quickly morphed into adjacent residences' backyards. "This is thought-through stuff, Crys. It's creepy shit. Following Charlotte around, knowing about this little park . . . setting up an ambush."

My sister nodded. "They had Charlotte and her grandmother surrounded, in kind of a pincer move," she said. "Until you showed up."

After I'd phoned Crystal, I jogged across the field and waved into the woods to let the two know the coast was clear, that the cavalry was on its way. Charlotte's grandmother then carried Charlotte from their hiding spot among the trees. The little girl was trembling, doing her best to stop crying. I admired the kid's determination as she did this silently. Charlotte stared at me for a long second before her eyes shot to Alice and Rex. After hasty introductions were made—I was reminded Charlotte's grandmother's name was Teresa—there came a cacophony of squealing tires and car doors. Suddenly, Crystal and Claypool were flying down the walkway, sprinting across the grass, heading in our direction. A moment later Paul Shortridge and his father came jogging down the hill, looks of dread smeared across their features. A minute later the squad car arrived.

The beasts hadn't jogged our way in a bit, so I glanced about and . . . there the two of them were, next to the park bench, Charlotte kneeling on the ground with an arm around Alice's neck while Rex licked at her fingertips.

Sure, now it was time for therapy dogs.

"Cory." Though we were too far away from the park benches to be heard, my sister whispered. I turned back and we locked eyes. "Someone is targeting the family."

I raised an eyebrow. "Not Charlotte, but the family?"

"It's the only thing that makes sense, right? First, her brother is killed and his body is hidden. The killers had to think Patrick wouldn't be found for decades."

I followed my sister's logic. "They want to hurt the family because the *unknowing* will eat away at them," I said. "It'd eat away at them forever."

"But Patrick's body was discovered. These men didn't get what they wanted—to make the Shortridges suffer the horror of a missing child—so they moved on to the next target," Crystal said. "They moved on to Charlotte."

"OK, but didn't the SVU detectives spend all summer looking into anyone who had a beef with the family?"

Crystal nodded. "They couldn't find anyone with a motive to hurt Patrick and suspected it was a random perpetrator or stalker, but considering what happened today—this family is being targeted." Crystal thought for a second. "There's something else you should know, Cor. It wasn't in the news out of respect for the Shortridges," she said. "They had an older son, but he took his life two years ago."

I was stunned. "He did?"

Crystal nodded again.

"You're thinking he—"

"Shh," Crystal cut me off and peeked down the pathway.

The police had, evidently, finished questioning Charlotte and were now busy talking with her grandmother, likely asking more somber questions. Charlotte headed our way, with Alice and Rex trailing in her wake. Up close I noticed how her pink leggings had light red hearts on the knees. Not exactly something I'd be able to pull off, but they looked awfully cute on her. I also noticed her blue eyes and freckled nose.

As she approached, I knelt down to greet her at eye level. "Hey, Charlotte," I said.

"Hey."

"Did I tell you this was my sister?"

She looked up at Crystal and shook her head.

"Yeah, Crystal is my older sister and she's a police detective."

Charlotte then said, "How much older are you than Cory?"

"Six and a half years," Crystal replied. "I babysat Cory when he was your age."

"You did?"

"Oh, yes. Cory needed a babysitter like no one you've ever seen."

I sighed and left it at that.

"I had older brothers," Charlotte said. "But I don't anymore."

My sister joined us at eye level. "I know, honey. I am so sorry to hear about that. They sounded like great brothers."

Fresh tears began to flow and I thanked God Crystal was here. This is the part where I start to bumble and fumble and mumble as I gauge how quickly I can make it out the exit door and to my truck. I felt my pulse quicken as Charlotte turned her attention back my way.

"My grandma said I should thank you."

"Don't give it another thought," I replied. "Glad to help."

Charlotte's voice caught. "I was so frightened when those men showed up."

"We all were."

"Alice and Rex weren't."

I looked at the two hams as they circled about us. "Well—Alice and Rex are pretty special," I said. "They're hero dogs."

She glanced at the beasts and then back my way. "Hero dogs?"

"Well, most of the time," I said. "But not when they make

me take them out in the middle of the night to do their business."

Suddenly, there was a grin among the tears. Her voice shook again. "Can I give you a hug?"

"Of course you can," I replied. Charlotte wrapped her arms around my shoulders and gave me a squeeze. Not used to this, I patted her on the back, awkward-like, and glanced at my sister. Crystal smiled and looked away. Thoughts of saying stupid things or bolting for my pickup melted along the wayside as I hugged Charlotte back.

What's that Chinese proverb? Something about if you save someone's life, then you're responsible for them forever. I don't know if it was that or if, Grinch-like, my heart grew three sizes, but I knew one thing for damned sure.

Nobody was going to hurt this little girl.

No one.

"I love Alice," she said as I slowly stood up. "Rex, too."

"I do too, Charlotte," I said. "I do too."

TWENTY-TWO

Past Days

Though seated inside, on a cushioned bench in an otherwise sterile corridor, Olive still wore her winter jacket. In fact, it remained zipped to her neckline. When she'd flown out of O'Hare, Chicago had been blustery, dusted in snow, not an atypical February morning. When she'd touched down at the San Francisco International Airport, the pilot mentioned it was currently fifty-seven degrees outside with a high of sixty-one expected later in the afternoon. But Olive's mind was far from caring about her winter attire or California's milder climate.

No, Olive's mind was on what awaited her on the other side of the doorway across the bench from where she sat.

Olive had taken a cab from San Francisco International straight to the coroner's office.

"Miss Cripps," Detective Martel said gently. The detective was one of the tallest men Olive had ever met in person. He'd towered above her as they walked down the hallway. Currently, he held open one of the steel doors leading into the morgue's interior. "The medical examiner is ready for you."

Once inside, the detective led Olive down a short set of concrete steps onto the morgue's main floor and then over to an examination table on the far side of the room. Across the table stood the ME, an older man dressed in surgical scrubs. He had kind eyes and gave Olive a somber nod before he lifted the sheet shrouding the face of the deceased.

Olive's rasping sob served as her response in the affirmative. Detective Martel held onto her arm in case Olive fainted or slid to the floor.

And though she'd not seen her daughter in well over two years, it was her.

It was Darlene.

PART THREE

The Death in the Dorm

A bone to the dog is not charity. Charity is the bone shared with the dog, when you are just as hungry as the dog.

—Jack London

TWENTY-THREE

The older brother's name was Reed Shortridge. He'd been a tremendous athlete in high school—a star swimmer—who met the qualifying times at Sectionals in the fifty, hundred, and two-hundred-yard freestyle events in order to advance to the State Final in both his junior and senior years. Though he hadn't placed in either State Championship, Reed scored a partial scholarship to compete on the swim team at the University of Illinois Chicago—Go Flames. Halfway through the season reality sunk in that, unlike at high school, Reed was not Poseidon of the pool at UIC. In fact, the competition was next level fierce, and Reed quietly quit the team in early January.

Financially, it didn't matter as his parents had enough money to float the full tuition . . . and then some.

Crystal sat at the kitchen table, sipping bottled water, her half-eaten bowl of split pea soup pushed to the side, a distant memory. It was nearly midnight. Cory had hung in with her, pretending to highlight sections in a textbook, until an hour ago when he had tossed in the towel, let Alice and Rex out for their final sniff and pee, and headed downstairs, presumably to hit the hay.

Crystal wondered, after what happened at the playground in Kenilworth, if her brother would be catching any Zs tonight.

Crystal wondered if she would be.

Even after the adrenaline had worn off, Cory remained one part cocky to two parts frazzled on the drive home from Kenilworth. Unfortunately, the frazzled shares served to drown out his self-assurance as the evening wore on. Even her pinky promise of treating him to dinner at The Cheesecake Factory come Saturday night didn't do too much to deaden his apprehension.

"The guy said he'd *be seeing* me," Cory had told Crystal

when she'd stepped outside the Shortridge residence to check on him. Even though the Kenilworth PD squad car remained parked in the driveway, Cory and Alice and Rex had spent the time since the *incident* pacing back and forth across the family's front lawn as though they were on sentry duty. Crystal and Detective Claypool finished working the phone lines; arrangements had been made to get the Shortridges into a three-bedroom, split-level safe house in Park Forest.

"He was angry you got in his way," she'd replied. "If I wanted to hurt Person A and Person B kept me from doing so—I'd be fuming, too, but I wouldn't add Person B to my list."

"He seemed really pissed off."

"You have that effect on people, Cor. I've been pissed off at you plenty of times, yet I've opted to let you live."

Crystal took another sip of water and returned to the folder in front of her; the folder she'd received from Detective Claypool. It contained information stemming from the University of Illinois Chicago Police Department's investigation into Reed Shortridge's death. Claypool had obtained this material from UICPD as, during the initial stage of her inquiry into Patrick Shortridge's disappearance, the SVU detective had to determine if some flavor of domestic abuse may have caused Reed's depression or sense of hopelessness, and if similar mistreatment at home might have led Brother Patrick to run away. Claypool struck out on the abuse angle—close friends of both Reed and Patrick said, outside of the occasional family spat, the two boys got along well with their parents. And there were none of the telltale signs of child abuse—no sudden changes in their behavior, no withdrawal from friendships, no unexplained bruises or broken bones, and, clearly, no malnourishment.

After today's event, though, Detective Claypool had passed the report on to Crystal.

Investigators inside UICPD concluded that Reed Shortridge's death had indeed been a suicide. The Cook County Medical Examiner's Office also ruled the cause of death as suicide and recorded that decision on the young man's death certificate. It appeared to be an open-and-shut case, as Reed had hanged himself from inside his locked dorm room—as such, no autopsy was required to determine cause of death—and a suicide note had been left on the scene. His dorm room was in Commons North, on the east side of campus, close to both lecture halls and the Student Recreation Center.

Reed had been nineteen years old at the time of his death. He had been found deceased in his dorm room when his roommate returned to the university on a Sunday afternoon after spending the weekend at his parent's home in Madison, Wisconsin. Reed Shortridge had used a short strip of rope to hang himself; a simple slipknot secured around his neck with the other end wedged between a closed closet door and the upper door frame. Reed's twin bed had been pulled several inches away from the wall for its use as a makeshift stool from which to take his final step. It was not unlike how a famed comedic actor had checked out some years earlier. Reed's roommate had unlocked the door to discover his classmate twisting slowly, some kind of perverse piñata—his neck stretched, his eyes bulging, his lips bloated.

Detective Claypool's folder included a photocopy of Reed's suicide note, which had been found in the output tray of Reed's HP DeskJet printer. The note was short and sweet.

> Dear Mom and Dad,
>
> This is not your fault.
>
> Everything has spiraled away from me and I can no longer pretend.
>
> I love you two (and Patrick and Charlotte) with all my heart.
>
> Reed

On the dorm room floor lay Reed's yearbook from his senior year of high school, opened to a full-length picture of himself in his swimsuit at an afterschool practice; smiling and looking vibrant, full of life, with a twinkle in his eye.

Better days.

Six empty beer cans lay in a half arc around Reed's high school yearbook.

Crystal knew the stats, how suicide was the third leading

cause of death among people between the ages of fifteen and twenty-four. She understood how an overriding sense of futility and disappointment, rejection, and heartbreak could take a toll on the very young, and that undiagnosed mental health issues at such an age certainly didn't help the situation. UICPD's report touched on how Reed had broken up with his girlfriend a month earlier, shortly after Valentine's Day.

Per body temperature, the ME placed Reed's time of death between eight o'clock and eleven Saturday night. UICPD interviewed two freshman males who had been in Reed's wing in the Commons North dormitory during that time frame, but nothing had come from their input. One freshman had been ill and, with the aid of NyQuil, was comatose by nine p.m. The other student mentioned some girls had stopped by but, alas, they were looking for his roommate, who wasn't there at the time. He'd also chatted with some fellow male students in the elevator atrium as he headed out for a late-evening party.

UICPD also talked with the resident adviser on shift that night. It had been an uneventful shift for the RA—*quite pleasant for a Saturday night*, he'd informed them, as there were no noise complaints or whiffs of cannabis he had to deal with and no other dorm rules for him to enforce. More significantly, he'd not heard or seen anything suspicious as he made his nightly rounds through Reed Shortridge's wing of the dormitory.

Crystal leaned back in her chair and finished what remained in the water bottle. Then she underlined the name of Reed's girlfriend, as well as the name of the freshman who had not been comatose on the night of Reed's death.

TWENTY-FOUR

Paul Shortridge sighed. "We've been over this," he said. "We spent all summer going over this."

"I apologize," Crystal said. "Detective Lahlum and I are doing our best to get up to speed. We've read through Detective Claypool's notes on the investigation, but we'd appreciate if you could provide a *Reader's Digest* condensed version."

Paul slowly nodded. "OK," he began. "First, I was a financial analyst at Northern Trust for the bulk of my career, nearly twenty years. While there, I created financial models; I ran risk assessments—pretty much behind-the-scenes market analysis stuff, you know, the ho-hum grind," he said. "I did not defraud investors. I did not Ponzi scheme the elderly in nursing homes. At NTRS, they have policies and procedures in effect, so, quite frankly, I couldn't rip anyone off even if I wanted to."

Crystal felt Shortridge no longer possessed that thousand-yard stare. Perhaps, after yesterday's occurrence at the playground, the man had it reeled back to half that distance.

Paul continued his curriculum vitae. "Then, for the past four years I've been self-employed. I work from home, in my PJs, where I manage the family's portfolio"—he glanced at his parents—"and I've only pondered bilking Mom and Dad on a handful of occasions."

Paul Shortridge, his parents, and, in a rare appearance, his wife, all sat on one couch in the living room of the Park Forest safe house. Across the glass coffee table from them, on a matching love seat, sat Crystal and Mark Lahlum. SVU Detective Claypool sat in a wingback chair, her head pivoting back and forth between the sofas based on who was speaking. Even though a patrol car passed by the safe house on the hour, every hour, Claypool had stayed overnight, sleeping on the sofa. The detective looked as though every minute of it had been spent tossing and turning.

Cory and Alice and Rex were in the backyard with Charlotte. Crystal hoped her brother was doing OK, as she knew how awkward and gawky he could get in certain situations. She also knew her brother had bonded with the little girl; how he identified with the poor kid's sense of loss. Cory was familiar with loss, on a first-name basis, stretching back to the night their parents went out for a dinner date and never returned. Crystal hoped things were going well in the backyard.

Fortunately, the pups were there to soak up any tears.

Detective Lahlum cleared his throat and the Shortridges turned his way. "Detective Pratt and I recently arrested a middle-aged man who had been stalking his college girlfriend," he said. Crystal was glad her partner was sensitive enough to leave off the part regarding what the man had done to his ex-girlfriend's husband. Lahlum continued. "Were either of you involved in any previous relationships that may have ended on a sour note?"

Paul sat quietly but shook his head.

"No old paramours harboring any grudges or anger, perhaps resentful over how things turned out?"

It was then Jennifer Shortridge spoke for the first time. "Paul and I began dating halfway through our senior year at Northwestern. I'd recently broken up with my boyfriend. He was another student at the university, and he was not happy about it. Some choice words were left on my answering machine." Mrs. Shortridge was no longer the haggard woman hovering in the doorway to her son's room Crystal had met yesterday. Her hair was combed, her eyes were sharp, and she now wore makeup. Crystal figured she'd snapped out of her stupor the instant she heard her daughter had nearly been assaulted. Her internal mama bear had awakened and Crystal hoped it would stick. "But," Jennifer glanced at Detective Claypool, and said, "Lynne tracked him down and told us he got his bioengineering degree, but eventually tossed that aside and now owns an A&W in northern Minnesota that he runs with his family." Jennifer addressed Claypool directly. "You said he was working there the day Ricky went missing." She placed a hand on her husband's knee. "Paul and I—well, you know how people are—checked him out on Facebook. He doesn't have a page but we hunted down his wife's account. Lots of pictures. She looks like Angelina Jolie, so I doubt he's spent much time pining over me."

Paul and Jennifer Shortridge were in a dilemma. After the incident at the playground, they planned on skipping town; perhaps an extended vacation in the Florida Keys was in the cards. But today they had changed their mind and Crystal figured it had been a result of Jennifer's input. The family was going to stay in the safe house, at least in the short term, and pray like hell CPD was able to find out who'd been targeting their family. The Shortridges wanted to be around in case the detectives needed their help or answers to any questions.

As such, Crystal began today's meeting by stressing to all members of the Shortridge clan not to provide the Park Forest address to anybody—not to friends or neighbors, not to the extended family, not to any old colleagues . . . not to anyone.

Detective Lahlum then turned to face the grandparents and James Shortridge took the hint. "I've been retired for eight years. I play golf most days at the club. Sometimes I'll stop by the liquor store if we're having friends over." Grandpa Shortridge looked from his wife to Detective Lahlum. "No one I dated an eternity ago would be involved in targeting the family. That's ridiculous, on its face." He chuckled. "They're all retired now, or in nursing homes, or pushing up daisies."

His wife cleared her throat. "It's not a laughing matter."

"For Christ's sake—I know it's not a laughing matter, Teresa," James said, a little louder than he may have intended. Then he shook his head. "I'm sorry. It's been . . . very stressful."

Teresa stared across the room, as though focused on a spot on the far wall, before she spoke again. "I agree with my husband. First off, we've lived in Arizona for most of the past decade, not up here. And I've a meek existence. I scrapbooked for years until I got bored with that. Now I alternate my time between yoga and two book clubs. Outside of my mother, from years ago, I can't think of anyone I've angered. And Mom and I forgave each other long before she passed away." Her gaze turned back to the detectives on the love seat. "There's no one

I've wronged, or who would be obsessed with me at such a level, or at any level, quite frankly, that they'd target my grandchildren," she said. "And I've never seen either of those men from the park before in my life."

There was a moment of silence before her husband filled it. "I'm certain you've run all of us through whatever systems you run people through to see if they've got a criminal record, so you're aware none of us do." James shook his head again. "I've got nothing for you. If I did anything to antagonize someone twenty or thirty years ago, why would they wait until now? Huh? That makes no sense. And why go after our grandkids?" He shrugged and threw a hand in the air. "There were rumors my grandfather worked for Al Capone," he said, "so maybe bootleggers are involved."

Lahlum lit up. "Is that true about your grandfather?" Crystal knew her partner was a history buff, especially when it came to old-time Chicago and its storied mobsters.

"The rumors are true, but it's all BS. The years don't make sense, as Capone went to prison in the early thirties." James then commented, "I'm sure someone in the family said something a long time ago that was meant to be a joke and we've run with it ever since."

"What did your grandfather do?"

"Lionel was a tax accountant; hell—he would have kept Al Capone out of jail."

"Did you know him?"

"Not really. He passed away in the early sixties," James said. "I remember a stern-looking old man. To be honest, he kind of frightened me."

TWENTY-FIVE

"Can we marry them?"

I chuckled but noticed Charlotte's eyes were wide. She was serious. "You want to marry Alice and Rex?"

"It's obvious they love each other."

"Hmm—I'm not so certain," I said. "Sure, the two of them get along real well . . . but love?"

Charlotte and I snuck a couple cans of lemonade from the refrigerator and the four of us trotted outside, into the safe house's backyard, leaving the adults to speak of adult things. The house's deck was minimalistic; it might seat a family of four if you counted Mom and Dad's laps as patio furniture. It was also ground level; a single step got you down onto the lawn. The yard was enclosed via a chain-link fence, the perfect arena for Frisbee fetch. After explaining the ins and outs of the game—it took me all of three seconds—I'd surrendered the Frisbee to Charlotte. She then spent ten minutes flipping the disk, alternating between Alice and Rex, before she paused, slowly turned my way, and embarked on this crazed notion of canine matrimony.

"But not everyone loves everyone a hundred percent of the time," Charlotte replied. Then she whispered, "Sometimes, when I can't sleep at night, I hear my parents arguing."

I wasn't sure how to respond so I went the clichéd route. "I'm sorry to hear that."

"It's been happening more and more since my brother disappeared last summer." Her voice shook. "And now that he's . . ."

She didn't finish her thought, and I said, "I can't imagine how hard it's been on them, Charlotte—how hard it's been on all of you."

She swallowed hard and nodded. "You can call me Char," she said. "My friends all do."

"Well, it would be a great honor to be considered one of your friends, Char." I took a sip of lemonade and we stared at our feet for a few tongue-tied moments before I added, "I think I know what you're going to be when you grow up."

"What?"

"You're going to be a wedding planner."

"A doggie wedding planner," Charlotte said, and we both chuckled.

It was good to hear her laugh. The poor kid needed some kind of release after the emotional carnage of the past few months as well as after yesterday's attack. She'd paid an impossible toll at such a young age. Heartbreaking. I was on the cusp of seventeen when my parents died. Charlotte is only seven. She just started second grade last month.

Anyway—long story short—that is how Alice and Rex found themselves betrothed.

It was a whirlwind affair; the marriage hastily planned. The couple had no time to send out invitations, to chase down a photographer—literally—or to find a caterer, or to buy a wedding cake. That was fine by me, though—I wouldn't know where to hunt down Alice and Rex's parents in order to carve up the bill.

The wedding itself was left to Charlotte and, somehow, she managed to shepherd the three of us to our appropriate spots. The ceremony was held where the deck met the yard. She had me facing the deck—facing the three of them—with my hands enclosed around the Frisbee as though it were the King James Bible. Charlotte then stood between my bloodhound and springer spaniel as the two sat on the grass and stared up at me, quizzically, no doubt wondering what the hell I was up to now. Charlotte was the maid of honor, best man, and flower girl all rolled into one. She stood with a palm resting lightly on the back of Alice and Rex's necks, likely to keep the two from bolting for the hills.

I began by speaking briefly about the power of sniffing out love in this crazy world of ours, as well as the magic of sharing doggie treats. Charlotte then interjected about how the two should never go to bed angry and never *raise a growl* against one another. When I asked if anyone present knew of any reason that the two should not be joined in holy matrimony and said that they should speak now or forever hold their peace, a squirrel scampered across the yard and ran up a tree. This caused Charlotte and me to break out laughing and Rex to stand until I told him to settle.

Then, I brought the ceremony to a conclusion. "By the power vested in me as a canine handler and dog trainer in the great state of Illinois, in the presence of God and the witness of friends and family," I said as I nodded at Charlotte, "it is my great privilege to pronounce Rex and Alice husband and wife." Please don't let anyone know, but I was having a blast, certainly more than anticipated. "Rex," I said, "you may now kiss the bride."

Rex awaited his nuptial kiss, but Alice stepped toward me and nudged the Frisbee with a wet nose.

"I think she wants it annulled."

"What?"

I glanced at Charlotte. "Nothing," I said. "Hey, do you think we can get some more lemonade?"

TWENTY-SIX

Past Days

"Here's where it gets a little sticky," Detective Martel said. They sat in a small conference room on the second floor of the coroner's office, pretending to drink bad vending-machine coffee. "Darlene told the woman in the next-door unit that her name was either Denise Anderson or Denise Henderson. The neighbor's forgotten the surname she was told as she took to calling her Denise. The name on the lease, though—a six-month lease—has Darlene listed as Karen Henderson, but"—the detective looked down at the open file on the table in front of him—"it's not the kind of neighborhood where landlords ask many questions or require any answers. Plus, the landlord told us Darlene never caused any problems, and that the rent was always paid, in cash, on the first of each and every month."

Olive listened to Martel who, even seated, towered above her. She nodded in all the appropriate spots and answered with a simple *yes* or *no* whenever questions were directed her way, but Olive's mind had taken flight—it was far away from the here and now. Olive's mind was on her mother, and how she had been the glue that held everything together. Even before Darlene was born, going back to when Olive's father had died, it had been her mother that kept the family together.

Olive recalled breaking down; sobbing as she told her mother she was pregnant, and the man she thought was going to stand by her side was now running as fast and as far away in the opposite direction as humanly possible. She even provided her mom with an abridged version of the threats that had been made.

In response, her mother wrapped Olive in her arms; she embraced her and told Olive it would be OK; that she'd be there for her every step of the way.

Yes, her mother had been the glue that held the world together.

And when her mother died of lung cancer in late November of 1963—literally the day after the president had been shot and killed in Texas—the glue curdled into weak paste. It no longer held, and what remained of the family split apart . . . and, in less than two years, the world came crashing down.

"Admit it—you never wanted me," Darlene said. "You resent the hell out of me because of him . . . and you always have."

"That's not true," Olive protested. "You're my daughter."

Darlene scoffed.

"If I didn't want you, I could have had—" Olive didn't complete the thought. She didn't have to.

Darlene stared at her a long minute, then went into her bedroom and shut the door.

"The neighbors saw a man coming and going from the residence and believed he was either Darlene's husband or boyfriend. He kept to himself; he never spoke with anyone. And Darlene never brought him up in conversations with the woman in the next-door unit, but they were mostly just nod-and-say-hi friends." The detective shook his head and continued. "This town is harsh on young women. I have two daughters of my own and it breaks my heart. I've lived in San Francisco my entire life and it's not the place it was when I grew up. There's this widespread use of drugs now; it's endemic—it's washed over the city," he said. "Cannabis and peyote and psychedelic crap like LSD are commonplace, and we have more than our share of the harsher stuff—cocaine and amphetamines and barbiturates. I don't know if there's a way to turn back the tide." Martel shook his head a second time. "It pains me to tell you this"—he paused a moment—"but your daughter died of a heroin overdose."

Olive's eyes glistened. Like their coffee, a box of Kleenex sat untouched on the tabletop. She continued to nod as the detective spoke. She knew Martel meant well, she knew his heart was in the right place, but Olive hoped to God the detective would wrap this meeting up so she could flee from the facility that housed her daughter's remains.

Olive wondered if the Golden Gate Bridge had a walkway for pedestrians.

She imagined it did.

> Olive,
>
> We can't go on like this. I'm almost seventeen, older now than you were when you had me. I've got the money Gramma left for me and I'll finish high school when I find a place to settle. Please do not go to the police or come looking for me as we both know this is for the best.
>
> Darlene

Olive held onto the note her daughter had left on the kitchen table for her to find; it was in her purse right now. She should have run to the police. She should have gone searching for Darlene. She should have screamed her daughter's name from the mountaintops.

Instead . . . Olive felt an overwhelming sense of relief.

Olive would never be able to take that back, nor would she ever be able to shake the image of Darlene, lying there, motionless, on the examination table. She had not only betrayed her daughter; she'd betrayed her mother . . . and her father's memory.

Olive had betrayed all of them.

Identifying Darlene's bloodless face on the mortuary table was the final nail in the coffin, and once Martel wrapped up whatever else he felt the need to tell her, Olive would take the nearest cab to the Golden Gate Bridge and find out for herself if there was a pedestrian walkway or not. It would not be Stump Acres—she was past the need for symbolism at this point—but it would have to suffice.

"We found birthday cards and notes and letters in a box under your daughter's bed," the detective said, glancing again at the folder in front of him. "Most were from Darlene's grandmother. This is how we tracked you down. There was a postcard your mother sent your daughter from Yellowstone National Park some years back that had your address on it." He looked up. "Your mother must have vacationed in Yellowstone and sent her the card."

Olive cleared her throat, hoping her voice wouldn't fail her. "My father always wanted to go there, but he died before the two of them could make the trip. My mother took a tour bus there to honor his memory." Olive finally reached for a tissue and added, "It was the only vacation my mother ever took."

It was the detective's turn to nod. "I've never been there myself," he replied, "but I hear it's beautiful." He nudged his coffee cup with a forefinger. "Miss Cripps—once we knew Darlene's real name, we found out she had a record. Nothing major—she was picked up twice for vagrancy, once for possession, and another time for . . . well, for something else we don't need to talk about."

Olive knew exactly what the detective meant by *something else*. He meant Darlene selling her body. Olive wanted to scream at the top of her lungs. She wanted to throw her cup of coffee against the wall. She wanted to smash her fists through the conference room's window.

Olive wanted to die.

The meeting couldn't end soon enough. Darlene's brief life had been nothing short of tragic . . . and Olive was to blame. A mother's singular responsibility in life is to keep her children safe. Olive failed at that obligation every step of the way. Olive had not only been an absentee mother to Darlene all those years; she'd been an unspeakable one—she'd been horrid and vile.

Olive hung her head in shame and sadness.

Martel leaned back in his chair. "Like I said, this town chews girls up and spits them out. It's not the place I grew up in at all." He then went on to explain. "We suspect the man who came and went from your daughter's apartment to be a drug dealer. It makes sense considering the rent being paid in cash every month, as well as with the heroin that was involved."

If Olive were able to form words, she'd query Martel about bridges and walkways. Of course, the man was a detective; he'd connect the dots and try to stop her.

"I know this won't provide any comfort," he continued, "but we tracked down a treatment center Darlene had been active with. She attended meetings there throughout much of last year. Clearly, Miss Cripps, your daughter was trying to turn her life around—which is honorable for someone as young as nineteen. Unfortunately, heroin steals everything from you. It's opium—very potent, extremely addictive. It takes control of your life. And if a person relapses, their system may not be strong enough to tolerate a fix." Martel looked at her with moist eyes. "We do not believe your daughter's death was intentional. Your daughter's death was not a suicide, you know, for obvious reasons."

Olive didn't know what Detective Martel meant by *obvious reasons*. It didn't matter, though, nothing mattered anymore—and she'd come to the disheartening conclusion this meeting was never going to end.

"The drug dealer—the unidentified male seen coming and going from your daughter's apartment—is likely the man who called nine-one-one. I suspect he knew Darlene had OD'd; that she was dead, as he was long gone by the time the squad cars and ambulance arrived at the scene. He likely supplied Darlene with the dope, the bad fix, and knew he would be arrested on the spot." Martel then added, "I assume the only reason he hung around long enough to make the phone call, as opposed to leaving it to neighbors or the landlord to find the body, was because of the baby."

Olive lifted her head.

Suddenly, she was on high alert.

Darlene had a baby?

TWENTY-SEVEN

"I've never seen her that livid."

This time the twins sat in a dive bar in Rogers Park, one of the northernmost communities along the shore of Lake Michigan. They sat in a dark corner, drinking cheap beer, keeping their voices low and minding their own business. It was the first time they'd been there; another joint Garrick had heard of and suggested they try.

Wade agreed with his brother. "She was livid," he said and then shook his head. "We should have gone for it at the park . . . and then it'd be over."

"That fucking werewolf was amped to chew my face off," Garrick said. "You had that little-bitty terrier."

"It wasn't a terrier and it wasn't that little."

"Do you think she's right, though?" Garrick asked. "What she went on about?"

"You mean all that Nietzsche crap about *gazing into the abyss?*"

Garrick set his empty glass down on the table. "Yeah."

"I don't give two shits if the abyss gazes back into me. And we're not monsters, not even close." Wade shrugged. "I just want to finish what we started and get on with my life."

"How do you propose we accomplish that? I'm sure the cops have them in hiding somewhere."

"I imagine they do." Wade held up two fingers at a passing waitress; another round. "But we know someone who might know where they're at."

"Who?"

"The dog boy. And we know all about him—he's the same prick from the grade school that made us move things along."

Garrick frowned. "I'd just as soon not see the werewolf again."

"He got the jump on us," Wade said. "This time we'll be prepared. We'll get the jump on him."

His brother nodded slowly, grudgingly. "OK," he said. "Fuck the abyss."

"That's the guy I grew up with."

The two sat quietly as the waitress set down two tap beers, picked up their empty glasses, and then worked her way back to the bar.

Garrick returned to his original concern. "When she hears about the girl, she's not going to forgive us," he said. "There'll be hell to pay." He caught his brother's eye. "She said she'd go to the police if we didn't stop."

"It's an empty threat to scare us, to get us to back off. She hasn't gone to them yet and, at this point, she'd be considered an accessory. Plus," Wade said as he reached for his glass, "do you honestly believe Mom would send her boys to prison?"

TWENTY-EIGHT

Crystal was at her desk when the phone rang. She glanced down at her iPhone before realizing it was coming from her lesser-utilized landline. She picked it up and said, "Detective Pratt here."

"Hi, um, this is Jake Benson," a voice replied. "Are you the officer who's been calling me?"

"Yes," Crystal said. She'd initially contacted the University of Illinois Chicago student using her work phone, so he'd see CPD on the caller ID and not think he was being pranked by a classmate. "I was hoping to talk to you."

"It's not about the parking tickets, is it?"

"Parking tickets?" Crystal said, confused.

"Having a car on campus is hard enough without getting these stupid tickets every other week because I parked two inches away from the curb instead of one, or whatever," Benson said. "I haven't paid the last couple because I'm going to contest them in traffic court. I even took some pictures with my phone."

"I'm not calling about parking tickets," Crystal assured him.

"Good. Tuition's high enough without this BS tacked on."

Crystal smiled to herself and then dove in. "There was an incident that occurred in your dormitory during freshman year."

There was no hesitation on Benson's part. "Reed Shortridge."

"Yes. You were questioned at the time, but I have a few follow-ups I'd like to ask."

"Does this have to do with what's in the news? You know, about his younger brother?"

"Tangentially," Crystal said. She needed to handle this delicately. "I was going through UICPD's investigation into Reed Shortridge's suicide. UICPD were the officers that interviewed you."

Benson cut to the chase. "Was Reed's death not a suicide?"

"There's nothing to indicate that." *Not yet*, Crystal thought to herself. "And I apologize for any miscommunication. This is of a sensitive nature, as I'm sure you understand."

"I understand."

"There's a family involved, and I'd appreciate if you kept this call between the two of us. Any rumors or gossip at this point could open wounds."

Benson said, "One hundred percent."

"Good," Crystal replied. "Now, I've got your interview in front of me, Jake, but could you walk me through what you remember from that evening in the dorm?"

"You realize that was over two years ago, right?"

"Yes, but I'd appreciate anything you can remember."

"OK, I was stuck in good old Commons North that night, instead of having a life, because I tossed a load of laundry in the washer that afternoon and forgot about it. When I finally went down to check, some asshole had dumped all my wet stuff in the sink," he said. "So I was hanging around and waiting for my clothes to dry before I could head out."

"Then what happened?" Crystal said, prodding him along.

"I took the elevator down every ten minutes to see if my stuff was dry. There was a shirt I wanted to wear. So I passed Steve Dorsch a couple of times. Steve was the RA on duty that night. He was in that little office they have. You guys talked to him, as he did that walk-around thing they do every hour, or whenever."

"Yeah, Steve got interviewed."

"That's pretty much it," Benson said. "When my clothes got dry, I tossed on the shirt and headed out to a house party."

Crystal scanned the lines she'd underlined in the UIC student's interview. "You mentioned you bumped into some other people in the dorm."

"Um, yeah," he said. "A couple of girls stopped by looking for my roommate. I told them where he went, which was the same party I planned on going to. And they took off to find him."

"Did you know them?"

"I knew the one asking, as she was friends with my

roommate. They wound up dating but it didn't work out too well, and now they aren't friends anymore."

"That happens sometimes," Crystal said. "Did you see anyone else?"

"Hmm," Benson replied. "Hey, if you've got the report in front of you, can you drop me a hint?"

"You mentioned seeing some guys in the elevator."

"Oh, yeah, that's right."

"Do you remember anything about them?"

"Yeah—they were all decked out in UIC Flames hoodies and baseball caps," he answered. "A lot of school spirit."

"You didn't know them?"

"No, but it's a big school," Benson said. "A big dorm, too. I remember the two guys looked alike."

"What do you mean?"

"From what I could tell from their faces, they could have been brothers."

Crystal thought of the two men who'd accosted Cory at the Kenilworth playground. "Do you remember how big they were?"

"Oh, they were definitely big guys. Taller than me, too."

"Over six feet tall?"

"Yup, over six. I'm five nine and they were a chunk taller."

"Were they big as in muscular-big or obese-big?"

"They were muscular-big. If UIC had a football team, I'd have asked if they were on it."

"So football player-big, huh?"

"Well, not offensive line- or offensive tackle-big, but big enough."

"Did you speak to them?"

"I think we all said 'Hi.' I looked at their hoodies and caps and said, 'Go Flames' and they smiled and nodded. They seemed like nice enough guys. Then the elevator door opened and that was that."

"Had you ever seen them before?"

"I don't remember. It was so brief."

"Were they your age?"

"I assumed so because they were in the dorm, but I only saw a bit of their faces on account of the hats and hoodies."

“But you didn’t recognize them from Commons North?”

“No, but UIC has about ten residence halls. And I’ve been in most of them looking for friends or a party or for something to do.”

Crystal scribbled in her notepad and said, “Just one last question, Jake. Did you know Reed Shortridge?”

“Not really. I mean, I knew him from being on the same floor at Commons and seeing him in the cafeteria.” Benson cleared his throat before he spoke again. “And at parties. I saw him at some of the parties I went to. He always seemed to be having a fun time, which is why I was shocked to hear he took his own life.”

TWENTY-NINE

"What are you talking about?" I protested. "An all-meat pizza is a *specialty pizza.* It holds a very special place in my heart."

Despite her aired grievances, my sister slid two slices of my favorite pizza onto her plate; she wasn't crazy. "Next time," Crystal said, "could you pick up that artichoke one for me?"

"OK," I replied, grudgingly. I shook a blizzard of crushed red peppers onto my jumbo slice, grabbed a Rolling Rock from the fridge, and joined her at the kitchen table. "So, two big guys were seen in Reed Shortridge's residence hall on the night of his death?"

"Yes," Crystal said. "I wound up spending the afternoon talking to several of Reed's closest friends."

Alice and Rex sat in the living room. They'd both been fed their dinner, yet they stared our way, longingly—where there's life, there's hope. I'm positive the two would concur with my dissertation on all-meat pizzas. I'm not quite sure what either would do with an artichoke.

"And?"

"His best friend from high school told me Reed had burnt out on swimming by senior year. He told me Reed took the scholarship at UIC because—well, because he was offered a college scholarship. He'd have been a fool not to. Reed confided in his friend how big a relief it was to find out he'd not be setting any collegiate swim records. It made it OK for him to drop out of the program."

"So you're thinking the shrine set up in his dorm room could have been rigged?"

Crystal shrugged. "It got a little strange when I talked to Reed's freshman girlfriend, only to find out she wasn't really his girlfriend."

"How the heck does that work?"

"The two of them dated for a month or so, with an emphasis on *dating*, you know, getting to know each other," Crystal said and pointed at her plate. "Mostly they went out for pizza. Evidently, they did a little necking—PG-rated, she said. He started pushing for a more restricted rating and it made her uncomfortable. She pulled away."

I took a sip of beer. "They were not star-crossed lovers?"

"Not even close. Last time she saw Reed, he was at a party chatting up another girl." Crystal added, "She felt awful about what happened—shocked—but she didn't feel their brief romance or fling could have triggered such a horrific reaction. She left her resident hall after Reed's death, moved back home, and finished the school year from there."

I didn't need much more convincing. "The guys from the park could have killed older brother Reed and made it look like a suicide." Crystal kept nibbling at her pizza, so I continued. "A nearly abandoned dorm on a Saturday night and Reed gets a knock at his door. He thinks it's one of his college buddies; instead, these two big guys are in the doorway. A punch to his gut shuts him up and by the time he recovers there's a noose around his neck," I said. "I mean—you can't really scream for help if you're being strangled, right?"

My sister nodded her agreement and set down the remaining pizza crust. Crystal doesn't eat the outer rim. Sometimes, when she's not looking, I'll flick those pieces to Alice and Rex. She wiped her mouth with a napkin and added to my scenario. "The cord drops over Reed's head and gets yanked. It's taut around his throat, ever tightening, the slipknot lodged behind his ear. These are big guys—football-big. Maybe the cord goes over one of their shoulders and Reed gets wrenched up over their back. Reed bucks and twists in an attempt to loosen what's stealing his oxygen . . . what's killing him . . . but by then it's too late." Crystal then said, "They use the cord to move Reed's bulk. The poor guy's a marionette—all dead-weight—and they bring him over to his closet, toss the other end of the cord over the door, and slam it against the frame. And there the poor guy hovers, half a foot above the floor, until his roommate returns the next day."

I put down my beer. "I see you've given this a little thought."

My sister nodded again. "They could have torn through his room, looking for anything to back up their narrative—Reed's high school yearbook, empty beer cans, where to put the suicide note they brought along with them."

"I bet those doors can be set to lock automatically, you know, as you shut them."

"Yeah, pretty typical—the college wouldn't want to make it easy to get into a student's room if they forget to lock their door on their way out to class."

"Which explains the locked dorm."

"Yes," Crystal said. She crossed to the refrigerator, took a beer out for herself, and returned to the table. "I figure Reed was dead within a few minutes of opening his door. Then another five minutes go by as they move his bed and rig everything up to make Reed look like he hung himself. Another minute to press his fingertips against sections of the cord and the suicide note. Add in a few more to arrange the yearbook and beer cans. Add three seconds to toss the note in Reed's printer tray and maybe a final minute to audit their work, to see if there's anything's missing or out of place."

"Two good-sized guys could have done all that in less than fifteen minutes," I said. "Can you reopen the investigation into his death?"

"Not at this point."

"Why not?"

"It's all conjecture," Crystal replied. "And what's not—a witness seeing a couple of big guys in hoodies and caps in a dormitory elevator and you, a couple years later, getting into it with two guys at a park—isn't enough to change UICPD's finding that Reed's death was a suicide."

"But both incidents involved members of the Shortridge family."

"I know, but think about it for a second. Even if we had caught the men from the park, their attorney would say they met up for an afternoon stroll and your dogs nearly attacked them."

"That's BS, though."

"I know it's BS, but it would sell in court." Crystal sighed. "There are five manners of death, Cor, and I'm taking suicide off the table. We can also say goodbye to natural and accidental and undetermined. So we're left with homicide. Reed's case is reopened in my mind. He was murdered and it was made to appear as though he killed himself. And then his brother Patrick is killed and squirreled away in what should have been the perfect hiding spot for a generation or two, right?"

I nodded. "Reed's suicide rips the Shortridge family apart. Then Patrick's disappearance destroys whatever's left."

"Yes—the motive appears to be that of prolonging the Shortridges' misery, to make them suffer, to make their lives a living hell." Crystal frowned. "Once Patrick's body was found, they knew they wouldn't get the drawn-out, soul-crushing agony that comes from a missing child. It didn't bleed the Shortridges as much as they wanted it to." My sister caught my eye. "So now they're coming after Charlotte."

I glanced down at my plate, realizing I'd yet to touch my pizza. "And no one in the family has a clue who could be doing this to them?"

Crystal shook her head.

THIRTY

Past Days

"Hi, Beverly," said the woman behind the reception desk.

"Hello, Annette." The elderly woman signed the visitor sheet at Golden Gardens. "Another beautiful day, isn't it?"

"It sure is," Annette replied. "And it's so nice of you to spend part of it visiting with him again. He so rarely has visitors."

"The family comes, don't they?"

Annette thought for a second. "I've only met his grandson on a couple of occasions. He'll bring the great-grandkids along, but they only stay a few minutes or so."

"Such a shame," the elderly woman said and shook her head. Then, using her cane for support and balance, she headed toward the wing of the assisted living facility that comprised the specialized care units, the rooms for those suffering with Alzheimer's and dementia.

"Hello, Lansing," the woman said as she entered the SCU. "I see you've started *Wheel of Fortune* without me."

Lansing smiled and nodded her way. Smiling and nodding along with the periodic mumbling of "Yes" were Lansing's go-to responses.

The room was small and simple. A green lounge chair and matching green couch lined one wall, separated by a side table with a remote control sitting on its glass surface. Further along this side of the room lay a twin bed with adjustable controls she doubted Lansing had ever utilized. The other wall possessed a mounted flat-screen television on which the game show had commenced. In the corner sat a smallish bathroom, rigged up with grab bars and rails, as well as a raised toilet to keep residents from falling and injuring themselves. There were no kitchenettes in these specialized care units, for obvious reasons.

Lansing sat on one side of the sofa, his customary perch, with an elbow on the armrest and a palm on the side table. The elderly woman settled into the lounge chair, leaned her cane against the wall, reached across the table and patted the top of Lansing's hand. "How are you doing today, old friend?"

Lansing smiled again and said, "Well, you know." It was another one of his Pavlovian responses.

"Good," she replied.

Lansing was slipping away; it was more and more telling with each and every visit—his hippocampus irreversibly damaged by Alzheimer's. Sure, he had the occasional good day; the occasional spark of recognition. To be honest, though, the elderly woman thought, Lansing's good days had been whittled down to infrequent moments. He might mention a name from the past, typically the name of a long-dead family member or perhaps a childhood pet. Now and again Lansing might even blurt out a *Wheel of Fortune* answer, but his phrases were for the most part incorrect, not even close.

Lansing did not remember her, but he was affable enough and appeared to enjoy her visits. He was dressed in gray sweatpants and a gray sweatshirt today, and it dawned on her that was what Lansing wore whenever she stopped by. In the world of assisted living, Golden Gardens was fairly swanky—she'd checked—and Lansing never smelled of body odor, not once, so she assumed they generally took good care of him.

Lansing was at the ass-end of the middle stage of Alzheimer's, the moderate dementia stage. At least he was amiable and not irate, she thought, like some of the other residents in this ward of Golden Gardens she'd bumped across. Severe dementia was the third and final stage of the disease; after this stage, well, it was all-aboard time, as the train was soon to leave the station.

"A barrel of laughs." She blurted out the winning phrase a second before the contestant. She glanced over at Lansing. "I should be on this show, don't you think?"

Lansing nodded and the two watched *Wheel of Fortune* until it ended. At that point the woman picked up the remote control and pressed the mute button. He looked her way.

"Lest I forget," she said and dug into her purse. "I brought you a present. Don't ask me how, but I somehow managed to hold onto a packet of these." She set a single coaster down on the side table, next to his hand. "You can use it for a glass of water if you want, when you take your pills, or if you're allowed to drink a can of pop." She leaned back in her chair. "I know it's not much, but I thought you might get a kick out of it."

Lansing looked at her and nodded again. This time he said, "Yes."

They sat together another minute before she spoke again. "I've certainly enjoyed our time together, our little visits, Lansing, but I'm afraid I won't be able to stop by anymore. I know your mind isn't what it once was—and that hurts my heart, it really does—but everything I've been telling you in our chats on families and bloodlines is proceeding as planned. And it wouldn't be terribly bright of me to keep stopping by." She reached for her cane. "I sure wish I'd begun our visits a couple of years ago, back when you were in better shape, but believe me, I have certainly cherished our time together." She stood and stepped toward the entrance, but then turned around. "I hate to be the bearer of bad news, Lansing, but your great-grandson Reed hit a bit of a rough patch at the university this past weekend." The woman who was known at the facility as Beverly opened the door to the SCU and added, "I imagine words of condolence are in order, old friend. How does this sound—you and your family are *forever in my thoughts*?"

Lansing continued gazing at the silent flat-screen several minutes after his guest had departed, before glancing down at the side table. He picked up the coaster that had been left there for him. It was made of cork and contained the name and logo of a long-since shuttered establishment . . . the Wexford Hotel.

Something scratched in the fog that was Lansing's mind.

"Olive," he said.

But then it was gone . . . and Lansing returned his attention to the TV set.

THIRTY-ONE

Crystal figured *what the hell* and made the call on her cell phone.

"Hello." A male voice answered on the first ring, his tone soft, more of a hum than whisper.

Crystal greeted the voice and introduced herself.

"How did you get this number?"

"Did you miss the part where I said I was a CPD detective?"

"I did not," the voice replied. "Might you have a pen at hand?"

"Why?"

"Because I'm going to give you the number of Mr. Lanaro's attorney."

"Could you do me a favor?" Crystal said. "Please tell Mr. Lanaro that Detective Crystal Pratt is calling." A lengthy pause ensued, so she continued. "I worked on the cold case involving the death of his cousin earlier this year."

"Why would that matter?"

"Can we leave that up to Mr. Lanaro?"

Another long pause before the voice replied, "One moment, please."

New York has its five families, but in Chicago, organized crime—the mob—is called the Outfit, and there is only one family involved—the Lanaros. And the current head of the Lanaro crime syndicate is an icy snake by the name of Mattia Lanaro. Crystal had not only worked on, but solved the decades-old murder of Lanaro's first cousin. Unfortunately, she was unable to bring one of the killers to justice because—Crystal knew; every detective at CPD knew—Lanaro had gotten to them first.

The moment turned into a minute and granted Crystal time to question her judgment. What exactly did she hope this phone call would accomplish? What did she hope to gain? They were grasping at straws in the Patrick Shortridge investigation, looking at what little they knew from every possible angle; but why was Crystal wasting her time chasing down this loose end?

Even if it were true . . . so many years had passed that it meant nothing.

She considered disconnecting when a different voice spoke over the cell phone.

"Hello, Detective Pratt," the different voice said. "What an unexpected surprise."

"Is this Mattia Lanaro?"

"In the flesh."

"Thank you for taking my call, Mr. Lanaro," Crystal said. Talking to the man made her skin crawl, but she needed to show proper deference—well, at least adequate deference—if she expected to obtain any information out of Chicago's mob boss in return.

"To what do I owe the pleasure?" he said, his tone dry.

"I was hoping to ask you a question regarding a case I'm working on."

"You may ask," Lanaro said. "I can't promise you I'll answer, but you may certainly ask."

"Fair enough," Crystal said. "Though I can't imagine any of this being able to come back and bite you."

"Well then, Detective—consider me all ears."

Crystal began, "An elderly gentleman informed me that, per his family folklore, his grandfather worked for Al Capone."

After a beat, Lanaro began to chuckle. Even his amusement was dry. He finally said, "I did not see that coming, Detective Pratt."

"I know—the gentleman himself thinks it's one of those crazy rumors that got passed on down the family tree."

"Capone would be going back a hundred years," he said. "What, is the gentleman descended from Baby Face Nelson or John Dillinger?"

"Nothing like that," Crystal said. "His grandfather was a tax accountant."

There was more dry laughter. Then, "If his grandfather was a tax accountant for Al Capone, he was not a very good one."

Since Capone had been convicted of income tax evasion, Lanaro had a valid point. "The gentleman mentioned the timing doesn't work with Capone," Crystal replied. "Like I said, he thinks it's a myth. Hearsay, an urban legend, what have you—but there might be something to it."

"What's the name of the old-time accountant?"

"Lionel Shortridge."

"Shortridge? I know that name from something more recent than Al Capone," Lanaro said. "How?"

"Do you follow the news?"

"Religiously." Then he added, "The boy they found inside the school wall?"

"Yes."

"That has to be a difficult case to be working on, Detective Pratt."

"It is."

"When would this Lionel Shortridge have passed away?"

"1962."

"I wasn't even born yet," Lanaro said. "And it was before my father's . . . *tenure*."

"Like I said, there's no way this bites you."

"Not when the statute of limitations ran out eight or nine decades ago." Lanaro cleared his throat. "Tell me, Detective, how does this factor into what happened to that poor boy?"

"I can't get into specifics," Crystal said. "But we're looking at motives, trying to see if someone could have been targeting the family. Quite frankly, I'm just trying to run down this rumor to see if it's true or not."

"OK," he said. "Let me check around. I'll ask some old-timers who may remember old-timers." Before he hung up, Lanaro added, "I'll call you back at this number."

THIRTY-TWO

"I better head out, Apple Core," Brielle said.

Brielle had taken to calling me *Apple Core*, some variation of Cory. I found it kind of cute. I found Brielle cute. Plus, I've been called plenty of worse names, often by Crystal. "I can't thank you enough for all the help. The next two at Cockrell are on me."

Cockrell was the cafeteria at Harper's. Brielle refused any compensation for assisting me with my canine obedience class tonight—said she was doing it pro bono—but I insisted on springing for a lunch or two. And Brielle had been of tremendous service collecting forms and payment from the new dog owners in attendance and helping haul in the gear and cones and canine treats, as well as handing out said treats to puppies that performed accordingly, or at least close enough for government work.

"I'll blow off my usual salad and see if Cockrell has lobster or filet mignon," Brielle replied. She'd really come along to see what the hounds could do. And they hadn't disappointed. "Alice and Rex were amazing."

At the sound of their names, the two wiggled over and licked at Brielle's fingertips as she knelt down to voice her goodbyes. Brielle normally dresses up for school; not in a ballroom dress or anything grandiose, more smart casual—certainly better than the rest of us slugs at Harper. But tonight she sported blue jeans, a sweatshirt and a pair of old sneakers. I had warned her not to wear more fashionable attire, the good stuff, in case any of the twenty-odd canines in attendance decided to shower her in slobber; to baptize Brielle in drool.

As I watched her scratch at necks and shake paws, I realized Brielle looked just as gorgeous in jeans and a sweatshirt as she did in her college attire. Of course, she'd always been a stunner; I'd noticed her in the hallways at Harper before we ever met.

How could I possibly miss that wavy copper hair and side-swept bangs, those inquisitive eyes and slender nose, that playful grin of hers?

I'm not blind.

She stood and smiled. "See you tomorrow, Apple Core."

Were we dating, this would be the part where I leaned over and kissed her on the lips. Instead, I said, "Say hi to Adam for me."

The two were meeting up for a late dinner.

I watched Brielle depart, out the entry door and off into the night, leaving me alone in the packaging warehouse. Fortunately, the evening's obedience class had taken place in Wheeling, a few miles southeast of Buffalo Grove. I'd be home in no time flat.

Brielle had been able to hang out long enough for the horde of novice puppy owners to dissipate, to assist me in rounding up the gear and doggie treats, and to walk me through how she handled tonight's paperwork. I thumbed through the forms and checks and peeked inside the money envelope, from those who paid in cash. Brielle had all the documentation alphabetized and itemized; more organized than I'd ever been. She'd also listed the names of the clientele who paid using my credit card reader, as well as those who went the Venmo or PayPal route, so I could double-check their remittances against the payment apps on my smartphone. I was delighted to see there was only one customer I'd have to chase down in order to settle his tab, and Brielle had his name, phone number, and home and email address jotted down to help me in that quest.

For all her help, two meals at Cockrell Dining Hall was a bargain.

The evening had gone swimmingly.

So why then was I standing here, on the chipped concrete of a warehouse floor, feeling a tad melancholy?

Perhaps Crystal was right. She'd not spoken it out loud, just talked around the edges, but I knew my sister and I knew what she was driving at. Can you be *just friends* with someone you have feelings for?

Brielle and I had this light flirtatious thing going. Nothing weird or warped or anything that could get me called before some disciplinary board at Harper's. She loved Alice and Rex, absolutely adored the two, and had taken to referring to them as though they were her dogs.

And she did seem to get some kind of goofy kick out of me.

But I had these feelings for her . . . much deeper than *just friends* feelings.

Aw, hell—who was I kidding?

I was smitten.

If I couldn't sleep at night, my thoughts turned Brielle's way. If she missed a day at Harper's, I trudged about the campus all by my lonesome self, a social leper, and, more often than not, cut out early. And if not for Brielle . . . I'd have likely dropped out of the community college last summer.

Nevertheless—can you be *just friends* with someone you have romantic feelings for?

Can you be *just friends* when those feelings went unrequited?

That was Crystal's unspoken concern: my being the ashtray in a romantic triangle.

I shook the thought away. There was too much going on right now to get my guts all twisted up and tangled. Maybe I'd talk to Crystal about it, over a beer or two . . . but probably not.

I took the paperwork, tucked it inside a monster-sized envelope, and slipped it into one of the plastic buckets I carried the gear and treats in. I stacked the orange cones and scanned the warehouse floor in case there was anything I'd forgotten or any mess that needed cleaning up. Fortunately, no little gifts had been left behind. The owner of the warehouse offers me a great deal on renting out this facility for my after-hours training sessions, on one condition. Said condition being the warehouse remains unsoiled. Lest I face his wrath, the last thing I needed would be for him to scrub up any kind of waste or clutter.

The warehouse owner also had me set the entry door to shut and lock after everybody left, and to triple-check it was locked when I headed out for the evening. But the guy lives a few blocks away and, knowing him, I suspect he swings by to make sure everything is A-OK and ready for the morning crew before he's able to slip between the sheets and get a good night's sleep.

I picked up two buckets, stuffed with gear, by the handles, then I heard a knock at the front door. It was soft at first, and then a little louder.

"Yes," I called across the chamber, setting the buckets back down. Perhaps Brielle had returned. I stepped across the cement of the warehouse floor, the beasts following in my wake. "Who's there?"

"Hey, Cory, I think I left my keys inside," a man's voice floated through the steel door. "I looked everywhere and can't find them." He added, "I'm not able to get into my car."

I glanced again around the warehouse as I'd done a moment earlier and spotted no keys. I reached for the push bar just as Alice began to growl.

THIRTY-THREE

Crystal got home at half past eight; an early evening. She wished Cory was home with the fast-food tacos or burgers or chicken he'd picked up, but knew he had a canine obedience class tonight. She was worn out and didn't feel like cooking, whether it be healthier than Cory's cuisine or not. So she slipped upstairs—her domain—changed into sweats and returned to the kitchen, with thoughts of garlic pasta with peas floating about her mind, when her cell phone vibrated.

She recognized the number and answered immediately. "Crystal Pratt."

"Hello, Detective."

"Mr. Lanaro?"

"Yes," he replied. "Are you free to talk?"

Crystal knew a negative response was not on the table. "I am."

"Excellent. I checked around regarding our friend Lionel Shortridge. And, no, Mr. Shortridge did not work for Al Capone," he said. "But let me ask you this, Detective—how conversant are you regarding Chicago's checkered past?"

"I wouldn't win any awards," she said. "I'm probably at a CliffsNotes level."

"Then you might recognize the names I'm going to bandy about, because Lionel Shortridge's accounting services did, in fact, come into play in the post-Capone era."

"So it's true?" Crystal sounded surprised because she was.

"Yes, Detective—it's true. Lionel Shortridge worked predominantly for a gentleman by the name of Tony Accardo," Lanaro said. "Do you recognize that name?"

"I do."

"And if Shortridge worked for Tony Accardo, that meant Shortridge also worked for a man by the name of Paul Ricca," he said. "I trust you recognize Paul Ricca's name as well."

Crystal almost dropped her iPhone. She knew both names. Tony Accardo and Paul Ricca were the de facto leaders of the Outfit for several decades following Al Capone's imprisonment. Crystal decided to push her luck. "Did you know those men?"

A dry laugh drifted through the cell phone and then Lanaro said, "Certainly by reputation, but Ricca died in 1972. I was a toddler, Detective. I met Accardo once or twice at some events in the late eighties, but he was an old man by then."

Crystal pushed her luck further. "I imagine the IRS would have been breathing down their necks during that time frame," she said. "Would Shortridge have been brought aboard to deal with any tax implications?"

Another dry laugh. "What do you think?"

"I think a good tax accountant would have been in high demand."

"A reasonable person might suspect Lionel Shortridge did more than count beans or perform light bookkeeping."

Lionel Shortridge may not have performed any *light bookkeeping*, but Crystal read between Lanaro's lines . . . Shortridge kept books. And, she thought, *a reasonable person* might be highly skeptical vis-à-vis the accuracy of Shortridge's books. Yes, he kept books, all right—Lionel Shortridge laundered them. Crystal then thought about the financial portfolio Paul Shortridge managed for the family and said, "Would he have been highly compensated for his services?"

"I know nothing of Shortridge's *arrangement* with Accardo or Ricca. And I probably wouldn't tell you if I did, but generally speaking—yes—the man would have gotten a taste." There was a short pause before Lanaro continued, "Quite frankly, Detective, I got lucky regarding your request. A dear friend of the family—in fact, my father's right-hand man—is a bit of a historian. Even though he himself is up in years, he had to hunt down some real old-timers in order to get you your answer."

Crystal stared at the floor and considered how figures and finance appeared etched in the Shortridge family's DNA: it flowed through their veins. "Would you know if Lionel's son—Lansing Shortridge—did similar work for Accardo or Ricca?" she asked. "He was an accountant as well."

"No, my *historian* friend only tripped across Lionel. No Lansing, no other Shortridges. Trust me; more current names would have been easier to track down." Lanaro then said, "This has been an interesting stroll down memory lane, Detective Pratt, but tell me something—what can you possibly make of this ancient history?"

Lanaro had a point. Crystal shrugged and said, "I doubt anything, beyond letting the Shortridges know that, except for the piece about Al Capone, their juicy bit of family trivia is true."

"I wish you luck, then," Lanaro said. "Horrible thing, what happened to that boy, but I don't see how any of this can help. Like I said, though, I wish you luck."

"Thanks," Crystal said. She knew her allotted time had come to an end; she'd be getting nothing more from the head of Chicago's mob.

"One last thing, Detective. I do appreciate your role in resolving what occurred with my cousin. I loved him dearly. But if you call this number again," he said, "you will be referred to my attorney."

"I understand." In truth, Crystal hoped the next time she spoke to Mattia Lanaro would be to read him his Miranda rights as his hands were cuffed behind his back.

"Well then, Detective Pratt, have a good remainder of the evening," Lanaro said and disconnected the phone call.

Crystal set her iPhone down on the kitchen countertop. Hard to believe she'd spent the last several minutes with a man who had calmly, matter-of-factly, provided her with the information she'd requested, but would also calmly and matter-of-factly order her death if she ever became an impediment.

Notions of garlic pasta had vanished from Crystal's mind as she pondered the meaning of this riddle . . . or if the riddle had any meaning at all. If Lionel Shortridge worked for Tony Accardo and Paul Ricca as their tax accountant, then Lionel was a heavy hitter. It was like Lanaro said: he would not have been there to count beans or perform light bookkeeping.

Crystal's cell phone vibrated again. This time it was Cory.

He must be finishing up the night's training. She tapped the Accept button and said, "Hey, Cory."

"Open the fucking door!" she heard a voice scream. It wasn't her brother.

And then shots were fired.

THIRTY-FOUR

I jerked back from the push bar as Alice growled her warning. Something had tripped her trigger. My bloodhound focused on the door in front of us as though studying for a final exam. Rex stepped forward, his snout at the bottom of the entry frame, a guttural buzz deep in his throat.

Danger.

I stared at the warehouse entrance door as hair rose on the back of my neck. The pups were alerting me to a threat, outside, on the front walkway. If they spoke English, they'd demand the door remain locked shut, not opened to some guy fussing about lost keys. His voice was dimly familiar, but I'd spoken to dozens of puppy owners tonight.

Suddenly I caught Alice and Rex's meaning. I caught their meaning loud and clear.

And I knew what awaited me if I pushed open the entry door.

Death.

"I'll be seeing you," the man at the Kenilworth playground had told me.

"Are you still there?" the voice called out, breaking my trance.

"Settle," I whispered to Alice and Rex. Then I spoke to the man behind the warehouse door. "Yeah, I'm here." I then added, "I just looked around and I don't see any keys."

There was a short pause before the man said, "Can I come inside and check? I know where I might have dropped them during class."

I slipped my iPhone out from my pocket. "The owner's got these locks on a timer," I replied, grasping at straws.

"What?" he said, a pinch of irritation in his tone. "That can't be. If there's a fire, you shove the push bar to open the door."

"You'd think." I tapped my phone app. "But I tried that and it's not working."

His irritation raised an octave. “Well, how the hell do you get out?”

The man had a point. My heart caught in my throat as I tried to think. “Let me grab one of the janitors.”

“Janitors?” The voice was now one part exasperation to two parts anger. He was on the verge of piecing it together. “There aren’t any other vehicles out here,” he said, not pleased—not pleased at all. “Look, let me in so I can get my damned keys and go home.”

“Hey, Jake,” I called across the empty warehouse floor and tapped at Crystal’s cell phone number. “How do you get this stupid door unlocked at night?”

This time there was a longer pause before he said, “Open this door right fucking now, Pratt.” He realized I’d been deceiving him and spoke in the same manner he had at the playground. “Or I’m going to kill you.”

All pretenses had melted away. I said nothing and prayed my sister would pick up the phone. A second later she did. “Hey, Cory.”

“Open the fucking door!” the man screamed.

Then shots rang out as he blew away the keyhole.

THIRTY-FIVE

Crystal was in her HR-V in a flash. On her sprint to the garage she'd checked Cory's website and noted tonight's training was at an address in Wheeling. Good. It was ten minutes away; she'd be there in five. She tapped nine-one-one, hit speaker, and tossed the iPhone on the dashboard as she tore out of the driveway. Crystal identified herself to the dispatcher who took the call, reported there'd been shots fired at a warehouse in Wheeling where her brother had been running a dog obedience class, provided the facility's location, and informed the dispatcher she was on her way there. Crystal took a final moment to describe Cory, so officers arriving at the scene could tell him apart from any bad guys, and stressed to the dispatcher that her brother was unarmed.

She then tried Cory's cell phone again, but it went straight to voicemail. Dammit! She feared his cell was still active from when he'd called her. Not a good sign, Crystal thought as she gunned it along Buffalo Grove Road. Crystal had initially shouted into her phone, begging her brother to reply as she grabbed her car keys, badge, and gun.

What the hell was going on at that warehouse?

Only a few of Cory's customers paid him in cash; most clients go cashless, swiping their credit card or cutting a check. Was somebody robbing her brother over a hundred dollars? It was dumb as hell but, sadly, the way of the world—it happened each and every day in Chicago.

Screaming for Cory to *open the fucking door* made Crystal think the bad guys were more interested in something inside the warehouse and Cory had phoned her when the altercation got heated. Whoever owned the warehouse, or whatever business they had going on in there, had to have something worth more than Cory's cash take from his training session. Raw materials or finished goods? Equipment? Could they have been casing the place and spotted an opportunity when Cory's class ended, after the dog owners and their puppies had funneled out for the night, while her brother was inside finishing up?

Crystal had no idea what she'd do or where she'd be if anything happened to her little brother. Cory *was* her family—her only immediate family. The two of them had somehow found a pathway back after the death of their parents. Cory would say she was the one responsible for getting them through the dark nights, for pulling him out of a deep funk of depression and despair, and Crystal had done the best she could at the time for someone in their early twenties . . . but that wasn't the complete truth.

As big a hot mess as Cory had been at the time, the dirty little secret was how he'd been there for her, too—in a certain manner, anyhow. Having to care for her little brother helped to keep her moving; it kept her distracted. It took a small portion of Crystal's mind off the dismay and gut-wrenching horror of having lost both her mother and father.

Crystal shook away those thoughts. Right now she needed to focus. She zipped past a Jeep Cherokee, her siren blaring, doing eighty in the right lane—thank God there wasn't much traffic at this time of night. Shots had been fired and she wasn't able to get back in touch with Cory because . . . well, because he was busy; fleeing to safety tends to demand one's full attention. Plus, he had Alice and Rex in there with him. The pups were Cory's secret weapons. They had saved his life on more than one occasion. The two would protect him even if it cost them their own lives. Rex would put on a hell of a show, all bravado and up in your grill, and Alice—well, Alice would kick ass and take names.

Alice would draw blood.

Crystal heard the Doppler effect of sirens joining hers as she closed in on the warehouse, now just a block away. If the squad cars beat her there, it'd be by seconds.

THIRTY-SIX

I dove to the side, bounded hard off the cement floor, and tore ass across the warehouse, a bat out of hell—hoping I'd make the double doors leading to the storage and shipping area and, ultimately, the loading docks.

"Run," I screamed, knowing Alice and Rex would be on my heels.

The front entryway shattered inward as though struck by a grenade. I smashed into one of the double doors, glanced back, spotted the man from the playground—same dark hoodie, same Bears cap—stepping inside, raising his arm, a pistol in hand. But then I was through the doorway and cut left into the storage zone, now out of his sight. I flashed on an idea and sprinted the length of the floor, toward the manager's office. The office lay beyond a second set of double doors; only this pair was wide open and led back into the frontage room I'd just fled. What I had in mind would leave me exposed for the briefest of seconds, but it might be a game changer.

I stuck my head and arm around the open door and spotted the playground man who now stood in the center of the front room; unfortunately, his partner was at his side. The two saw me, their guns raised as I slapped down the light switches on the wall plate, dropping to the floor as the warehouse faded to shadows. Bullets whizzed above my head, where I'd been standing, as I slithered backward, a snake in reverse.

Once clear, I leapt to my feet, squinted in the near darkness, and whispered, "Come."

I had another idea and the three of us dashed toward a string of pallets, stacked high with stretch-wrapped boxes that awaited shipping. They stood like dark foothills beyond the loading docks. In the murkiness they looked flush against the exterior partition, but I'd been given the nickel tour a couple times and knew there was a slight gap, maybe eight or nine inches we could squeeze behind before you hit the concrete wall.

With a hushed command for Alice and Rex to follow, I pressed myself behind one of the middle pallets and then my luck ran out . . . when the overhead lights kicked back on.

Dammit—the overheads worked on a three- or four-way switch, meaning multiple wall plates, and one of the men must have found the plate near the entryway door. Then I heard rushed footsteps as they came for us, now entering the shipping area. I crouched low as best I could, pulling in the pups, and silently cursing myself. I'd made a bad move, real bad—a deadly one. We should have flown past the office and hit the rear door in a mad scramble to get the hell out of the warehouse and off into the night. The blaring alarm from slamming open the door would have worked in our favor.

Instead, I'd jammed us into a dead end, stuck between a rock and a hard place; we were sitting ducks.

"Check in there." I heard the voice I'd come to know command his partner as he darted across the path I'd taken moments earlier, making sure we'd not doubled back to the front of the warehouse through the doors on the far side. I touched Alice's shoulder and felt her tension. She knew we were in trouble. My eyes grew moist as I realized I had but one move left. If they came to check the pallets, and it made all the sense in the world they would, I'd have to sic my dogs on them in some sort of last-second Hail Mary pass.

But the two men were armed. They'd pick off Alice and Rex like fish in a barrel.

I listened as the man in the office suite upended desks and smashed computers and kicked at tables and chairs. We'd not been hiding in there and he was busting stuff just to bust stuff. Then the main man jogged back to the shipping area and shouted, "Jesus Christ—knock that shit off."

"You see him?" his partner called back, frustrated.

"No—the prick's hiding in the loading docks, near them pallets." A second later he laid out his plan. "I'll start on this side; you come from there. Spray the goddamned dogs," he said, "and then we shoot the fuckers."

Spray, I thought. Mace or pepper or dog repellent? These guys had come prepared. Any one of those could send Alice and Rex spinning in circles, reeling blindly and bouncing off walls, easy for target practice. My eyes glistened with tears.

We were pinned down; mice in a trap.

And it was all my fault.

I'd managed to get us killed.

"You still want him?" his partner asked, sounding dangerously close.

"Yeah, I'll need him for five minutes, but not here," the leader replied. "We'll dump his ass in the woods by the golf course."

Tears slid down my face. Not for me, but for Alice and Rex. I was about to call out, to turn myself in and beg them to leave my dogs alone, when I heard a sound . . . it was off in the distance . . . police sirens.

"Fuck!" the leader said.

"What do we do?"

"Get the van."

I heard footsteps sprinting away when the leader added, "Grab the fucker's phone. He dropped it by the door."

I wiped my eyes with a forearm. It was seconds, but seemed an eternity as I waited for the man from the playground to leave.

He finally spoke, "I know you can hear me, Pratt."

I knelt motionless behind the pallet of boxes, heart pounding in my ears, as the police sirens became piercing, not far off. My hand remained on Alice's shoulder and I placed a calming palm on top of Rex's head. I'm not sure if the man expected a response, but he wouldn't be getting one.

"You can't hide forever." Then he said, "If you knew anything at all . . . you'd know how patient we are."

And with that the man was gone.

But the three of us remained huddled behind the boxes until I heard tires screech and car doors slam and finally a familiar voice calling, "Cory!" My sister was worried; she was frantic. "Are you here, Cory!?"

"Yes, Crys," I called back, trembling, my voice unsteady. "I'm OK."

Alice and Rex raced ahead as I paused a second to glance inside the destroyed office suite and then stepped across to the frontage room, the area where I'd been training puppies what now seemed like hours ago. My sister and several police officers clustered about the remnants of the shattered entryway, staring my way—their guns drawn, pointed downward. Something told me that even if I had the funds to pay for all this damage, I'd never be allowed to rent this place again.

"It was them, Crystal," I said and watched as her jaw slowly dropped. "It was them."

THIRTY-SEVEN

"They took my phone," I said after I'd explained what happened in the warehouse.

We were on the sidewalk out front. Crystal's partner arrived within minutes of Crystal and the two squad cars. The detective stood at her side; he'd been there long enough to catch the gist of the evening's event. A forensic unit was on its way. I doubted they'd be able to lift any fingerprints from what remained of the front entryway, what with its lock having been blown away and the door kicked in. I also doubted they'd get any prints from the manager's office as, from what I heard, it sounded like playground man's partner let his feet do all the talking, as he had gone apeshit and kicked at the furniture and computers in there. From the peeks and flashes I caught of the two men, I wasn't positive but fairly certain they wore gloves. It made sense, as they had them on at the playground.

"Wouldn't they need your password to get in?" Detective Lahlum asked.

"Couldn't they just bring it to an Apple store or something?"

"They won't hang onto your phone long," Crystal said. "They know we'll be tracking it." My sister recognized the look of concern on my face. "What are you worried about, Cor? What have you got on it?"

It would be a major pain in the rump to set up a new phone without a SIM card. I think I had data and stuff backed up on the cloud; I wasn't sure. Crystal figured I was tangled up over business or school or contact info that'd be lost. But that wasn't the case; far from it. There was something else involved . . . and I felt like an idiot. "You've got to get them tracking my phone right now, Crys—as in right now."

"What's going on, Cor?"

I felt sick to my stomach, as in puking-my-guts-out sick. "I plugged the safe house address into Maps so I'd know how to get there," I said.

I watched as Crystal's face worked its way through lighter shades of pale. Lahlum glanced at his watch, doing mental gymnastics on how much time had elapsed since the assault had taken place.

"If they're bright enough to get into it," I said, filling the awkward silence that ensued, "they'd have to check under Recents and then be clairvoyant enough to know what that address stands for, but . . ." I let the sentence trail off and linger.

Lahlum pulled out his cell phone. "I'll get the Shortridges out of there," he said as he headed toward his car. "And I'll get the trace going on your cell phone."

I shook my head. "I am so sorry, Crys."

"How could you have known they'd be coming after you?" my sister replied, trying to make me feel better and a little less like the village idiot. "Mark will have a squad car there in a minute." Then Crystal asked me, "Did you get a good look at them tonight?"

"A couple of glimpses. They were geared up in caps and hoodies again, just like at the park," I said. "But . . . but their faces, from what little I could see when they were next to each other in the front room—they looked alike, similar features."

"You think they're related?"

I shrugged. "I don't know, but they have the same thick build and height, too."

"Football-player big," Crystal nodded and said. "Maybe not offensive line or offensive tackle-big, but big enough."

"Yeah, and the main guy knew I was a dog trainer, Crys. He pretended he'd been in the class to get me to open the door."

"He'd know that from the playground."

"But he knew my name, too. He called me *Cory* at first, when he was trying to get in, and then *Pratt* when he got all pissed off."

"He knew you had an obedience class here tonight from your website, just like I did, but how would he get your name to begin with?" she said. "You weren't mentioned in the news reports—just *blah-blah-blah cadaver dogs found a body inside a wall.*"

"It gets worse," I said and swallowed hard. "Alice and Rex alerted me—they saved my life. They recognized his scent, maybe even his voice, as the threat from the park, so this definitely ties back to the Shortridge family."

Crystal looked off to the side, lost in thought, trying to unravel a troublesome knot.

"He also told his buddy he needed me for five minutes, and after that they could dump my *ass* in the woods by the golf course."

That caught Crystal's attention. Her head snapped back and we locked eyes.

I sighed. "I took it to mean they'd beat the safe house address out of me. And, if they got the safe house address out of me, they'd drive right over, middle of the night or not, and storm the place," I said, tossing a hand toward the warehouse, "just like they did here."

A question beat through my brain like a kettledrum.

Who the hell are these guys?

THIRTY-EIGHT

Past Days

"This place used to be called Stump Acres when I was young." The old woman sat on a webbed lawn chair that looked as if it'd spent half a century in a dusty attic. "People would come from all around to buy Christmas trees here. But for the rest of the year, Stump Acres sat empty." Her cane lay horizontally atop the chair's plastic arms, her wrinkled fingers curved about its shaft. "It'd originally been owned by a farmer all those years ago, but I read somewhere he'd sold it to developers, or rather, his heirs sold it to developers after his death. I don't know the ins and outs of the deal, but nothing ever came of it. There are no townhomes or condos or shopping malls—nothing here at all." It had been a lengthy hike for her from the SUV, a stroll made all the more difficult due to the uneven terrain. She would certainly sleep well tonight. "Anyway," she continued, "they stopped selling Christmas trees here at some time in the 1970s."

A jumbled sound arose from deep within the figure who sat in the dirt and underbrush in front of her—a series of moans, a soft grumble, and then a whimper, all struggling to escape—but the expressions failed in their fight for freedom, likely due to the wide strip of duct tape covering his mouth.

More strips bound his wrists and ankles.

"I know," she said. "I was surprised as well, but I imagine folks nowadays prefer those artificial trees you can reuse every year. My mother and I never came out here to buy a tree, though. Money was a scarce commodity when I was young and we put what few presents we had around a poinsettia." The old woman centered her attention on the figure before her. "Believe it or not, your great-great-grandfather, Lionel, and one of his *associates* nearly brought me out here once. It was quite the jaunt the three of us had that day," she said, "and it left me never wanting to come back."

Tears dripped down the young teen's face.

"Yes, a depressing story—there was no happy ending," Olive Cripps said and glanced about the forest. "I knew your great-grandfather Lansing as well. Or thought I did. Once upon a time he told me he was going to take care of me. And if I were to be honest with you, Patrick, truly honest with you—it was the greatest day of my life." Olive collected her thoughts. "But it wasn't in the cards. Yes, your great-grandfather did take care of me . . . just not in the manner I was expecting."

Patrick began struggling against his bonds.

"I did visit Lansing in his final year, while he was in that home; unfortunately, his mind had gone and he didn't remember me." Olive then cleared her throat. "I assume you're wondering who we are," she said. "Aren't you?"

Patrick struggled another second and then sat still, staring back her way.

"We are practically family, after all. The men who brought you here this evening—for our little heart-to-heart—are my great-grandsons. That would make them distant cousins or half cousins of yours; however that kind of stuff gets divvied up." Olive glanced at Wade and Garrick, who stood several yards away, arms folded against the night breeze, listening and letting her have her say. "They're identical twins, in case you haven't noticed," she said and returned her focus to Patrick. "I know they're delighted to finally meet you. Hopefully, the feeling is mutual." Olive leaned forward. "And guess what? Your brother got to meet them, too. He certainly did. The three of them had a nice little visit in your brother's dorm room." Olive rose from the lawn chair and leaned on her cane for support. "I am an elderly woman with little in common with you young'uns, so if you'll please excuse me, I'll work my way back to the SUV and let the three of you get to know each other," she said. "Don't worry about me, though. I'll rest awhile, maybe even nod off for a bit."

Patrick thrashed again against his bonds; now frantically, feverishly.

"Best let you get acquainted with your *long-lost cousins*, Patrick, without me being a stick-in-the-mud," Olive said as she wandered past the trio. "I know they've been dying to meet you."

THIRTY-NINE

"Can I talk to Alice and Rex?"

"Of course you can," I said. I'd spent a chunk of the morning farting around and retrieving data with the replacement iPhone Crystal picked up for me. "They're both loafing about in front of me—the slackers—so I'll put it on speaker and hold it between them."

Crystal and I had grabbed connecting rooms, a door in between us, at a Discount Inn and Suites in Elk Grove Village. It allowed dogs, so the two goofballs were on cloud nine. It was a new place for them to poke about, with me hauling them outside for long walks or sniffs and pees every few hours.

"Hey, super dogs." I heard Charlotte Shortridge speak to the beasts. "Cory says you two are Batman and Robin. I want to thank you again for the playground and for keeping Cory safe at the training class."

Since the two men had come for me at the warehouse, my sister and I feared they might also know where we lived in Buffalo Grove, and perhaps even knew where I attended college. So home and Harper's were currently off-limits. Crystal had a long chat with the Discount Inn's manager and paid in cash so there'd be no record of our stay, on the off chance these assailants had Lisbeth Salander-level hacking abilities. CPD would eventually reimburse my sister for the two motel rooms; at least I hoped they would.

I left the connecting door between our rooms open, not only to add additional square footage to my holding cell but also so Crystal could go Wyatt Earp in case the big guys somehow managed to show up here. Of course, my sister was away at work most of the day, so a lot of good that would do me if the two arrived before the sun had set.

"Can they hear me, Cory?" I heard Charlotte say and brought the phone back to my ear.

"Loud and clear, my little friend."

"Do you think they understood me?"

"Alice and Rex are pretty intuitive," I said. "They can tell you're happy with them. Their tails wagged as soon as they heard your voice."

"Good."

Charlotte and I had been on the phone for ten minutes, chatting about recent events. I did my best to keep what had occurred at the warehouse at a G or PG level—family friendly—but, well, her parents had to snatch the poor kid out of bed as they fled into the night, tucked between a caravan of squad cars, in search of another safe house. My sister was currently with the Shortridges at their new location. Char had asked Crystal if she could call me, and Crystal let her borrow her cell phone. I'd not queried Crystal on where the family was now residing, and my sister didn't cough up that information.

Quite frankly, I didn't want to know their new address. I would not be the weak link.

I still felt clumsy gabbing with a seven-year-old, so I defaulted to, "How are things going on your end, Char?"

"It's been very quiet here," she replied. "Except for setting out food, Mom and Dad don't talk much." There was a tremble in her voice. "My grandparents try to make it seem like everything will be OK . . . but their hearts are broken, too."

I felt my eyes begin to well up. "I am so sorry, Char."

"I miss my brothers so much."

"I know you do," I said. "What you've been through—I wish there were some magic words I could say to make all the hurt go away, but there just aren't any."

"Cory," she whispered through the phone line, "will the hurt ever go away?"

I glanced around my room, from the empty pizza carton and cups on the coffee table to the open bathroom door to the water dishes I'd set out for Alice and Rex, as I tried to think of what to tell her. "It never completely goes away, but—" I didn't complete the sentence.

"But what?"

I swallowed hard. "My parents were in a car accident when

I was young, Char. It was a pretty bad crash," I said. "And they both passed away as a result."

I heard a gasp over the cell phone.

"It felt like the end of the world for a long while. Crushing me. And I didn't handle it very well. Not well at all." I walked across the room and reached for the motel Kleenex. "But as time went by, Char, the pressure on my chest went away, little by little, until I could breathe normally again." I was being honest but didn't want to overwhelm the poor kid. "I carry them with me—always, even the hurt—but I mostly dwell on the good times we had together."

A few seconds passed as she mulled over what I was trying to tell her. "I'm sorry about your parents, Cory."

"I know you are, Char. And I'm not very good at talking about this, but what I'm trying to say is that time doesn't necessarily heal all wounds . . . but time makes the wounds a little more bearable." Charlotte seemed wiser than her seven years and I hoped to God I wasn't doing any damage. "There are people—counselors and therapists—you can talk to about the sadness and the pain. They know a lot more than I do."

"That's what Lynne keeps telling us."

I remembered SVU Detective Claypool. I knew she was staying with the family as an added layer of protection. "That's pretty good advice, Char," I said. Counseling and therapy hadn't worked for me. I was pretty far out there at the time. But I knew it worked for others and I hoped it would for someone of such a tender age. "Lynne knows her stuff."

FORTY

"Did you get to speak to Alice and Rex?"

"Yes," Charlotte said, returning Crystal's phone. "Can I give you a hug?"

Crystal was taken aback. "Of course you can," she replied. "I am a collector of hugs."

Charlotte wrapped her arms around Crystal, put her lips near her ear, and whispered, "I'm sorry about your mom and dad."

Crystal leaned back and looked at the child. Charlotte had been on the phone with her brother much longer than it took to say hello to the pups. Clearly, the two had covered other territory. "Thank you," Crystal said. "That's very sweet of you to say."

The family was residing in what passed for a safe house in Inverness. CPD wasn't in the business of providing hideaways but, in the mad dash to get the Shortridges the hell out of the compromised address in Park Forest, CPD had latched onto this two-story, at least in the short term, as the residence was currently undergoing foreclosure.

Crystal sat at a glass table a few feet outside the kitchen. She figured it served as either a kitchen or dining room table. She sat at the head, in the turkey-cutting seat, with Paul Shortridge and his wife Jennifer on one side and Paul's parents, James and Teresa, along the opposite edge. Lynne Claypool sat on a stool at the kitchen island; a battered paperback, a bodice ripper, lay closed in front of her as she listened to Crystal's update.

Crystal's update had been short and sweet. She informed the family and the SVU detective of what had occurred in the warehouse after Cory's canine obedience class had come to an end. She explained how her brother had ID'd the perpetrators as being the same two individuals involved in the confrontation at the playground near their Kenilworth home. When pressed by Grandpa Shortridge as to *what in hell* CPD was *doing about all this*, she walked them through how the principal and office administrator at Henry Horner had provided them with an extensive list of all contractors and subcontractors, all construction workers—electricians and plumbers, HVAC technicians and carpenters, city inspectors and appliance movers—that had stepped so much as one inch inside the elementary school during the summer remodel. The list also included the staff members and teachers who volunteered their time to spend a day or two sitting in the office, unlocking doors and being the point of contact in case anything came up.

Crystal also informed the family that her partner, Detective Lahlum, was leading the effort in background-checking the individuals on the compiled list to see if any had criminal records, which would include either felony or misdemeanor convictions as well as indicate if the person appeared on the national sex offender registry. Background checks also included credit reports, employment and education verifications, and driving history—license suspensions, traffic violations, or DUIs. The investigators were also pulling photographs from the Illinois DMV to see if any of the male construction workers matched the descriptions provided by her brother, as well as by Charlotte and her grandmother. As the perps involved in the assaults were over six feet tall, Lahlum was able to eliminate construction workers who were substantially shorter.

Crystal took a sip of coffee. Someone in the household had brewed a pot of weak dark roast and she'd been offered a cup upon arrival. Crystal compensated by dowsing it in half-and-half. She'd jumped at the chance to swing by their new digs, as she'd heard grumbles that, after the warehouse incident, the family might pull up stakes and go hide somewhere in Florida. Let the perps try to find them at the Magic Kingdom.

Lynne Claypool shuffled up from her stool, placed a hand on Charlotte's shoulder, and said, "What say you and I go play Jenga?"

"Sure," Charlotte replied.

"You going to let me win this time?"

"No."

Crystal watched as the two headed toward the family room and then turned to James. "I did follow up on your grandfather. It turns out Lionel Shortridge worked for the *gentlemen* that ran things after Al Capone."

James nodded. "That makes sense," he said. "It makes sense on more than one level."

Crystal was confused. "What do you mean?"

James looked from his wife to his son; something unspoken passed between the three. Then Grandpa Shortridge told Crystal, "My father, Lansing, was what you might call a serial adulterer. Today, they'd probably throttle back and say he was a victim; that Lansing suffered from some form of sexual addiction. But I'd say *screw that*, because my mother and my sister and I were the ones that had to live with it."

"Honey." His wife set a hand on her husband's forearm. "There's no need to drag up the past in front of the detective."

"I've got a point to make, Teresa." James placed a palm over his wife's hand, gave it a quick squeeze, and continued, "My father was a goddamned pervert. What he did to my mother was cruel and inhumane. It was torture. He was always home late from work, except for the nights he didn't come home at all. My sister and I once found a purse and lipstick in the back seat of his car; they didn't belong to Mom. And Mom would find condoms in his trouser pockets when she did the wash." James frowned as the memories washed over him. "Finally, one night when he didn't come home at all, Mom grabbed the two of us and left," he said. "By the time my sister turned twelve, she'd stopped talking to the asshole altogether. She was through with his bullshit."

Teresa added, "James's sister died of lung cancer five years ago."

"I'm sorry to hear that," Crystal said. Then she thought about how the Shortridges had been targeted and asked, "Did your sister have a family?"

"No—she never married, no family," James said. "She once told me she'd had enough dysfunction to last a dozen lifetimes." He blinked back moist eyes. "I miss her every day. My sister was tough; she had grit. Unlike her, I hung in with the bastard because I'm weak . . . because of all the goddamned money."

Teresa shook her head.

"No—it's true," James said. "I hung in and made our relationship work, even as he kept showing up with that big dumb grin on that big dumb face of his, holding hands with women that were younger than me."

The family's patriarch had something to get off his chest and, though Crystal felt as if she'd walked in on a soap opera, she wasn't about to stand in his way. Although this wasn't an interrogation and James Shortridge was not a suspect or person of interest, her training kicked in. When someone gets a head of steam going, don't get in their way.

"See—Dad was amiable enough for me to string along and make believe we had some sort of father-son thing going on. We were men, after all; we knew things my mother and sister couldn't possibly comprehend." James coughed into his fist. "It was such bullshit. And I shoved all that crap onto you, Paul and Jen," he said. "I dumped Lansing onto your plate."

"We've been through this before, Dad. Even as a kid I could tell there were issues," Paul said. "There was a void between the two of you; a cavern. But I was young and Grandpa was just Grandpa to me." The younger Shortridge shrugged. "Later, he was an old man. And then he got Alzheimer's . . . and shortly after that, he wasn't even Grandpa anymore."

"You were good to him, much more than he deserved." James pushed his coffee off to the side. "My point, Detective Pratt, is that my father didn't generate the kind of *affluence* that's been handed down to us. Whatever you call it—generational wealth, blood money—it came from my grandfather. The money came from Lionel." James then said, "What's that old adage? Behind every great fortune is a great crime?"

Crystal nodded. She'd heard the saying before.

"After Lansing got dementia, Paul and I took over the purse strings; the assets and the real estate." James Shortridge chuckled. "A quick audit showed just how much dear old Dad had pissed away on girls half his age. Quite frankly, Detective,

I'm surprised there was anything left." James nodded slowly and repeated, "The money came from Lionel."

Crystal asked, "When did your father pass away?"

"Not long after Reed's death," James replied. "It took Alzheimer's a decade to eat him."

"So Lansing was in his nineties?"

"He made it to ninety-six," James said. "Assholes live forever."

"Lansing lived at an assisted living facility in town." All eyes shifted to Jennifer as she spoke for the first time. "We had them donate Lansing's clothes and furniture to charity but they sent us a box of his personal stuff. We never opened it or peeked inside, but the woman from the facility told me it was mostly photo albums and trinkets and this or that." She looked across the table at her in-laws. "You said you weren't interested in any of his belongings, and I set the box in the attic. It's been up there gathering dust ever since."

"Hmm," Crystal said. "There's a box of Lansing's stuff in your attic?"

PART FOUR

The Photo in the Album

Heaven goes by favor. If it went by merit, you would stay out and your dog would go in.

—Mark Twain

FORTY-ONE

"But only your truck and my car were in the parking lot when I left," Brielle said over my replacement phone. "They must have waited until I was gone."

"Yeah." I sat on my bed, my back against pillows and the headboard. Rex loafed next to me with his head resting on my thigh. Alice, on the other hand, had trespassed through the open door between our rooms and selected Crystal's bed upon which to while away the evening hours—girl power. The TV was on; it had been all day, but the volume was turned down. "They probably watched as you walked to your car."

"Oh my God, Apple Core. When you put it that way—it's so creepy."

"I know. They knocked on the door about a minute after you took off."

Crystal was running late. Clearly. She'd texted several hours ago telling me she'd come bearing burgers for dinner. It was nearly eight o'clock and I was starving.

Eating is a major pastime in these new digs of mine.

"Do you think they know who I am?" Brielle connected some dots; she was now scared.

"No," I said, trying to reassure her, to place her mind at ease. And I was being honest. "They knew I was there from the schedule posted on my website. You stayed ten minutes after the training ended." I scratched Rex behind the ears as I spoke. "They would have figured you were there for the class or were maybe my assistant." Over the past year a couple of most unpleasant individuals had shown up at my door, uninvited. As a result, I'd scrubbed my home address off my canine training website. And, with Crystal's career in law enforcement, our home address had been unlisted in public directories for years. "Plus," I stressed to Brielle, "they didn't follow your car or anything like that. They tried to get into the building as soon as you left."

"So they wanted you dead?"

"No, that would have been a lot easier. If they'd just waited until I walked out to my truck, they could have driven by and shot me in the head. They wouldn't even have to get out of their vehicle or worry about the dogs."

"Then what did they want?"

"I'm really not supposed to talk about the case."

"Apple Core?"

"I'd better not," I said. "Crystal would pistol-whip me if she found out."

"Would you like to come over and study?"

"I'd love to, but I can't."

"OK—so how about if I come there with some sandwiches from Panera?" Brielle asked. "I can get that spicy chicken thing you like."

I glanced around the motel room that served as my detention center and said, "I'm not supposed to let anyone know where I'm staying."

"Even me?" I could hear the disappointment in her voice.

"I'm sorry, Brielle. It's only temporary, you know, until they get a break in the case."

"I get it," she said after a second. "I understand."

"Thanks again for texting your notes." Brielle had taken snapshots of her notes from class today and sent them my way. I'd yet to look at them. I glanced across the room at my closed textbooks sitting atop the dresser table. I'd yet to look at them, either, since beginning my exile at the Elk Grove Village Discount Inn and Suites.

Brielle and I took a minute to say our goodbyes. After hanging up, I found myself left with the same sinking feeling I had when she'd departed the warehouse after the training class. I was left with the same reservation as well.

Can you be *just friends* with someone you have romantic feelings for?

I scratched underneath Rex's jaw. "What do you think?" I asked my springer spaniel. "You ever find yourself in a situation like this?"

Rex glanced up at me and then peeked at the open doorway into Crystal's room, beyond which lay Alice.

"Seriously?"

Well, I imagine Rex was still moping over his failed nuptials.

I took a sip of lukewarm beer. It had been sitting open since before I called Brielle. My major outing for the day had been to a nearby liquor store, where I bought a twelve-pack of Rolling Rock. The remaining eleven cans lay in the room's bathtub, in a glacier of ice liberated from the machine down the hallway.

I guess I wasn't in the mood for beer.

My gut tends to get tied up in knots when I think about Brielle—the curve of her cheek, the softness of her neck . . . that smile of hers. And it hurts to know that we can chuckle and giggle and goof around at the community college but, eventually, she slips away to be with her boyfriend.

You grow up with a cluster of kids your age or thereabouts. As such, I climbed trees and played kickball and ding-dong ditch with neighbor girls when I was a little tyke, until I got to be nine or ten and realized girls were all yucky and icky. Then, a few years after that, I realized girls were actually the opposite of yucky and icky. And I went through junior and senior high saying "hi" to these old tree-climbing chums of mine in classes or in the hallway during passing time.

Were those girls I knew from way back then friends? Of course, I never got these crazy Brielle feelings—these warm fuzzies or whatever you want to call them—from any of those girls. Plus, outside of bumping into one or two of them at the mall or grocery store every now and again, I've not socialized with any of them since before my parents died.

Perhaps I could call one of them right now, out of the blue, and see if they're up for a good game of ding-dong ditch.

Crystal was right. This whole Brielle thing was driving me nuts.

Perhaps I could have Crystal talk to Brielle in my stead; my sister usually handles the turbulent stuff that heads our way. That would be something to see, wouldn't it? Having my cop sister break up with a girl I'm not even dating.

Somehow I doubted Crystal would do that for me.

As I took another sip of lukewarm beer, there came a muffled knock on the motel room's door.

"Who is it?" I barked, trying to sound like a gangster in a Martin Scorsese movie.

"Shut up and open the door."

Crystal had arrived. Rex and I jumped off the bed in unison and Alice merged with us on our trek to greet her. I threw open the door and there stood my sister—a Burger King bag and a couple of drinks sat atop a box Crystal gripped with both hands.

She must have knocked with her kneecap.

FORTY-TWO

"So you got a bunch of photo albums and junk like this?" I held up a set of brass salt and pepper mills or shakers or whatever the heck you want to call them.

"Hey, those are antiques, Cor. Too nice to use. I'm sure they've been in the family for generations," Crystal said. "I called Paul Shortridge when I opened the box and he mentioned Lansing had some collectors' items in his room, just to sit out on shelves and brighten up the place." Crystal retrieved the mills from my hands and set them gently back inside Lansing's box of keepsakes. "Paul was happy to hear these items hadn't disappeared or been stolen."

"Anything with the photo albums?" I returned to my chair at the coffee table, back to devouring my Double Whopper. We were in Crystal's room; the contents of Lansing's box had been laid out across her bedspread.

"Most contain old-time pictures of Lansing's parents—you know, Lionel and his wife. There's also an album of Lansing and his family." Crystal sat back down in her chair and stabbed a french fry into a mound of ketchup. "Family pictures from when he was married, but those peter out and then you see a few of an older Lansing with his son, James. There aren't many, but one or two were photos he had taken with his daughter before she wrote him off," Crystal said. "There's pictures of him with his grandchildren, plus a few of an elderly Lansing with the great-grandkids—you know, Reed and Patrick, and Charlotte when she was a toddler."

"A life in pictures, huh?"

Crystal nodded. "Here's the crazy thing, though. There's a small white box that contained a single photo album. The first few pages display a half dozen or so pictures, old black-and-white ones, of young women from—I don't know—way, way back in time. Lansing doesn't appear in any of these photographs; the women are pictured alone. But in later pages, there are several images of Lansing with younger women."

I wiped my fingers on a napkin, returned to the bed, lifted the lid off the little white box, took out the photo album, and began flipping through the various spreads.

"I snapped the pictures and texted them to James Shortridge. He didn't recognize any of the women from the old black-and-whites, you know, the individual pictures. He said maybe they could be long-forgotten cousins or neighbor girls, but he doesn't think so. James said the other photos, the ones that included Lansing, were likely the women his father began seeing after his parents got divorced."

After scanning through the album, I flipped back to the first page. "These pictures that have only girls in them; the girls look awfully young," I said. "I know these are pretty ancient, but the girls"—I glanced over at Crystal—"look awfully young."

Crystal now stirred a french fry in the mound of ketchup. "I know."

"They look *awfully* young, Crystal."

My sister shrugged.

"Did the family know about this white box album?"

"They don't remember it," Crystal said. "They helped Lansing put together the other ones. In fact, the other ones sat on a shelf in his room for visitors to page through."

"So maybe Lansing kept his *white album* private, hidden away in a sock drawer or someplace, where it remained out of sight and out of mind as his Alzheimer's progressed?"

I went back to the table and attacked what little remained of my hamburger. Alice and Rex sat on the carpet, keeping their distance but staring our way. They'd been trained not to beg for food; however, if an errant french fry tumbled to the floor . . . all bets were off.

"I know life was harder back in the day. I imagine it aged people a lot quicker. But the girls in those photographs, Crys, are the opposite of old." I tossed my wrapper into the empty Burger King bag. "Why would Lansing Shortridge hang onto those pictures all these years?"

My sister caught my insinuation and cut to the chase. "The girls in those pictures look as though they're fourteen or fifteen."

"That sounds about right. And Lansing hung onto these old black-and-whites in that *special little box* of his for a million years," I said. "Interesting mementos. The only pictures I've hung onto are me with you and Mom and Dad, or some with me and old friends. I don't have any pics of long-lost cousins or neighbor girls I was creeping on."

"Have you ever heard of hebephilia or ephebophilia?"

"No."

"We know pedophiles are sexually attracted to prepubescent children. Hebephilia knocks the age up a little bit. It regards adults with a sexual attraction to pubescent children; early adolescence, between the ages of eleven and fourteen," my sister explained. "Ephebophilia involves adults with a sexual attraction to those in later adolescence, you know, teenagers between fifteen and nineteen."

"Ugh," I said. Then I asked, "Was it common for adult males to date underage females in the forties or fifties?"

"Not too common. It raised eyebrows like it would today, but, you know—Jerry Lee Lewis married his thirteen-year-old cousin in the 1950s."

I looked at Crystal. "He did?"

"Yeah, it was a huge scandal at the time and hurt his career for a while," she replied. "As for actors in Hollywood, well . . . where to begin."

"So you're thinking Lansing Shortridge had that hebephilia or ephebo thing going?"

"I don't know what to think." Crystal shrugged again. "The man had a spotless record. He'd never been arrested for anything. If he was *intimate* with any of those *young women*, it never became a police matter."

"Of course, he came from money . . . and this was back in the day."

Crystal tossed a hand in the air. "A more likely explanation is that Lansing bought a camera and fancied himself a photographer."

My sister had a point. None of the girls looked under any kind of duress; none were cuffed or chained to a pipe in a basement lair, none were bruised or beaten, and all were fully clothed. In fact, most were smiling at the camera. "I guess it's just another oddity, like how his father was an accountant for the mob."

We sat in silence. I'd already burned through the fries that came with my combo. Crystal had eased off what remained of hers. I took it as a sign they were fair game, up for grabs, and slid her container my way.

There was no resistance.

"OK," I said, switching topics. "How are the background checks coming on the construction worker lists Principal Isaacson and that Suzanne office lady gave you?"

"Not much there." Crystal leaned back in her chair. "A few DUIs, an unrelated bankruptcy; one had a restraining order from his wife when they were going through a divorce; a handful of speeding tickets. Lahlum's heading it up, but no red flags so far." Crystal sighed. "Nothing to sink our teeth into."

Rex took the opportunity to hobble over to the coffee table with a *Brother, can you spare a dime?* expression on his face.

"You already had your dinner, Rex," I said and watched as he hobbled back to Alice with an *It was worth a try* look across his features.

I washed down the remaining fries with what was left of my lukewarm beer. Crystal had gotten me a Coke to go with my meal but it sat untouched on the coffee table, resting in a small puddle of condensation. I was reminded of something else I'd just seen. I stepped back to the bed, reached down, and this time picked up a singular drink coaster, another trinket from Lansing's box of souvenirs. It was in pretty good condition, seemed to be made of cork or something, and contained a black-and-white imprint of what appeared to be some swanky hotel somewhere. Spoiler alert—I knew it was a hotel because underneath the image it read *Wexford Hotel.*

I held it up. "If you catch me collecting coasters in my old age, Crystal," I said, "feel free to shoot me."

My sister stared at what I held in the air a long second and then said, "Let me see that."

FORTY-THREE

"I'm bleeding internally," Olive's granddaughter said. She looked from her grandmother, sitting motionless in her rocking chair, to her boys perched on opposite sides of the living room sofa. Her eyes were wet. She wanted to vomit, which might well have happened had she eaten anything in the past several days. "The three of you are killing me," she said. "You're killing me."

"We understand where you're coming from, Mom," Wade said softly as Brother Garrick stared down at the carpeting. "You were never supposed to be a part of this." Wade shook his head in emphasis. "Never."

They sat in the living room of Olive's condominium in Frankfort, Illinois—a village a dozen miles outside of Joliet and thirty-something miles from Chicago. It was a happy middle ground for the family meeting Olive's granddaughter had requested—no, Olive's granddaughter had demanded. Natural light coming in off the balcony betrayed the somber mood of the living room.

"I never knew about the older boy's *suicide* because the news media does not report on suicides; they respect the privacy of the families involved. But you thought I was such an idiot I'd miss the headlines last summer," she said. "You thought I wouldn't put two and two together about the younger boy's disappearance."

It had taken a couple of news cycles before she realized the missing boy's name was Patrick Shortridge. Then the lightbulb had flashed over her head as a bad feeling swelled in the pit of her stomach. She tried contacting her sons but both were incommunicado, not answering their cell phones. She then phoned their employers—Wade made a good living as a regional manager at a bearing supply company; Garrick made good enough money working in a warehouse—but discovered both of them had taken time off. She jumped into her car and sped toward Whalon Lake, where she and her ex-husband had, in happier times, bought an acre of land. Not on Whalon itself—the lake was too cost prohibitive—but a solid ten minutes from the public boat launch. You'd never find the place unless you incidentally happened to be the owner—twisty dirt roads through woodlands, no nearby neighbors. A rusting pop-up camper sat in the middle of the lot, further along lay a well-used firepit and, off near the tree line, a fish-cleaning shack, not much bigger than an old-time phone booth. The ensuing divorce put an immediate end to any thoughts of constructing a small cabin, but when the settlement was finally over, Olive's granddaughter wound up with the property.

She'd have gotten rid of the damned place years ago, but her boys loved it and went there for fishing weekends.

Upon arrival, she glided her car in next to Wade's Chevrolet Traverse and noted the camper had been cranked up. Yes—her boys were here. In fact, they came out to meet her as she stepped from her vehicle, surprise smeared across their features. The three stared at each other for several seconds in silence before she turned and headed across the yard, past the gray and black ashes in the firepit, marching over dead grass and dirt on her way to the fish-gutting shack. Her boys jogged to catch up but she picked up her pace and threw open the door before they could stop her.

And what she found inside the fish shack made her blood run cold.

Ice cold.

"What happened to our grandmother—to your mother, for Christ's sake—and great-grandma Olive is an ice pick to the heart." Wade spoke again, less softly this time. "Tossed on a trash heap as though they were human garbage." He shook his head. "Someone had to pay."

"Do you even hear yourself, Wade?" His mother then focused her attention on her grandmother. "You poisoned my boys . . . you poisoned them just like you did Darlene."

Olive returned her stare, unblinking. "That's not true, honey," she said slowly. "I was the one poisoned and it bled through every pore in my body; it bled through my tears, through every single breath I took. I *was the poison* when I raised your mother. Perhaps it would have turned out differently had I told Darlene the truth about her father and grandfather." Olive took a short breath. "Instead, I kept my mouth shut and my sweet, precious baby girl got poisoned, too," she said. "I was incapable of loving her . . . that'll haunt me to my grave." Olive wiped a sleeve across her eyes and added, "The only reason I'm even here is because of you. You gave me a second chance."

Olive's granddaughter sighed. "But look at what you've done with it. Look at what you've done," she said. "You've turned my boys into killers . . . you've turned them into murderers."

Olive closed her eyes and leaned back in her rocker. "I've done nothing but tell Wade and Garrick the truth, like I should have done with Darlene."

"No—you let the hatred simmer, like acid . . . until you fell in love with it. You had us in your life, Grandma," she said. "Wasn't that enough? Didn't we make you happy?" She gestured toward her twin sons. "Instead, this vendetta of yours—you nurtured it in them when they were too young to know better. Until it became a part of them, too; until it flowed in their veins."

"Oh, honey," Olive said, "I'm not that devious. You give me too much credit."

"Do I?" she replied. "Do I really? At least the Hatfields and McCoys were aware of the blood feud. The Shortridges have no idea what's happening to them." She swallowed hard. "It would have made more sense if you marched into Lionel Shortridge's office back in the day and shot him in the face," she said. "And the reason you kept me out of this wasn't for my safety or my well-being or whatever helps you sleep at night, but because you knew I would have put an end to it." She then added, "You don't make great-grandchildren pay for the sins of their great-grandparents."

"Mom, please, you have to stop," Wade said. "Garrick and I brought our plan to Grandma. Not the other way around."

"But don't you see," she replied, staring at her son. "Grandma groomed you to bring that *plan* to her. For Christ's sake—a plan to end a family's bloodline. Her need to tear them apart has destroyed us." Her head dropped to her chest and she folded her arms together as though curling into herself. "I want to scream."

"Mom." Garrick lifted himself up from the couch and spoke for the first time. He crossed the living room and knelt down in front of her armchair. "It's over, Mom." Garrick cupped her right hand in both of his. "It's over."

Her head slowly rose. "It's over?"

"Yes."

"The girl is safe?"

"Yes."

She caught Wade's eye as he nodded along. Then she glanced at her grandmother, but couldn't read Olive's features. She'd never been able to read her grandmother's features. Her gaze turned back to Garrick and then to Wade.

It's over.

It lightened her heart.

She felt as though she could breathe again.

Even though she knew it was a lie; even though she knew it was a siren's song.

She knew her boys.

Sure, Garrick looked sincere . . . and she believed he was sincere, in the moment, anyway. But the look on Wade's face was the same one he'd worn when denying having taken any of the bottles of whiskey that somehow disappeared from the liquor cabinet, or any of the beer that mysteriously vanished from the fridge, when he was growing up. It was the same look Wade wore when he explained away the fights he'd gotten into at school, or any of the other trouble he'd gotten himself into.

It was a look she knew so well after having raised him.

Wade had always been the brains behind the two, and—like a puppet on a string—he'd been able to control Garrick as far back as she could remember.

Yes, her twin sons may have been lying to her, but if she could find a way to believe their lies, then—like a spouse in an abusive marriage—perhaps she could find a way to breathe again.

FORTY-FOUR

"My father was the general manager at the Wexford when the owners opted to sell the hotel," Joyce Bauer told Crystal. "It broke his heart because the investors planned to tear it down and put up a shopping mall, which is exactly what they did."

"That was in the midsixties, right?"

"Yes. I was finishing high school, which was perfect timing because my parents then moved to Chicago, where Dad took a job at the Drake. He managed the front desk." Joyce took a sip of the green tea she'd steeped for them. "Although Dad enjoyed working at the Drake, he said it never felt like a family. Not like it felt from his years at the Wexford. Dad said the Drake was too big to have that family ambiance to it, but he liked the staff and stayed there until he retired."

Crystal had quietly done the math. Joyce Bauer was around eighty years old but, to look at her, the woman could pass for midfifties. Her hair was reddish-brown; dyed, Crystal assumed, but didn't look it. Joyce's complexion was smooth and blemish free. She had large blue eyes and a dainty nose, her teeth as white as ivory. Crystal figured it might be in her interest to stop by in a decade or so and solicit the secrets of Joyce's beauty regimen; perhaps come with a search warrant to see if she had the Fountain of Youth squirreled away in the basement.

But until then, she'd chalk it up to good genes.

The two sat at a small glass table outside the kitchenette in what Joyce referred to as her "mother-in-law suite." It took up the back half of the first floor of a Craftsman-style house in Lincoln Square. She lived in the residence with her son and daughter-in-law, as her three grandchildren had left the nest to begin lives of their own. Joyce said she began living there shortly after her husband passed away, which had been a little over four years ago.

The three got along great, Joyce told Crystal; possibly because of the mother-in-law suite; more likely because she couldn't have asked for a sweeter daughter-in-law. Before she moved in, a team of carpenters had banged together this back space so Joyce could have her privacy and not have to worry about taking any stairs, which, she assured Crystal, had yet to become an issue. The suite contained a bedroom, her own bathroom and, of course, the kitchenette near where they sat, though Joyce said she ate most meals with the family in the main dining room.

Joyce Bauer's father had been Donald Lehman. And Joyce informed Crystal that Donald—Donny, as he'd been known to family and friends—began working at the Wexford Hotel upon returning home from World War II. She told Crystal how her father had worked his way up the Wexford totem pole, ultimately becoming the hotel's general manager a few years before its sale.

Donald Lehman had passed away in the late nineties. It had taken Crystal a few minutes to track down his oldest daughter. She then contacted Joyce over the phone and was pleased to hear that the woman had all but grown up at the Wexford. Crystal asked if she could swing by Lincoln Square and ask her a few questions about her childhood there, and Joyce was more than willing to chat about the long-forgotten place.

Crystal set her teacup down on the saucer, glanced across the table, and cut to the chase. "Do you recall anyone from that time by the name of Lansing Shortridge?"

"Hmm," said Joyce. "It doesn't ring a bell."

Crystal removed several photographs of a youthful Lansing Shortridge, early in his marriage, as well as the pictures of an older Lansing Shortridge with the various young women, out of a large brown envelope and handed them to Joyce. "Does the man in these pictures seem familiar?"

Joyce took her time with each photograph and then handed them back. "No," she said. "I can't place him." She caught Crystal's eye. "What is this all about, Detective? I've never seen or heard of this gentleman, but his surname, Shortridge, has been all over the news of late."

Crystal nodded. She had to be very careful here. "I am one of many investigators working on the case," she said. "I'm chasing down a loose end—it's not really even a loose end—and it doesn't appear to have anything to do with the investigation." Crystal cleared her throat. "If you could keep our conversation private, out of respect for the Shortridge family, I'd appreciate it."

"Of course," Joyce replied. "Quite frankly, I'm not sure what I'd even have to say to anyone."

Crystal then shook the drink coaster out from the envelope and slid it across the table. "I bet you remember these?"

Her eyes lit up and a smile spread across her face. "Oh, my goodness," she said as she held up the drink coaster. "It's been ages since I've seen one of these."

"Brings back memories, I bet."

Joyce nodded. "Oh, yes. Pretty classy looking for the time." Joyce looked at Crystal. "These coasters were used in the main restaurant, at the bar, and even with room service," she said. "Where in God's name did you find this?"

"It was in a box containing Lansing Shortridge's belongings," Crystal said. "He died a couple of years ago."

"I'm surprised it's in such good shape." Joyce set the coaster back down on the table. "He must have kept it as a souvenir instead of actually using it."

"So he had to have picked it up at the hotel, right?"

"Yes. We wouldn't have cared if any of the guests grabbed a few to take home with them. Free advertising, my father would say." Joyce slid the coaster back to Crystal "My son collects model train cars. He purchases them off the Internet. Perhaps Mr. Shortridge could have bought this coaster on eBay or Craigslist, or some other place online."

Crystal nodded her head. That was certainly within the realm of possibility, though she didn't get the feeling Lansing was much of a Craigslister; certainly not as his dementia kicked in.

Crystal then shook the remaining photographs out of the envelope. "I've got a few more pictures to show you in case you recognize any of the young women that appear in them."

Joyce took the photos, examined each one, and then laid them face up on the table as though she were playing a card game. But she came to a stop at the fifth one; her eyes widened. "Oh, my God." She held the picture up for Crystal to see. "This girl used to babysit me when I was a child. Both she and her mother worked at the hotel," Joyce said. "I'll be darned—that's Olive Cripps."

FORTY-FIVE

"You should go over and say hi, and let her meet Alice and Rex."

"No," I said. I was telling Charlotte about the motel's front desk clerk. "I'm terrified of her. She scowls at me whenever I bring the dogs down to go outside."

"Is she a meanie jelly beanie?"

"A meanie what?"

"A meanie jelly beanie."

I'd never bumped across that term before and filed it away for later use. "I'm not sure."

"Maybe she doesn't know you clean up after them."

"I thought that might be it at first, so I held up a handful of waste bags so she'd know I wasn't leaving a mess in their courtyard."

"That's gross, Cory."

"No, Char—we were heading outside and the bags were empty, not full. She got my point but still looked all crabby and stern."

I listened as Charlotte chuckled over the phone line. I had called her to say goodbye, as Crystal told me the Shortridges were heading off to Florida. They'd decided to make it all but impossible for anyone with malicious intentions to find them. I felt a bit sad, not because I was bored out of my gourd sitting about the motel room all the livelong day, but because I'd come to enjoy our little chats.

"I'm not sure where you're going, Char, but if you happen to run into Mickey Mouse, please give him my best."

Charlotte snickered again. "I'll be sure to tell him that." There was a long pause as we grappled with how to say farewell before she added, "Can I come visit you and Alice and Rex when we come back?"

"You better," I said. "In fact, I have an immediate opening

for an assistant to help me out with my dog obedience classes, in case you're interested."

I sat at the coffee table, cell phone glued to my ear, while Alice loafed at my feet. Rex, on the other hand, strutted about, peeking into the closet, then peering into the bathroom, and finally staring into Crystal's adjoining room as though he were a bellhop awaiting a tip. But there'd be no tip for my springer spaniel; he'd yet to carry a single bag.

Charlotte asked, "What do I have to do?"

"Mostly you hand out treats to puppies that perform their tasks correctly."

"I can do that," she said. "Would I have to clean up any messes?"

"Well, sometimes the pups get a little excited, so there might be the occasional cleanup on aisle five. You'd just toss a couple of paper towels on top and, after class, I can spray and wipe down the area."

"I can do that," she repeated.

"Better yet, just hand a couple of paper towels to the puppy's owner and they'll take care of the rest."

The twice daily walks the beasts and I took had turned into prolonged excursions as we sought out different boulevards and sidewalks and avenues and walkways—mostly for my benefit. Plus, I snuck Alice and Rex by Crab Face at the front desk every couple of hours for their sniff-and-pees. Their bladders could last eons longer, certainly longer than mine, but it gave us something to do aside from sitting around a motel room, pondering what had become of my life.

Charlotte then asked me, "How much do I get paid?"

"Wow—you leapt right into salary, didn't you?" I replied. "Nicely played. Sadly, there are these pesky child labor laws, Char. Very difficult for me to get around. Perhaps I'll just have you hand out doggie treats and then we'll go get pizza and ice cream when the training's over."

"Chocolate ice cream?"

"You drive a hard bargain."

Charlotte went on to tell me her brother's memorial was being planned for some time down the road, when it was safe for her and her family to return to Chicago, so they wouldn't have to celebrate Patrick's life in secrecy. She invited me to attend; I promised I'd be there.

The two of us talked another minute and agreed that saying "See you later" was much better than saying "Goodbye," and that Alice and Rex and I would connect with her as soon as she and her family came back to town.

I'd joshed with Charlotte about needing an assistant for my training classes, but it wasn't a complete lark. You see, I'd come to the conclusion that Brielle's services would no longer be required. Not that she'd done anything incorrectly or anything bad; heck, I'd even write her a letter of recommendation if requested.

But here's the thing of it—when one sits around a motel room all day long, it gives one a ton of time to collect one's thoughts, which is what I'd been doing. And, as uncomfortable as the conversation would likely be, I had to tell Brielle that I like her in a carry-your-books-home-from-school manner and, as such, I'm too immature to *just be friends* and continue this pretense of doing things together outside the classroom setting. I'd discussed this with Crystal and she told me to keep the exchange short and sweet and, if possible, upbeat. Though, to be honest, I didn't think I'd be capable of pulling off upbeat.

My sister mentioned Brielle may have been through similar conversations in the past.

I'd not worked out any of the specifics yet, but figured I'd scribble down a few notes I could read over the phone that wouldn't make me sound all creepy and screwy and weird. Crystal said I should talk to Brielle in person, that I owed her that much, but if I did it in person there might be awkward silences or pained expressions that might prompt me into sticking the entire shoe store in my mouth.

There was also another reason—an overriding reason—that I didn't want to do it in person.

I was chickenshit.

However, by phone, I could have my notes splayed across the table in front of me. I could even have them sorted and labeled and color-coded. For example, if Brielle got frustrated,

I could say this sentence. If she had any questions, I could read off one or two of these sentences. And, if she got angry and hung up, well . . . there'd be no need for additional sentences.

My cell phone buzzed. I glanced at the caller ID. It was Crystal.

"Hey," I said.

"Hey yourself," my sister replied. "Guess what?"

"What?"

"I've got a lead on one of the girls in the pictures; you know, Lansing's private collection."

"OK."

"And she's still alive. She's in her nineties and lives somewhere near Joliet."

"Great. Hopefully, she can tell you what was up with those photographs."

"Yup, I'm heading there now," Crystal replied, "so I won't get back to the motel until later tonight." She then said, "You'll have to get your own damned dinner."

FORTY-SIX

The apartment door opened to an elderly woman who looked every inch of her ninety-plus years; white hair, weathered face—leathery and wrinkled, frail posture and stooped shoulders. She sported pink elastic-waist pants with a matching sweatshirt and leaned on a cane that implied gravity was winning in the war of attrition. Crystal saw no trace of the girl from the photograph in the woman answering the door, but figured eight decades could do that to a person.

The woman Crystal took to be Olive Cripps stared back at her through thick glasses that blurred her eyes and said, "Are you the detective that called earlier?"

"Yes," Crystal said and held her badge at eye level. "I'm Detective Crystal Pratt, with the Chicago Police Department?"

"The Chicago police?" the woman replied, confused. "You're not from Joliet?"

"I'm not." Crystal placed her badge back in her pocket. "Just an hour down the road, though. I made great time."

The woman smiled and opened the door. "Well, come on in then," she said. "I'm Olive Cripps."

The two sat at a wooden table in a cramped space that passed for the apartment's dining room. Olive set out a tray of chocolate chip cookies, small plates and napkins, and poured Crystal a cup of coffee. "It's decaf," Olive said. "Not because it's late in the afternoon, but because the doctors made me give up caffeine a decade ago." She set the cup in front of Crystal and added, "Evidently, it messes with my blood pressure."

"Decaf is fine," Crystal said and picked up a cookie. "Are these homemade?"

Olive nodded. "It's my mother's secret recipe."

Crystal nibbled at the cookie. She remembered Joyce telling her about Olive Cripps's mother, as the two Cripps women would tag-team babysitting her when Joyce was a wee little tyke. Joyce had some considerate words for Olive, but she absolutely adored Olive's mother. She told Crystal the woman had such a kind and gentle soul that, when Joyce was a child, it was like having an additional grandmother.

"It's very good," Crystal said. "Your mother's recipe stands the test of time, Ms. Cripps."

"Thank you," she replied, "but call me Olive. All my friends do." She added, "My mother spent most of her career as a cook. I imagine nowadays she'd be referred to as a sous or a station chef." Olive took the chair opposite Crystal, leaned her cane against the table, and took a second to stir cream into her cup of decaf. "So, a police detective coming to visit me," she said and smiled. "It's like being on a TV show."

"I hope my call didn't alarm you."

"Oh no, dear. If I'm being honest, you've made my day. Normally, I'd be doing laundry, but your showing up is much more *interesting*."

"Anything's more interesting than doing laundry, in my world." Crystal set the brown envelope on top of the table, unclasped one side, and said, "Have you ever met anyone by the name of Lansing Shortridge?"

FORTY-SEVEN

"Have you ever met anyone by the name of Lansing Shortridge?"

Wade squeezed at the handle of the butcher knife when he heard the lady cop's question. He leaned against the bedroom wall, beside the doorframe, and eavesdropped as the conversation in the dining room unfolded. The door to his great-grandmother's bedroom was open, which made for easy listening, but Wade was out of sight. No inquisitive glances about the small apartment by the CPD detective would pinpoint him.

Wade had been there when Detective Pratt called his great-grandmother's landline to ask if she could swing by and ask her some questions. As soon as Olive picked up the phone, she hit speakerphone so he could listen in. His jaw dropped and Wade doubted he could have handled such a call without stuttering and stammering his way through it, without arising suspicion.

But his great-grandmother was in top form, all calm and nonchalant; it was just another day in the park.

Wade had stopped by Olive's apartment alone because, let's face it, he and his great-grandmother were the brains behind the operation. Plus, there was no way either of them would be involving his mother in further activity. The only reason his mother became involved in the first place was due to her tripping over what he and Garrick had done at Whalon Lake.

Good God—what a nightmare that turned out to be; an afternoon no one in the family would ever forget.

And when it came to his twin brother—well, Garrick would drag his feet, hem and haw, and raise all the right questions, but ultimately he would go along with whatever Wade and their great-grandmother came up with. But for now, there wasn't much for Garrick to drag his feet about. Wade and

Olive had decided it would be best for everyone involved if they, like certain insects in winter—like yellowjackets or hornets—went dormant.

Time, after all, was on their side.

Even if I'm not around to see it, Olive had told Wade, *I know you and Garrick will finish the job.*

After his great-grandmother disconnected with Detective Pratt, Wade lobbied for the two of them to jump in his Traverse so he could get her the hell out of Dodge. He knew the lady cop was the dog-boy's sister, and that her showing up out of the blue spelled disaster. But Olive shook her head and said no. His great-grandmother told him the police would not call if they had anything on her. There would be no warning. The cops would just barge in and take her away.

Wade then phoned Garrick at the warehouse to verify his brother was indeed *at the warehouse* . . . and had not been picked up or arrested. Turned out his twin was just fine. "Jump in your car right now," Wade instructed him. "Tell work that Grandma had a fall and you're heading to the hospital. Go like hell. I need you in the parking lot before the detective gets here." After a few more seconds of instruction, he hung up.

Then Wade called his office under the guise of retrieving a client's phone number, but actually to gauge if the receptionist and his admin sounded as though everything at work was A-OK, and not as if a squadron of police officers was currently rifling through his desk.

"Let's just see what Detective Pratt has to say before we do anything rash," his great-grandmother cautioned him. "She mentioned she has some questions for me regarding years gone by."

"But I don't trust her, Grandma."

"Nor do I, honey," Olive had said. "Nor do I."

FORTY-EIGHT

"Lansing Shortridge." Olive Cripps repeated the name slowly, letting it roll off her tongue. "There's a story about a missing boy they found inside a school wall that's been in the news. I turn off the television because it makes me want to cry. I think the boy's last name was Shortridge, but I forget his first name," she said. "I don't believe it was Lansing."

"The boy's first name was Patrick."

"Is Lansing his father?"

"No," Crystal said. "Lansing is the boy's great-grandfather. He passed away a couple years ago."

"My memory's not as good as it once was." Olive returned Crystal's gaze. "Could the man have gone by Lance?"

"I'm sure Lance could be short for Lansing," Crystal replied. Quite frankly, Crystal hoped she'd be as alert as Olive Cripps if she happened to make it into her midnineties. Crystal found the woman sharp as a tack. The cookies weren't bad, either. "Did you ever know a Lance Shortridge?"

"I've known a few men named Lance—I lived next door to Lance and Maggie Hellervick for years and years—but I'm sorry, none of the Lances I knew had Shortridge as a last name."

Crystal dipped a hand into the brown envelope and fished out the photographs of Lansing Shortridge, both the earlier ones with his family as well as the later ones taken with the younger women. She set them down in the middle of the dining room table, one by one, facing the elderly woman, and watched for any type of reaction. "These are pictures of Lansing Shortridge," Crystal went on to say, "from when he was in his midtwenties on up through his forties."

Olive hovered forward, over her coffee and cookie plate, a finger pressed against the bridge of her eyeglasses as she studied each photograph as though she were a nearsighted anteater inspecting an anthill.

"Possibly you knew him, but he went by a different name."

Olive nodded slightly at Crystal's comment and continued examining the line of photographs until she reached the final image. Then she leaned back into her chair and stretched her back. "I'm sorry, Detective Pratt—I don't recognize the man."

"Thank you for taking the time to look, Olive," Crystal said, and then she swept the photos into a stack and returned them to the envelope.

"Were those later pictures of Shortridge taken with his daughters?"

"No," Crystal replied. "They were women he was dating at the time."

"Ooh," Olive said. "I thought that might be the case." A smile worked its way across her face. "In my day they called it *robbing the cradle*."

"I think they still do."

Olive lifted her cup of coffee. "I apologize for not being of much help, Detective," she said. "Perhaps you can tell me what this is all about?"

Crystal nodded. "First, let me show you a handful of additional pictures," she said, her hand dipping back inside the envelope. Crystal retrieved the dated black-and-whites of the individual women and flipped through them to make sure she had them all. Then she laid the photos out in front of Olive Cripps in the same manner as she'd done with the pictures of Lansing Shortridge. "Do you recognize anyone in this set of photographs?"

Olive set her cup back down and leaned forward again, this time a nearsighted anteater probing rotting wood for termites. She made it halfway through the row of pictures before her head popped up, her mouth open in surprise. "That's me, Detective Pratt," Olive Cripps said and pointed at the middle picture. "My God, that's me."

FORTY-NINE

"That's me, Detective Pratt. My God, that's me."

Wade heard the excitement in his great-grandmother's voice and slid his head an inch beyond the doorframe so he could see what was taking place in the dining room. If Pratt somehow spotted him, well—then Pratt was dead. But the two were on opposite sides of the dining table, a string of photographs between them, eyes locked, staring at each other. He slid back into concealment and lifted the butcher knife.

Wade was pleased that Pratt had come alone; pleased her detective partner or pipsqueak of a brother had not come along for the ride . . . he was relieved there'd be only one dead cop for him to deal with.

If Detective Pratt so much as began reading his great-grandmother her Miranda rights, she'd be dead before she finished the first sentence. If Pratt handcuffed Olive, she'd be dead before they locked in place.

Goddammit!

The detective was being all crafty and cagey; she was playing cat and mouse. First, the woman starts in quizzing Olive about Lansing Shortridge. Then, she's pulling out pictures of Lansing and his jailbait girlfriends, and now she's taken out an old photograph of his great-grandmother herself.

And if the picture of Olive had Lansing in it with her, then they'd be totally screwed—the game over—but Detective Pratt would be just as dead. Wade almost wanted it to play out in that manner; he could practically taste it. Every fiber in his soul wanted it to head in that direction as payback to that little shit of her dog-boy brother.

And when it came to Pratt's little shit of a brother, the kid's smartphone had been a complete bust. Wade and Garrick had fiddled with it for ten minutes after rushing from the warehouse in Wheeling, trying to unlock the goddamned thing. Then they worried about cops using the iPhone to track their location and decided to cut their losses. They wiped it down with Mountain Dew and old napkins and then dumped it in a storm drain off Dundee Road.

Yes, Wade thought as he listened to what was playing out at the dining room table . . . the next few seconds would tell whether Crystal Pratt survived or got a kitchen knife sunk deep into her jugular vein.

FIFTY

"Where on earth did you get this picture?"

"It was with these other photographs"—Crystal pointed at the row of black-and-whites on the dining room table and then tapped the brown envelope—"in one of Lansing Shortridge's photo albums."

Olive stared at Crystal in bewilderment. "But this Shortridge gentleman never took my picture."

Crystal cleared her throat. "Would you have any idea where it came from?"

"We didn't own a camera when I grew up." Olive set the photograph beside her coffee cup, her eyes still glued to the image of her younger self. "Too expensive; Mom and I had enough trouble making the rent each month."

"Was there anyone you knew who had a camera that could have taken this photograph?"

"I'm sorry," Olive said. "My memory isn't what it once was and any pictures of me from back then were few and far between." She finally looked up, a bobber returning to the surface. "I can't believe I was ever that young," she said. "Can I keep it?"

"I'll take a picture of it and text it to you."

"I'm old," Olive said, grinning. "I don't own a cell phone, and I've never texted in my life."

"I'll make sure to get this picture to you once we've finished with our investigation." Crystal jotted down a reminder in her notepad.

"That would be awfully sweet of you," Olive said, "but getting back to your question on who took this photo. I went to movies with my father when I was a little girl, before he died, and I got it stuck in my mind I was going to be a world-famous actress."

"You wouldn't be the first to think that."

"Alas, except for talent and looks, there would have been no stopping me."

Crystal pointed at the picture in front of Olive. "You look pretty stunning in that photograph."

"Bless you, dear," Olive replied. "I do remember an ad in the newspaper back then, doubtless because I cut it out and taped it to my mirror. A talent agent was coming to town and setting up auditions. I forced my mother to drive me there, nearly bent her arm to do it. The agent snapped a few pictures of me, but then he started talking about his *fee*." Olive dipped a cookie in her cup of coffee. "It became awkward. We had no money . . . and we slinked away."

"It sounds like the talent agent was a fraud."

"Mom and I thought the same." Olive nibbled at the moist end of her cookie and then continued. "But his pictures were taken inside, not like this one." In the image on the table in front of her, a young Olive Cripps sat on a blanket, sharing a toothy smile with whoever snapped the photograph, a line of trees in the background. "I had a small part in a school play—*The Tempest*. That was when I realized I lacked the skills to pursue acting, but a photographer took several pictures of the cast members. Of course those were shot inside as well; we all stood in a row on the stage."

Crystal nodded along as Olive reminisced about deceptive talent agents and high school theater. She wasn't certain what she hoped to accomplish with today's visits; chatting with elderly women about long-ago times. Neither Joyce Bauer nor Olive Cripps held any earth-shattering recollections that ripped the Patrick Shortridge case wide open. Crystal hadn't expected much of anything to pan out; to be honest, she was amazed the young girl in the old photograph was still alive. But Crystal was committed to following every lead, no matter how weak or irrelevant they turned out to be. She'd write today off as just another loose end tracked down, not unlike discovering the rumor of Lionel Shortridge working for organized crime was, in fact, true.

Crystal's partner had intimated she should drop this flight of fancy and return her attention to more current events.

Detective Lahlum was right, without a doubt, but Crystal had logged enough hours at the precinct that pursuing this particular *flight of fancy* was, in gambler terms, a push.

But then Olive's eyes lit up. "I know. That picture was taken at one of the Wexford Hotel's summer picnics." She paused in thought for a long second. "Of course it was."

Crystal smiled, fished a hand back inside the envelope, and retrieved the drink coaster from the old hotel. She set it down beside the picture of young Olive Cripps.

Olive's jaw dropped open. Even through the thick spectacles, Crystal saw tears form in the corners of Olive's eyes. "I haven't seen these coasters in . . . it has to be at least sixty years," she said. "I was a waitress at the Wexford. I must have placed a million of these down on tables." She looked at Crystal. "Can I have this?"

"You'll have to arm wrestle Joyce Bauer for it?"

"Joyce who?"

"I believe you knew her as Joyce Lehman."

Olive's eyes widened. "Joyce the Voice."

"Joyce the who?"

"Her father, Donny, had nicknames for everyone at the hotel. He called me Olive Oyl—you know, like the woman in *Popeye*—but mostly he called me Oyl. I babysat Joyce all the time and when she began to speak, Donny started calling her Joyce the Voice, or just Voice."

"Her father sounds like he had a good sense of humor."

"I loved Donny; everyone at the hotel loved Donny." Olive dabbed at a tear with her napkin. "Whenever I think back on the Wexford, I think of him." She lifted her eyebrows. "You met with Joyce."

Crystal nodded. "She's the one who told me that was you in the picture."

"How is she doing?"

"She seems well. She's living with her son and daughter-in-law. She even has her own suite set up in their house."

"Can I get her phone number?"

"I'll pass your number onto Joyce," Crystal said. "That's CPD's procedure, but I'm sure she'll give you a call."

"Joyce the Voice," Olive said again and dabbed at her eyes. "Your visit, Detective, is a stroll down memory lane; you've made my day . . . you've made my week. I'll even buy a cell phone if that's what I need to get that picture of me and a shot of the old drink coaster."

"Let me see what I can do before you go purchasing anything," Crystal said and then steered the conversation back to the picture of young Olive Cripps. "Tell me about these summer picnics the Wexford put on."

"Well, they were thrown at a nearby park, which explains why this photograph was taken outside. They were held midweek, maybe on a Tuesday or a Wednesday, when the hotel wasn't at full occupancy. And they'd hold them in the afternoon, after the lunch rush, so most of the staff could find a little time to sneak away and stop by. They put on a great show of it—barbequed chicken and hamburgers and pink lemonade, and"—she glanced down at her plate—"my mother's cookies, and we'd play all different sorts of games and they'd raffle off prizes. They were so much fun that I hated cutting out early to return to the Wexford, to allow other staff members to attend."

Crystal scribbled a sentence on her notepad and asked, "And the hotel brought along a photographer?"

"Well, not a professional or anything fancy like that. One of the managers, or maybe even Donny himself, had a camera and they'd go around the park snapping pictures. After the pictures were developed, they'd post them on one of the bulletin boards in the lobby so all the employees could come and look at them."

"The pictures were posted in the Wexford's lobby?"

"Just for a week or so because the boards or lobby displays were needed for hotel events."

"Were the pictures kept behind glass or secured in some manner so no one could take them?"

"No," Olive replied. "If you were in a picture, they wouldn't mind if you took it. In fact, you could probably just pocket it without asking anyone."

Crystal nudged the black-and-white of young Olive with

a forefinger. "But you don't remember this particular photograph."

"It was a long time ago, Detective. I may have seen it on the display board and forgotten. I wouldn't have appreciated the picture as much back then as I do now," she said. "But since it was taken outside, I'm sure it's from one of the picnics."

"So if a guest saw a picture on the lobby display board, they could have just taken it, right?"

"I guess," Olive replied. "It'd be easy if no one spotted them. Donny might have had something to say if he caught a guest taking photographs off the board." Olive frowned. "Do you think that's how this Shortridge gentleman got my picture?"

Crystal shrugged. "I have no idea." She glanced around the room, thinking about lifting another chocolate chip cookie; perhaps ask if she could take an extra one home for her brother. Crystal noticed a framed picture of a green countryside on the far wall; next to it was a picture of flowers in a vase. Another frame depicted a melancholy clown, but Crystal didn't spot any family pictures on display. She turned back to Olive and said, "Joyce mentioned you had a daughter."

FIFTY-ONE

"Joyce mentioned you had a daughter."

Wade filled the bedroom doorway. His great-grandmother was speaking but he couldn't focus on what she was saying. He was incensed—a living, breathing pressure cooker—his face red, his temples beating in time with his heart. All of Wade's attention lay on the detective at the dinner table. If the cop turned her head so much as two inches, she would spot him, certainly in her periphery . . . and it would hasten her death.

The knife would sink deep into the side of Pratt's neck as she attempted to stand, as she fumbled for her holster.

Fuck this noise! Fuck this charade!

Wade was sick of the cat-and-mouse bullshit. Pratt had gone from quizzing his great-grandmother about Lansing Shortridge, to pulling out some ancient photograph of Olive as a child, to showing her some goddamned drink coaster from the hotel where she'd first met Lansing, to now questioning her about her dead daughter. Darlene—the grandmother Wade had never met, who'd never had a shot at life. He'd seen enough true crime documentaries to know how interrogation games played out; how you get the suspect talking, how you give them enough rope and—eventually—they hang themselves from the rafters.

No more!

Pratt didn't bring backup, which meant this was a fishing trip. The detective had nothing on his great-grandmother, but stopped by uninvited to find out if any of her queries got the old woman to implicate herself. And if Olive implicated herself . . . that would be all she wrote.

He wasn't about to let that happen.

Not tonight. Not ever.

The two conversed as Wade made his plan. He'd rip up the carpet as well as anything else tainted by blood splatter. He'd make sure to get all that DNA shit out of the apartment and dispose of it accordingly. The firepit at Whalon Lake came to mind.

Olive would have to call Detective Pratt's cell phone in an hour or so and leave a message, asking, all sweet and innocent-like, when the detective planned on arriving, as it was getting late and her bedtime was fast approaching.

He'd get Garrick's ass up here as well, to help out. They'd plunk the lady cop into her own trunk once the sun went down. Perhaps check for cameras in the underground garage in case sneaking Pratt out that way worked best. Then, in his SUV, he'd follow Garrick as they both drove to some shithole section in Rockford to dump the woman's car. They'd leave the doors unlocked with the keys on the dashboard and let nature take its course. Of course, the cop's purse and credit cards would be missing on account of Wade's pocketing whatever cash she had on hand and tossing the purse and the rest of its contents into the first lake he spotted on their late-night excursion to Rockford.

Let her dog-boy brother spend the rest of his miserable life stewing over what happened to his precious sister.

Wade took a deep breath and readied himself.

He could do this. It was going to be a long night, but he and Garrick could pull it off.

Then came a flash of movement at the dining room table. His great-grandmother must have sensed his presence in the bedroom doorway, as she'd not glanced his way, not once, but her right hand now hung down by her lap, beneath the tabletop, out of Pratt's view. Olive flicked her fingers in his direction; it took him a second to catch her meaning.

She was waving him off, shooing him away as though he were a backyard fly. Olive was telling Wade to get his ass back inside the bedroom, to get out of sight right this instant; that she had everything under control.

His great-grandmother was the smartest woman Wade had ever met in his entire life and, even though it rubbed against every fiber in his body, he'd give her five more minutes to get Pratt out of the apartment.

As Wade slipped back into the bedroom, a floorboard creaked.

FIFTY-TWO

"My daughter died many years ago," Olive Cripps replied, setting down the remnants of her chocolate chip cookie.

"I am so sorry," Crystal said and sat upright. She felt as though the tip of a nail had scraped against a blackboard. "I didn't know, Olive. Joyce didn't mention that."

"Joyce wouldn't have known. They'd moved to Chicago a few years before Darlene died. By then the Wexford had been torn down, replaced by a shopping mall I've never set foot in." She stared down, but Crystal knew her focus wasn't on the tabletop. "Hard to keep in touch back then; there was no Facebook or email." She glanced up and caught Crystal's eye. "My daughter moved to San Francisco and fell in with the wrong crowd. She became addicted to drugs, the kind that kill . . . and, as a result, my little angel died of a heroin overdose."

"Oh, Olive," Crystal said. "I have no words."

"I spent a good part of the 70s and a bit of the 80s speaking at substance abuse groups, mostly Narcotics Anonymous, doing my best to tell Darlene's story in the hope that other children wouldn't be lost." Olive swallowed hard and leaned back in her chair, her hands dropping to her lap. "I don't know if I made a difference." She shook her head. "I doubt I was of any help."

Crystal said, "I'm sure you were. NA is still active." Working at CPD, she was well aware of the different substance abuse groups. "They still bring in speakers to tell their stories in order to get through to people." Crystal looked down at her coffee. "I wish we could just snap our fingers and make it go away."

"It seems to go on and on, doesn't it?" Olive sighed. "It sounds like fentanyl's the latest craze to sweep in and destroy lives."

Crystal opened her mouth, ready to step up on her opioid soapbox, but she heard a nearly-imperceptible sound—the floor creaking in another room. She cocked her head a second, then glanced toward the apartment's hallway, toward the bedroom's open door, but saw nothing. "I'm sorry," Crystal said. "Am I interrupting company, Olive? Is someone else here?"

The elderly woman shook her head. "Just the world's fattest cat," she said. "Bailey tends to run and hide whenever company comes over."

Crystal smiled. "I live in a canine household. I bet she smelled the dogs on me and dove under the bed."

"It's funny because once Bailey gets to know you, she'll never leave you alone."

"Would you like me to try and pry her out from wherever she's hiding?"

Olive shook her head. "You'd spend the rest of your life trying to coax her out. If Bailey gets to be too much of a hermit, or refuses to leave her hiding spot, I'll crack a can of Purina and watch her come running." Olive folded her hands on the dining room table. "Like I said, she's the world's fattest cat."

Crystal checked her watch. "I've taken up way too much of your time, Olive." She then glanced at the plate of cookies. "Don't ever lose your mother's recipe," she said, and thought of her brother. "Can I steal a couple for the ride home?"

"Take as many as you'd like, dear."

FIFTY-THREE

Olive held her great-grandson's eye. "Have another cookie, Wade."

Wade sat in the chair Detective Pratt had vacated moments earlier. "I'm sorry, Grandma. I wasn't sure how many more *items* Pratt was going to pull out of her grab bag of bullshit."

"She came here because Donny's daughter picked me out of Lansing's *trophy* pictures," Olive replied. She recalled him snapping the photograph of her as though it had occurred only yesterday; it was the afternoon she told Lansing she was pregnant. He wanted to immortalize the moment . . . and he certainly had. "There was no need to take it to the next level."

Wade took a deep breath. "Well, you handled it brilliantly," he said finally. "If I didn't know you were making stuff up, I'd have bought everything you told her."

"Yes," Olive said, nodding, though she was anything but pleased with Wade hovering in the bedroom doorway where he could easily have been spotted; his almost marching out and butchering the cop at the dining room table, as though her home were a slaughterhouse. Olive had the *Detective Pratt situation* under control, under her full control, and her great-grandson damn near ruined everything.

For the love of God, she had to ad-lib being a cat owner.

And she hated cats.

But Olive's mind spun elsewhere. She was placing every nook and cranny of her conversation with the CPD detective under the microscope. She thought about Pratt's packet of pictures and sighed. "I went through all of Lansing's photo albums at the nursing home. They sat out on a shelf, but the pictures of me and those other girls were not in them. He must have kept those concealed, from back when his brain still worked and told him those pics should remain hidden." She looked across the table at her great-grandson. "I imagine he had the photos buried away somewhere until his brain fried and he forgot they even existed."

"Probably stuffed away in his underwear drawer or under the mattress, wherever—and his family found them after he died and passed them on to Pratt?"

Olive nodded again. That made sense. She also agreed with Wade that she'd managed herself quite well with the detective from Chicago; more than passably. Olive may not have had the required looks to go to Hollywood, but she certainly had the acting chops, as she'd heard them referred to in the biz.

But Crystal Pratt was bright.

She was not one to underestimate.

Olive did her subtle best to see that the detective left empty-handed. Pratt would be forced to put the picture to rest; to tack it up as irrelevant . . . just another dead end. Olive even sprinkled breadcrumbs for Pratt to follow, a trail that envisioned Lansing lifting the photograph of young Olive from the hotel's lobby, possibly during an overnight stay at the Wexford.

Lansing's obsession with midteen girls couldn't let him walk away from an image that struck his fancy, that aroused him. *Who knows,* Detective Pratt would think, *maybe he first spotted young Olive as she served diners at the hotel's restaurant.*

Olive frowned. She sure wished Donny's daughter hadn't brought up Darlene with the detective. It opened a door Olive would have preferred kept shut. But she couldn't imagine the detective pursuing the matter any further. It held no relevance to the present-day case. And, should Pratt decide to keep digging, Darlene's birth certificate would be another dead end.

No, Olive thought, it wouldn't make any sense for Detective Pratt to keep digging. After all, Olive Cripps was just an elderly woman, into her ninth decade—and quite frankly, there wasn't much runway left for her.

Olive Cripps couldn't possibly be considered a threat.

"Wade," Olive said, reaching across the table to take her great-grandson's hand in hers. She knew her other great-grandchild was a helper; Garrick would be there for support and cleanup; however, he lacked the stomach to perform the dirty work. Brother

Wade was a different breed. As such, Brother Wade was the only one that truly understood—and approved—of her plan. "You do know this is not because of Lansing Shortridge? He did betray me; he stabbed me in the back when I was at my most vulnerable . . . and the man was a predator. But it was Lansing's father who destroyed me, Wade. It was his father. One hour in a car with the man and I was ruined. Your grandmother Darlene was ruined as a result. She fell, too, like a string of dominoes. It's Lionel Shortridge I've always been after." She stared into her great-grandson's eyes. "I realize it's splitting hairs, but it's Lionel's lineage I'm after."

"I know, Grandma." He squeezed her hand. "I know." Then Wade leaned back in his chair, looked at her a long second, and asked, "Did you really speak at substance abuse groups?"

Olive slowly smiled. "Of course not."

There came a knock at the door. Wade was there in a flash, peering through the peephole, hoping the cop hadn't returned. But it was Garrick and he quickly opened the door.

"Pratt drives a Honda HR-V," Garrick said, sounding winded. He must have jogged up the staircase instead of taking the elevator. Garrick glanced from his great-grandmother at the dining room table back to his twin brother and added, "I popped the tracker in the wheel well. We'll know wherever she goes."

FIFTY-FOUR

"Did you know most people are right-eye dominant?" I asked Crystal as soon as I opened the room door.

She raised her eyebrows. "OK."

"It's kind of like how more people are right-handed."

"Another long day of sitting, I see."

Crystal was right, of course. I talked to the dogs, but that only went so far. Alice isn't a big fan of pop culture or sports; Rex only listens to country music and is more of a Trekkie than a *Star Wars* fan. Yup—I was in desperate need of basic human interaction. The attached rooms had become my holding cell. Wall panels instead of vertical bars, strolls about the neighborhood in lieu of spending time in the yard, and fast-food drive-throughs as a substitute for meals in the chow hall.

At least none of the other guests at the Discount Inn and Suites had tried to shiv me.

"I'm proud of myself," I said. "I got to wondering if there was such a concept as having a dominant eye, so I googled it and, sure enough, there was—ergo, I'm highly intelligent."

Crystal asked, "Would it hold true if you're twenty-twenty in your left eye and twenty-forty in your right?"

I froze for a second. "OK, I didn't dig into it that deeply, but seventy percent of folks are right-eye dominant. Just ask the Internet—they're never wrong. And I bet that includes your twenty-twenty thing." I then changed subjects so I could continue feeling all brainy and intellectual. "I found a Chinese takeout place a few blocks down the road and got you beef and broccoli," I said. "It's on ice in your sink, but you may want to microwave it."

"Thanks, Cor."

It was nine o'clock at night and, by Crystal's demeanor, I could tell there were no major breakthroughs in the case and that I'd not be getting pardoned by the governor, or let out of stir for time served or good behavior. I'd continue sitting about all day again tomorrow. Hard to believe, but I was beginning to miss my programming courses.

Crystal spent a minute with her two biggest groupies, scratching behind Alice's ears and rubbing Rex's belly. Then she cut through the open door to dump her stuff inside her suite. A few seconds later she returned, carrying a large white box, a smaller one of rice, and a plastic fork. She sat at my coffee table.

"You're going to eat it cold?"

"Yeah," Crystal said. She did that sometimes. My sister examined the two boxes. I knew what was cycling through her mind and started to fidget. "You always get eggrolls," she said. "Don't these combos come with an eggroll?"

"I wasn't sure when you'd be getting in tonight," I said. "And I didn't think the eggroll would keep very well on ice."

"So you ate it?" she asked. "You ate my eggroll?"

"I waited an hour or two until I thought it might be going bad."

Crystal sighed. "You're much too kind." She lifted the lids on both boxes. "So, what other grand thoughts have you had today?"

"I got to thinking about Mom and Dad."

Crystal speared at a piece of beef. "You did?"

"Yeah, I was thinking back on how they met. Remember, Dad was starting out as a veterinarian and Mom was still working on her master's?"

"They bumped into each other at a brunch buffet."

"One of those first-class buffets in downtown Chicago. Dad was there for a conference and Mom and her roommate had a coupon or gift certificate or something."

Crystal nodded and speared a large piece of broccoli.

"So Mom is sitting at a nearby table and she watches as Dad bumbles his way through the buffet line, slopping grub onto his plate. Then Dad gets all confused because no one's at the prime rib station; it's empty," I said. "Dad hasn't eaten at many of these places, so he figures it's like the other entrées;

you serve yourself. He grabs the carving knife and chef's fork and starts cutting himself a big slab of rib roast."

Crystal stuck her fork in the box of rice and says, "Then an elderly couple comes by and asks Dad if he can cut some slices for them."

"Right. Normally these places give you a slice so thin you could shine a flashlight through it, but now a line is forming and Dad finds himself cutting these one-inch slabs for the customers. He makes it through a half dozen people before there's a tap on his shoulder. He turns around and it's either the manager or chef, and the manager-or-chef says, 'What are you doing?'"

"Meanwhile, Mom, who's been watching all of this play out in real time, is laughing her ass off."

"Yeah, the chef probably snuck off to the restroom or the kitchen for more horseradish sauce or whatever. And even though Dad is getting chastised, he spots Mom laughing . . . and falls instantly in love."

Crystal finished the story. "So Dad gets up the nerve, walks over to Mom's table, and asks, 'Do you mind if I sit here? It won't be for long, as I'm about to be arrested.'"

"Dad said he must have cut about seven inches of prime rib that day."

"Best meet-cute story I've ever heard."

"And from that day onward, Mom and Dad rarely left each other's side."

"Right up to the end," Crystal said. "What made you think of that?"

"I don't know," I replied. "I've been thinking about the talk I'm going to have with Brielle and that popped into mind." I'd shared with Crystal how once this case was settled, and some sense of normalcy returned, Brielle and I would have that conversation. I'd even finished writing my crib notes.

"It'll be an awkward five minutes," Crystal said, "but it'll be OK."

I shrugged. "As a police officer, Crys, you've got that *protect and serve* thing going, right?"

She nodded.

"Wouldn't this conversation fall under protect and serve?" I asked. "Can you have the chat with Brielle for me?"

Crystal chuckled. "No, Cory—that won't be happening. I won't be talking to Brielle."

"It doesn't fall under protect and serve?"

"Not in the least," she said and returned to her takeout.

I glanced at Rex, asleep on my bed, snoring lightly, no doubt dreaming his country-music dreams. Rex was my personal space heater at night. Alice had taken to crashing on Crystal's bed, keeping my sister warm and cozy. While sleeping, our suites became segregated, like locker rooms.

"Hey," I said. "She's not here this late in the evening, but have you met the clerk on the day shift?"

"You mean Pam?"

"You know her name?"

"Yes," Crystal said. "Why do you ask?"

"Because I'm afraid of her," I replied. "She scowls at me whenever I bring the dogs outside."

Crystal stirred at her Chinese food. "Pam's a sweetheart, Cor. She shows up early for her shift, so we say hi every morning as I head out."

"She doesn't look all crabby and scowl at you?"

"Not at all."

"How come I always have to deal with stuff like that and you get to waltz through life whistling 'Zip-a-Dee-Doo-Dah'?"

My sister chuckled again. "Yeah, right, because that's so true."

"Maybe Pam has RSF—resting scowl face."

"I don't think so," Crystal said. "And since it appears we're going to be extended guests, you should introduce yourself and let her meet Alice and Rex."

"That's the same thing Charlotte said."

"Out of the mouths of babes."

FIFTY-FIVE

Garrick returned to the SUV, flicked his Marlboro onto the pavement, stubbed it out with the toe of his work boot, and then opened the passenger door.

"I thought you gave those up?" Wade said.

"I've quit several times." Garrick climbed inside and shut the door. "But if someone spots me skulking about the parking lot at this hour, they'll think I'm sneaking a smoke before heading back inside to the little missus and the rug rats."

Wade nodded. "I can't argue with that logic."

"The GPS tracker is on the kid's Silverado, so we've got him covered as well in case he leaves here."

"Nice little device—always know where your kids are, catch a cheating spouse . . . track cops."

Wade's Traverse was parked along the outer edge of the Discount Inn and Suites' parking lot. It was half past one in the morning. Ninety minutes earlier they'd cruised the motel's lot, slowly, confirming the detective's HR-V was there as well as finding where her dog-boy brother stashed his pickup truck. The twins also kept their eyes peeled for any vehicles the Shortridge family owned in case they hit pay dirt, but no such luck on that front.

Chances were the cops had the Shortridges tucked away in a safe house somewhere, Wade figured, or, more likely at this point, the family had fled the continent.

After scoping out the parking lot, the twins left the Discount Inn. Wade felt a slight intermission was due in case the night clerk or any guest got suspicious concerning the black Chevrolet Traverse roaming the parking lot for minutes on end. A few miles down the road, they tripped over a Denny's that was open all night. The two ate pancakes, drank coffee, and chatted quietly before returning to the motel to plant the tracker.

Upon their return, Wade dropped Garrick off near dog-boy's

Silverado and then parked his vehicle in the back of the lot as though he were just another lodger returning after a late night of whatever. Garrick's planting the tracking device and moseying over to the SUV took all of two minutes.

There was no need for Garrick to run.

Running made you the center of attention.

"I'm thinking of taking a little time off from the office," Wade said as he turned right out of the Discount Inn's parking lot.

"Really?" Garrick said. "Shouldn't we be going about business as usual?"

"It's no big deal," Wade replied. "I can work remotely from anywhere in the world; check emails, work Excel sheets, make some phone calls."

"You fuckers with the *work remotely* bullshit," Garrick said. "You know what I heard working remotely stands for?"

"What?"

"Full-time pay for part-time work."

"Shh," Wade said. "We're trying to keep it a secret."

"I knew it." Garrick shook his head, and then he asked, "So what do you mean by *taking a little time off*?"

"You know, get away for a while." Wade steered the SUV down the frontage road but glanced back at the Discount Inn and Suites. "Now, if I only knew of a good place to stay."

His twin brother stared at him in silence.

PART FIVE

The Trainer in the Trap

The more I see of the representatives of the people, the more I admire my dogs.

—Alphonse de Lamartine

FIFTY-SIX

"You good staying here, Cory?"

I shrugged. "I'm getting hooked on soap operas, but it beats getting shot at."

"How are the dogs holding up?"

"Don't worry about Alice and Rex," I replied. "This is summer camp for those two rascals. They keep wondering when I'm going to break out the s'mores."

Detective Lahlum chuckled. "Sorry I didn't bring you a Starbucks."

"Hey," I said, "it'll give me a chance to sneak out and give you two a chance to talk."

Lahlum had arrived at Crystal's room bearing two medium roasts with cream: one for him, one for my sister, and, of course, nada for yours truly. My sister had warned me last night her partner would be stopping by in the morning to see if they had better luck thinking outside the box by, well, being outside the box—which meant being outside of the police precinct.

They'd not approached that point yet, but here's the deal. When CPD detectives cannot solve a case, it's usually closed and considered "cold" even though it's still *officially* "open." However, there is no active investigation in play unless new evidence emerges, because there are no active leads to pursue. That sucks out loud, not only because the bad guys dance away scot-free while their victims get screwed out of justice, but also because—in terms of Charlotte and her family, as well as little old me—we're left to float about in limbo.

Of course, I happen to have a sister who won't let that occur. Crystal would moonlight this investigation for as long as it took to get the perps tucked safely behind bars.

Even though the Discount Inn and Suites had bad coffee in a side room off the lobby, I hustled the beasts past the front desk without glancing in Pam's direction. I felt I'd exhausted the number of times I could meet the day clerk's glare before getting turned into a pillar of salt. As we trekked out to my pickup, Alice watered a patch of grass before we hit curbside, while Rex saved his tank for the front tire of a Mazda3.

After purchasing my daily dark roast, with minimal cream and a few shakes of cinnamon, I sat at a table outside the coffee house, sipping away and watching as the goofballs basked in the attention and adulation radiating off a never-ending blast of patrons lining up for their morning cups of java. It wasn't exactly summer camp, as I'd led Crystal's partner to believe. I'd kick it up a couple of notches and say the pups were on holiday. After a gaggle of suburban moms *oohed* and *aahed* over the twosome, I'd had enough of their being treated like royalty, so I herded Alice and Rex away from their adoring fans and the three of us headed back to the motel.

"Please join us," Crystal said, all businesslike, as soon as we entered my room and I slipped through the open door into my sister's less-cluttered suite. Crystal and her partner had set up shop at the room's coffee table. Two were already a cluster in such small space, so I perched on Crystal's bed, which she made first thing each and every morning, as opposed to the one in my room. "Mark and I are making a mental list of every step we've taken in the investigation so far."

Not sure what they expected of me, I nodded and said, "OK."

Lahlum then caught my eye. "Your sister and I have been pursuing the investigator's trinity, Cory. It may not be holy, but MMO—means, motive, and opportunity—solves a shit ton of crime. As such, we've backgrounded every single name on the lists of construction workers provided by Henry Horner Elementary School. This seemed promising at first because these were lists of means and opportunity—the tradespeople that had the ability and chance to hide Patrick Shortridge's body. For example, we'd be idiots not to look into the masonry workers who built the damned wall to begin with."

I nodded again.

"Then, as we struck out with the masons, we worked our way through the lists of all the others involved in the construction because, you know, how hard would it be to sneak a body into the school if you spent a chunk of the summer working there?"

I nodded a third time. It occurred to me I was here to act as some kind of sounding board for the two CPD detectives; here to listen as they laid out their investigation, in case it helped them find gaps in their sleuthing or bring to light any Perry Mason revelations.

"Especially since the school locked away their valuables in rooms that were not being touched, and they had Principal Isaacson, her VP, and a staff member or teacher on-site every day to answer questions, open any doors required for plumbers or electricians to gain access, and lock it all down after everyone left for the day."

Crystal commented, "Though these construction workers had means and opportunity to commit the crime—hiding Patrick's body—we've been unable to ferret out a motive."

"The lists of contractors and tradespeople provided by the office administrator, Suzanne Nickless, have been extensive. In fact, I received a finalized list of subcontractors from Suzanne yesterday and contacted Paul Shortridge. It turns out he employed an electrical contractor a few years back and that same contractor did subcontracting in the grade school remodel. However, a different electrician was sent to the Shortridge's house and there were no conflicts with the electrical work he performed." Detective Lahlum shook his head. "Such has become my lot in life. Unfortunately, we haven't been able to find any other links to the Shortridge family—no motives, no reason for killing Patrick. When it comes to chasing down the names on these lists . . . we got zilch."

I raised my hand as though I was in class and Lahlum smiled. "Questions?" he said and glanced about as though we were in a schoolroom instead of a motel suite. "Does anyone have any questions?"

I lowered my hand. "I follow the nightly news and I rarely hear of any rational or thought-through motive when it comes to killing someone."

"Correct," Lahlum replied. "It could be a random act of

violence, it could be a thrill kill, or maybe the perp was under the influence of alcohol or illicit drugs. Most homicides don't make a lick of sense." He added, "It could have even been some asinine road rage incident that went south. Maybe the perp honked at Patrick and got the middle finger in response, and he said, 'Not today.' And suddenly the killer's left with a body to dispose of."

"While we worked the Henry Horner lists"—Crystal picked up the ball—"we also turned our attention on the *personal* lives of the adult Shortridges. We were looking for motive, possibly revenge—you know, like an affair that didn't end well."

"It's extremely difficult for a marriage to rebound after the unexpected death of a child, Cory, or, in this case, the death of two children. We drilled into the Shortridges's cell phones, their text messages, the numbers incoming and outgoing on their landline, and we didn't find a thing—not a single unexplained phone call or text, no fatal attractions on either side of the equation." Lahlum shrugged. "Quite frankly, if your child dies, I don't think you'd give two shits about holding anything back. If someone kills your kid, you'd say, 'I had an affair with John Smith and it went bad. John's made threats and he's been following me. I know John did it.' You'd come forward because your child"—Lahlum's eyes glistened—"has been murdered and you no longer care how bad having an affair is going to make you look."

Mark Lahlum had grown on Crystal. Originally, she'd pegged him as a family man doing all he could to twist the life of a CPD detective into a forty-hour work week, as though he were day manager at a shoe store. But, as my sister grew to know him, she realized Lahlum brought the cases home with him at night for review, after everyone else had gone to bed, and when attending one of his kids' soccer games, Lahlum wasn't really there. Sure, he cheered and fist-pumped at the appropriate moments and got excited if his kid did well or scored a goal, but his mind was often elsewhere, miles away, lost on a current investigation.

I could see why Crystal had changed her assessment. The man seemed solid.

"We talked to Paul and Jennifer's friends, their best friends, subtly—and, at times, not-so-subtly—probing their knowledge of any potential affairs the spouses may have had," Lahlum said. "We told them that any information, no matter how awkward a position it put them in, could help in the investigation. But none of them were aware of any extramarital matters Paul or Jen may have had."

Crystal then said, "Another major motivation could be financial gain or, considering Paul's profession—financial loss. In recent years, he's devoted himself exclusively to managing the family's portfolio, their assets and investments. The guy is no Bernard Madoff." Bernard Madoff had been the financier who'd perpetrated the largest Ponzi scheme in history. It didn't end well: he died in prison. "No complaints have ever been filed against him with the SEC or FINRA, the Financial Industry Regulatory Authority, not even stretching back to Paul's early years as a financial analyst."

"So," Lahlum said, "zilch on any marital affair or on Paul Shortridge ripping off investors. We've got zilch on motive. Both their sons are dead and an attempt was made on their daughter's life, and the Shortridges have no idea who could be doing this to them." Lahlum frowned. "Unfortunately, neither do we."

"What else have we been up to?" Crystal said to the room while looking my way. "We've had officers canvassing the neighborhood around the grade school, Cory, knocking on doors and talking to homeowners, but again . . . zilch. Sure, the neighbors saw workers coming and going all summer long; sure, the neighbors were mildly interested in the remodel, but . . . not much beyond that to offer." Crystal took a sip of her coffee and continued. "In the past couple of days we've turned our attention to the Shortridges's Kenilworth neighbors, to see if there was any bad blood. Basically, we repeated what the SVU detectives had already done when Patrick disappeared in June."

This time I didn't bother raising my hand: interrupting my sister came with the territory. "Remember that crazy guy from last year?" I said. "He shot his neighbor from his bedroom window because he didn't like that his neighbor was pruning a tree on the property line."

Crystal nodded. "That was nuts. His neighbor was lucky the paramedics arrived in time to keep him alive. But there are no such property disputes in this case. The neighbors seem fond of the Shortridges. They've known them for years and are brokenhearted over the recent events." Crystal sighed. "We've even looked at neighborhood teenagers to see if a pack of bullies could have attacked Patrick. Again, we're following in the footsteps of what the SVU detectives did last summer, but"—my sister shook her head—"we're grasping at straws here, Cor. How could a pack of midteens transport Patrick's body across town? It's a half hour drive from Kenilworth to Arlington Heights. Hard to do if you just got your driver's permit a week earlier. Not to mention the teachers or principal manning the shifts at Henry Horner would have wondered why a bunch of fifteen-year-olds were wheeling in some kind of tarped-over equipment."

And with *tarped-over equipment*, their presentation came to an end.

Unfortunately, I don't think I'd been of much use as either a sounding or listening board and we sat in Crystal's motel room in silence.

"I hate to keep repeating myself," Lahlum said finally, "but the word of the day is zilch."

FIFTY-SEVEN

"Their fitness center's not that big—a couple of bikes, a rowing machine, an ancient treadmill from back when dinosaurs roamed the earth, and a few of those exercise balls I have no clue what to do with." I was walking Detective Lahlum down to his car as Crystal applied any finishing touches before she, too, headed out for the day. My quota of human interaction was nearing an end and I planned on milking it down to the very last drop.

"They've got a swimming pool, right?"

"It's broken; a part is missing or something." The elevator chimed and the doors slid open to the first floor. I added, "Otherwise, I'd spend half the day in there."

"That's too bad," Lahlum replied. "I'd bring the kids over if it were open."

I'd been a Chatty Cathy since we'd left our adjoining rooms and was amazed the detective didn't flee for his vehicle once the elevator let us out. My blood pressure edged up a notch as we crossed the lobby. Fortunately, some guy in a suit and tie and a GQ buzz cut was hunched over the front desk, blocking Pam from view. I seized the opportunity to grab a handful of granola bars from a glass bowl on a side table. They intermittently filled the dish with treats; a real hit-or-miss affair, as I'd yet to decipher when it got replenished.

I tossed a bar at Lahlum, stuffed the rest of them in my pocket, and nearly called out "thanks" to the businessman, but the guy seemed occupied, no doubt pleading with Pam for an early check-in or asking to extend his stay or whatever, and was no doubt greeted with a disapproving glower in response.

As we approached the detective's Kia Telluride, he came to a stop and said, "You know, Cory, your sister's very special."

I nodded. "She gets that from me."

Lahlum ignored my quip and took out his key fob. "She's

the best cop I've ever worked with," he said. "Hands down." Then he caught my eye. "Hard to admit this, but she's made me better at it." Lahlum opened the driver's door. "Don't tell her, though. It'll go straight to her head."

FIFTY-EIGHT

All of Wade's senses were on high alert. He heard the elevator chime somewhere in the background and, a second later, spotted dog-boy and a middle-aged man stepping into the lobby. He turned his attention back to the front desk clerk, the woman with *Assistant Manager* and *Pamela* etched on her name tag.

"That's too bad," Wade heard the older man say. "I'd bring the kids over if it were open."

The first thing Wade had done when he woke was grab his cordless clipper from the hall closet, where it'd been gathering dust since the time or two he'd previously used it. Then Wade buzz cut his hair, using different cutting sizes for the sides and top. It wasn't as good as they'd do in a hair salon, but it was passable. Then Wade used a shampoo-in hair color kit, sandy blond hair, and showered. He dressed in his best business suit—navy blue, white dress shirt, red tie. Finally, he slid on a pair of black glasses with clear lenses and stood in front of his bathroom mirror.

Though he hated the new look, absolutely hated it . . . Wade wouldn't be able to pick himself out of a police lineup.

And all dog-boy had ever seen was the center of his face, a few inches max, and perhaps a wisp of black hair.

Then Wade got in his Traverse and drove to the Discount Inn and Suites in Elk Grove Village.

Wade watched as dog-boy and the older man departed the motel through the entryway and onward into the parking lot.

His great-grandmother would have told him not to do this, his mother would have threatened to go to the police, and even Brother Garrick had stared at him as though he'd lost his mind.

And perhaps he had.

But when it came down to it—whether dog-boy gave him information on where Charlotte Shortridge was hiding or not—dog-boy would not be leaving the Discount Inn and Suites of his own volition.

They'd be carrying the little prick out in a body bag.

FIFTY-NINE

"That was nice of you to walk Detective Lahlum to his car," Crystal said when I returned to the room. She was slipping files into her briefcase with Alice and Rex at her feet, observing, in case she needed help with the latch.

"Mark said I'm very special and you're lucky to have me."

My sister glanced up. "I'm sure he did."

"I may have gotten it switched around."

"So what's on the docket today, Cor?" she asked. "More pizza for lunch?"

"You say that like it's a bad thing."

"How can you eat the same stuff day after day?"

"I don't." I objected. "I switch up the toppings. Today is double sausage."

"No need to save any for me." She slipped the briefcase strap over her shoulder. "I may be back late; don't wait up."

"Hey," I said, wanting a pinch more social interaction before I spent the next twelve hours hectoring Alice and Rex with endless meditations on reality and existence. "You know the old lady you talked to last night? The one in Joliet?"

"Yeah, Olive Cripps," Crystal said. "What about her?"

"Well—the traveling salesman must have gotten to her."

"What?"

"You mentioned she had a baby, even though she lived with her mother, and they all had the same last name—so the traveling salesman must have passed through Joliet back in the day."

My sister stared at me as though I'd sprouted a new head. "What did you say?"

"It was a joke, Crys," I said, thinking I'd somehow pissed her off. "You know—like the ones Dad used to tell about the traveling salesman and the farmer's daughter. This old Cripps lady probably wasn't a farmer's daughter, but, you know, she did get knocked up by someone."

"She wasn't a farmer's daughter," Crystal replied slowly, distracted now and glancing upward, yet I knew her focus didn't lie in the ceiling's drywall finish. "But she did get knocked up by *someone*."

SIXTY

"You're not that late," I said as I opened the door for Crystal. She held a transparent container of salad in one hand and a pregnant briefcase in the other.

"It's been a long day," she said, dropping her briefcase in the entryway between our adjoining rooms and taking a seat at my coffee table. "It's been a long week."

"A salad, huh?"

"I can't eat junk food anymore, Cor."

"That cuts to the quick," I said. "And here I went and picked up that Mediterranean veggie sandwich you like from Panera."

"You did?"

I nodded. "What kind of salad do you have there?"

"Romaine and spinach, some cucumber and tomato, a little vinaigrette."

"Oh, wow," I said. "Be still my heart."

My sister looked at her container and then back at me. "Where'd you hide the sandwich?"

"So did you find out who the baby daddy was?" I asked after Crystal retrieved the sandwich that sat in a Panera bag atop a bucket of ice in her bathtub. Turned out my sister was famished and alternated between chomps of the Mediterranean veggie and nibbles from her salad.

"What a pain that turned out to be. I had to play twenty questions with Vital Records at the Department of Public Health." She shook her head. "They finally sent a copy and no father is listed on Darlene Cripps's birth certificate. The field was left blank." Crystal stabbed at a piece of romaine. "Olive Cripps was born in 1932. Her daughter was born in 1948, when Cripps was sixteen."

"So minus nine months means she got pregnant at fifteen," I said. "Those traveling salesmen—they do get around."

Crystal switched over to her sandwich for a minute. After a bite, she asked, “Don’t these come with a bag of chips?”

“I thought you didn’t want any more junk food.”

“So you ate them, right?”

I looked away. “After all of your squawking about junk food, I thought I’d do you a favor and get rid of the temptation.”

“How terribly considerate of you.” My sister caught my eye as she stabbed hard at a cucumber with her salad fork.

“OK, already—there’s no need to be a meanie jelly beanie.”

“A meanie what?”

“Never mind.”

Crystal then shifted gears and asked, “Have you talked to Brielle yet?”

“She’s been sending me her class notes every day and I text back my thanks.”

“So you’ve not talked on the phone?”

“It’s been a few days,” I said. Just thinking about Brielle gave me the jitters. I knew I could only put off our *conversation* for so long. “She understands our current *predicament* . . . but I suspect she thinks something else is up.”

“I imagine she does,” Crystal replied. “You know, if you’re not going to tell Brielle how you feel in person, you should make that phone call.” She set down her fork. “The sooner the better.”

SIXTY-ONE

Wade leaned back in his chair, only two of its legs touching the ground. A pair of mini binoculars sat on his lap; the heels of his shoes rested atop the heating and cooling unit mounted below the motel room's only window. He sat in the darkness, blackout curtain a quarter open, staring off into the Discount Inn's parking lot. He'd requested a room on this wing so he could view a wide slice of the motel's main lot. It allowed him to keep tabs on guests who came and went, as well as keep an eye on dog-boy's piece-of-shit pickup truck.

A notepad and pen had been left on the dresser; a standard amenity, Wade figured, and he'd used them to record both times and direction headed as he observed Pratt taking his dogs out for walks, as well as the times when Pratt took them out to do their business. In the latter case, dog-boy marched them across the parking lot so they could empty bladders on a patch of grass that divided the inn from a neighboring bar and grill. Wade wondered if the inn had requested Pratt not have the mutts take their leaks out front, in the grass around the entryway, as guests checked in for their stays.

Wade had also noted the times dog-boy left the motel in order to pick up food; 11:30 for lunch, six o'clock for dinner. Both times he brought the dogs along with him. Pratt probably didn't want the yappy fuckers raising a ruckus in the motel room while he was away. And on both occasions Pratt returned with food to eat in his room: a box of pizza for lunch, a bag from Panera Bread for dinner. Pratt appeared territorial when it came to parking. When he returned to the motel's lot after picking up lunch, he backed his pickup into the exact same spot he'd vacated or, when a visitor had taken his spot during his dinner run, he backed the Silverado into a neighboring space.

It was nearly twelve o'clock and Wade was about to call it a night.

Both Pratts were in for the evening. Dog-boy's pickup sat in its preferred area and he'd watched as Pratt brought the mutts out for their final piss at nine o'clock sharp. Shortly after, he'd watched Pratt's cop sister—bitch that she was—drive her HR-V into the parking lot, lock it down, and then head into the motel.

He imagined by now they were both as snug as bugs in a rug.

The two best enjoy it while they could.

SIXTY-TWO

"She had no cat."

I lifted my head, thinking this was a dream, but in the light glowing off her room, I spotted my sister in the open doorway, wearing her nighttime sweats and staring my way. Alice stood guard at her feet. I glanced at Rex, motionless atop the bed, snoring lightly and refusing to stir—he'd placed no wake-up call.

Then I squinted at the alarm clock on the nightstand.

It was quarter to three in the freaking morning.

"No cat?" I muttered, wondering what the hell she was talking about.

"Olive Cripps said she had a cat, a big fat one." Crystal trespassed into my room and Alice followed suit. She took a chair at the coffee table and switched on the lamp. "I got the sense someone was in the apartment with us—there was a creaking noise in the bedroom—but Olive said she had a cat that hides whenever company comes over."

"OK." Like a vampire at the first light of dawn, I squeezed my eyes shut against the table lamp. "Maybe it jumped off a bed or something."

"No, Cory, that's not what I'm saying," Crystal said. "I'm saying there was no cat to begin with. There was no litter box, no food or water bowls sitting out, no toys, and no cat bed, either."

"Did you look in her bedroom?"

"No."

"What about the bathroom?"

"No," Crystal repeated.

"I think you're supposed to keep the litter box away from the food, so it could have been in one of those rooms." I slid up in bed, my back against the headboard, eyes still shut. "What's going on, Crys?"

I listened as she tapped her fingertips on the tabletop, something she did when frustrated. When the tapping stopped, she said, "We know Cripps's daughter, Darlene, died of a drug overdose in San Francisco in the late 1960s."

"You mentioned you'd stepped in it by bringing up her daughter?"

"I stuck my foot in my mouth and Cripps explained how her daughter died. What Cripps failed to mention was how she returned to Illinois with Darlene's baby in tow and raised the child as her own."

"What?" I said. I'd not heard this part before.

"It was in the San Fran PD report on Darlene's death. She had a baby girl. Olive was the only next of kin SFPD could find. As such, Olive brought the child home to Joliet to be with her."

"OK." I turned away from the table lamp and slowly opened my eyes. "But if the police show up to ask me questions, I doubt I'm going to drag out the family tree." I turned her way. "If it comes up that Mom and Dad are dead, I'm not so sure I'd bring up having a sister unless they started quizzing me about that."

"Gee, thanks for thinking of me," she replied. "Look, I get it, Cor—but the only pictures on her living room walls looked like what you'd buy at a garage sale for a quarter."

"Isn't Cripps almost a hundred?" I said. "Where do you think those garage sale pictures come from? An elderly relative passes away and the family tries to unload that junk."

Crystal shrugged. "Could be, but I'm thinking she hid her real pictures, her family pictures, in case a cop like me showed up and maybe recognized someone."

"Or she could have the family pics in photo albums, like normal people. Like Lansing Shortridge did, well, except for the molester stash he kept hidden." I rubbed at my eyes, doubting I'd be getting any more shut-eye tonight. "If Cripps was lower middle class or part of the working poor, she couldn't afford a family portrait. I don't know—maybe getting family portraits wasn't that common way back then."

My sister scratched at Alice's neck. "Do the pups make floorboards creak?"

"I guess I've never really noticed." I stared at my bloodhound. "Alice might be heavy enough to make them creak; maybe not so much with Rex."

"So if a cat weighs ten pounds," Crystal said, "let's say a chubby one weighs twenty-five pounds. Rex weighs double that amount."

"Well, like I said—the cat could have jumped off the bed and made it creak. If I jump, I come down harder than if I took a step. Or maybe her apartment building's a cheaply made dump," I said. "My God, Crys, it's the middle of the night and we're debating floorboard noise and how much cats weigh."

My sister raised her palms and sighed. "It's not my mind playing tricks on me, Cor, or us spinning our wheels because we can't figure out a motive. I think Olive Cripps played me." Crystal stood and stepped across the length of the motel room. "First, she leads me through some talent agent snapping pics of her, and then to pictures taken for a high school play, before she lands on these hotel picnics the Wexford threw for their employees." Crystal did an about-face and returned to the coffee table. "Cripps knew the picnic pics would raise red flags . . . and I bought it. I assumed she served Lansing Shortridge meatloaf in the hotel's dining room and he took a shine to her. I figured Lansing was a little obsessed with Cripps because of that young thing he had going, so he saw his opportunity and pocketed her photograph."

A thought occurred to me. "Wouldn't a hotel have their annual get-together in one of their own conference rooms? Why haul food all the way out to a park when you could cart it to a conference room in about eight seconds?"

"Exactly. Plus it'd be easier for employees to attend and they'd be on-site in case a guest needed help, or if anything else cropped up."

I started to see Crystal's point. "There's no father listed on her daughter's birth certificate," I said. "So you suspect her father is Lansing Shortridge?"

Crystal stopped pacing the room long enough to nod.

"OK," I said. "I get it. It's a good hunch, but it's a bit of a leap. The father could have been another kid at her school, right? Someone Cripps's own age." I thought for a second. "Maybe Darlene's father was even younger than Cripps. Her dad could have been thirteen or fourteen and that's why his name doesn't appear on the birth certificate."

"Maybe," Crystal said, not convinced.

"Or, like Dad's old jokes, a traveling salesman was staying at the hotel, he bumped into Cripps, and one thing led to another and she became pregnant. But the salesman lives three states away and, back in those days, she's shit out of luck even trying to get diaper money from the guy."

"Maybe," Crystal repeated, tossing me another bone.

"Who knows? A salesman could have given Cripps a fake name. It wouldn't be the first time a guy lied about something like that."

Crystal said nothing.

"OK, Crys, let's say there's a third of a chance it's a boy from her school, another third of a chance it was a traveling salesman that blew through town, and," I said, "a third of a chance it was Lansing Shortridge."

"I'd go with it being two-thirds Lansing Shortridge to one-third your other scenarios." My sister shook her head. "I've been lying in bed thinking about it. Cripps is good, Cor. She's real good." Crystal sat back down in the chair. "I thought I was talking to the grandmother . . . but I may have been chatting with the wolf."

Now I was wide awake. Even Rex began to stir. "What can you do with any of this? Even if Darlene's father was Lansing Shortridge, Darlene's been dead a long time," I said. "And what does any of this ancient history have to do with Reed's or Patrick's death?"

"That's why I've been tossing and turning all night . . . trying to noodle it out."

SIXTY-THREE

The San Francisco Police Department's report on Darlene Cripps's overdose death was short and sweet and to the point. It had been written by an SFPD detective by the name of David Martel. The bottom line, Crystal noted, was that Darlene Cripps, per the medical examiner's postmortem drug test—the death toxicology report—had died of a heroin overdose shortly before her twentieth birthday.

Crystal had glanced through Martel's report yesterday, but after last night, she now went through it with a fine-tooth comb. There were additional facts in Martel's report that caught her eye but, ultimately, made her feel sad and depressed. Darlene Cripps's story was not uncommon. And San Francisco in the 1960s had been anything but a safe haven for teenage girls. The poor kid had been picked up twice for vagrancy, once for possession, and another time for prostitution.

And these were only the times Darlene had been processed through the system.

Detective Martel mentioned that Darlene Cripps had provided her next-door neighbor with a false name. In addition, the name on Darlene's apartment lease was listed as Karen Henderson, a different name than what she'd given her neighbor. The report also noted how Darlene's monthly rent had been paid entirely in cash.

Paying entirely in cash, Crystal inferred, could point toward Darlene making the month's rent from selling drugs or, heartbreakingly, her body.

Martel went on to document how a Caucasian male, believed by tenants in the neighboring units to be Darlene's husband or live-in boyfriend, was frequently seen coming from and returning to Darlene's apartment. Evidently, the mystery man never bothered socializing or introducing himself to anyone in the neighboring units. As he was the only male seen coming and leaving her apartment, Martel didn't believe Darlene's unit was used for prostitution. Rather, the detective was on a similar wavelength as Crystal; he strongly suspected Darlene's mystery man to be a drug dealer.

Though a copy of Darlene's daughter's birth certificate was not attached to Martel's report, he noted the name of the father as it appeared on the birth certificate was *Tim Dow*. However, SFPD was unable to track down anyone by that name, which the San Fran detective put down as being yet another fabricated name.

This also screamed to Crystal that the mystery man in Darlene's life was involved in drug trafficking and wished to remain anonymous, hidden in the shadows.

Martel believed the nine-one-one phone call regarding Darlene's overdose stemmed from this mystery man, this drug dealer who cohabitated with Darlene Cripps and was exceedingly likely to be the baby's father.

The report revealed how Darlene had attended a nearby treatment center throughout the year before her daughter's birth. Detective Martel took this to mean she was trying to do the right thing—to stay clean and sober—while she was pregnant. Sadly, Martel also noted, Darlene's relapse may have hastened her death, as Darlene's body couldn't have adjusted quickly enough to the heroin and thus shut down.

Crystal understood the detective's reasoning. Drug overdoses are not uncommon after undergoing treatment.

Detective Martel concluded his report by stating how Darlene's mother, Olive Cripps, had come to identify her daughter's remains. As next of kin and the baby's grandmother, she had hired an attorney and was petitioning the court in order to be appointed legal guardian so she could take Darlene's daughter with her back to Joliet, Illinois; which, ultimately Crystal knew, had come to pass.

Unfortunately, there wasn't much in Martel's report on Darlene's death for Crystal to run with. She reached for her phone and hoped that acquiring a copy of Darlene Cripps's daughter's birth certificate from the Vital Records Division in the California Department of Public Health would not be as arduous as it had been obtaining Darlene's birth certificate in Illinois.

SIXTY-FOUR

The Frisbee hung by my side as the beasts and I lurked about the Discount Inn and Suites' lower-level hallway. First, we checked the swimming pool. The Out of Service sign still hung in the window, the door remained closed and locked, and there were no indications of any repairman screwing the thingamabob into the doohickey in order to make the darned thing work. The night clerk—a pleasant fellow by the name of Ronald something-or-other—informed me the part had been back ordered and that the pool would be fixed any day now, which, at this time, translated into *any week now*.

I'd pester the day clerk about thingamabobs and doohickeys, except for, well, as you know . . . I'm terrified of her.

We paused momentarily at the window to the motel's fitness center on our march toward the elevator atrium and onward through the lobby—checking to see if the treat bowl had been replenished—and then outside for Alice and Rex's third stroll of the day. A few days ago we'd tripped over a park not too far away. We were heading there now and I fully planned on Frisbee fetching the two goofballs so that tonight they'd sleep like Rip Van Winkle.

The businessman I'd seen checking in yesterday morning was the only guest in the exercise room. He worked the rowing machine as though he were escaping a tsunami. Instead of a suit, though, he had donned gym shorts and a Green Bay Packers T-shirt—sacrilege—and had built up a lather of sweat, likely working off the stress of whatever meeting he'd come to town for.

I wondered, if I ever began working as a programmer, if I'd be sent out of town on business trips. I wouldn't mind because I'd heard all about these daily per diems. Brielle told me her father gets about seventy-five bucks for meals every day when he travels for work.

Hey—I could easily gnaw my way through seventy-five bucks a day.

The businessman caught my eye and nodded. I said "Hey" through the window as we picked up our pace.

Guy talk.

Alice gave a short growl, guttural, which served to hype up Rex, who sputtered yowls as though he were a muffler backfiring. My head shot forward, thinking Front Desk Pam was stomping our way, a grimace across her features, coming to get to the bottom of just what the hell was going on in *her corridor*. Instead, I spotted a husband and wife heading our way, dragging luggage, with three kids in tow. I hustled the dogs along, wanting to slip past the family before the inevitable occurred, but, like paparazzi cornering a movie star, we wound up spending a couple of minutes where the hallway emptied into the lobby, so the little ones could meet and greet and pet and scratch the pups.

I watched as Alice and Rex hammed it up for the travelers. Must be rough, I thought. Yup—life at the Discount Inn and Suites was like being on holiday for the two goofballs. All that was missing were mai tais and tanning lotion.

SIXTY-FIVE

Wade caught dog-boy in his peripheral vision.

He watched as Pratt slowed to a stop at the window to the fitness center. In response, Wade rowed faster, throwing his shoulders into it, waiting to see if there was any sense of alarm on Pratt's part; to see if Pratt did a double-take or, God forbid, grab his smartphone and start punching in numbers. But there was no hint of recognition, as Wade expected, and he glanced Pratt's way and gave a quick nod, like one guy in a gym to another. Dog-boy mumbled "Hey" and returned to shuffling down the hallway.

This had been a test, a dry run to see if he and dog-boy could coexist in the same motel. Knowing Pratt's afternoon stroll was soon approaching, Wade positioned himself in the workout room an hour ahead of time. He didn't sport a business suit, clearly, but he did have the sandy blond buzz cut and black glasses thing going. Wade even sported a Packers T-shirt, to make dog-boy think he was visiting Chicago from out of state.

The dry run had been a success. The smile on Wade's face twisted into a smirk, but then came a growl from what he suspected was Pratt's bloodhound, followed by a series of yowls and yaps by what he assumed was Pratt's smaller dog.

Fuck!

Wade's heart caught in his throat. He ceased rowing. It wasn't Cory Pratt he was worried about; it never had been. Pratt was nobody without his canine entourage. It was the goddamned dogs Wade feared. It was the dogs he'd been thinking about all day, how to get around them . . . and he sure as shit prayed they weren't now warning Pratt of his presence.

Wade hoped the cheap cologne he'd doused himself in, as well as the closed fitness center doors, would conceal or alter his scent . . . but these were sniffer dogs, after all.

Then Wade heard friendly noises, further down the hallway;

he heard cheerful exchanges. He heard the eager voices of children, he heard the more cautionary tones of their parents, and he listened as dog-boy introduced the two mutts and informed the parents it'd be just fine if their little ones petted the puppies.

Wade resumed rowing. Pratt had been fooled; however, the verdict was still out on his cadaver dogs. He'd have to find a way to avoid them. Wade knew he'd do whatever it took, but the last thing he wanted to do was engage Pratt's canine companions.

Some primeval fear of creatures with sharp teeth that bite.

Wade shook his head. It was a damn shame the swimming pool was closed. If the motel was too cheap to spring for cameras, then perhaps Cory Pratt would suffer a cramp in his leg or inhale a lungful of water and, with no lifeguard on duty or other swimmers to pull him to safety, well—accidents happen every day. People drown all the time, often in shallow water. Wade imagined it wasn't an *uncommon* occurrence, if you added up all the hotels and motels and resorts across the country.

And if the Discount Inn and Suites had cameras, perhaps Wade could find a way to slip around those and have a *come to Jesus* meeting with dog-boy in the sauna or restroom.

Unfortunately, these scenarios were moot, as the motel's pool was currently out of order. Also, it'd be equally impossible to strangle the little prick in the workout room, what with the constant stream of visitor traffic in the hallway and with guests coming and leaving at all hours of the day. Christ—there'd be enough witnesses to sway the Nielsen ratings.

Yes, dealing with Pratt's dogs would be problematic; however, Wade had a canister of bear repellent in a bag in his motel room. And if the damned stuff worked on six hundred pounds of charging grizzly, well . . . food for thought. Perhaps it might make sense to trail Pratt back to his room, at a distance, of course, so as not to startle the guy or make his presence known—that is, until Pratt swung open the door to his suite and began to step inside. Then he'd rush dog-boy from behind, drench all three of the fuckers in bear spray, kick Pratt's ass into the bathroom, slam the door on the dogs, and strangle the little prick with a hand towel. He might even have a moment or two to squeeze some Charlotte Shortridge intel out of Pratt before wrapping the towel around his scrawny neck.

Vendetta or not, taking care of dog-boy would feel just as good as when he'd taken care of the two Shortridge boys; their eyes bulging, tongues hanging out, knowing their end had arrived. It was something Brother Garrick would never experience or understand as he stood nearby, yet looked away and let Wade do all of the dirty work.

Brother Garrick lacked the stomach to see the job through to completion.

Wade did not.

But Pratt's dogs would blow their tops—barking and baying and howling and raising holy hell until guests in neighboring suites called the front desk or spilled out into the hallway to see what the uproar was about.

That would make it impossible for Wade to slip from Pratt's room unnoticed.

Wade wiped the sweat off his forehead with a bath towel he'd brought from the room. His workout for the day was over. Plus, it just dawned on him what the easiest way to deal with dog-boy would be. Since Pratt took his mutts out for lengthy walks several times a day, as he was doing right now, Wade could smear mud across his license plates and hang out in the motel's fitness center until Pratt and company clomped by in the hallway, as they inevitably would. Then he could sneak out to the Traverse, follow Pratt from down the block and, if dog-boy and the mutts turn onto a secluded street, well . . . seize the day.

A midmorning hike would be best—adults were at work, children in school—and Wade could find out if his SUV truly went from zero to sixty in six seconds, as he'd been led to believe at the dealership.

Then he could witness exactly how high dog-boy could bounce off the asphalt.

He wouldn't even have to get near the goddamned dogs; that is, unless one or both happened to go under the tires.

To be honest, Wade would root for Cory Pratt's recovery; perhaps he'd even send the dog-boy an anonymous plant. After all, it's amazing how far medical science had progressed when it came to dealing with spinal cord injuries and head trauma.

And Wade could only imagine how much Pratt's bitch-cop of a sister would enjoy her weekly visits to whatever facility her little brother would be spending his days in, spoon-feeding him Jell-O while he chortled at Cartoon Network for the rest of his quadriplegic, cognitively challenged life.

SIXTY-SIX

"Hey, Cory!"

I lifted my head off the pillow. This time Rex was wide awake and staring my way. I got confused, as I'd been in a dead sleep. Was this a dream? How else could Rex be talking to me in my sister's voice?

"Cory, get your butt in here."

I didn't see Rex's lips move and realized it wasn't a dream. "What time is it?" I called out.

"Almost five," she called back.

"Why you keep waking me up so early?"

"You've got to check this out," Crystal replied. Light from her table lamp emanated through the doorway between our bedrooms. "The clerk in California's Vital Records sent a copy of Darlene Cripps's daughter's birth certificate last night."

"I'll come check it out later."

"Cory!"

"OK, already." Rex and I tumbled off the side of the bed and trudged into my sister's suite. Alice was up, sitting at Crystal's feet and staring at the two of us as if to say, "Are all the Pratt men slackers?"

I almost nodded in affirmation.

"See how her father is listed as Tim Dow." Crystal pointed at the birth certificate on her laptop screen as I leaned in over her shoulder. "Tim Dow is Darlene Cripps's mystery man—the father of her child and likely drug dealer who bolted after Darlene OD'd."

"We already knew that." I squinted at Crystal's monitor, hoping my eyes would adjust to the light.

Crystal pointed to the main name on the birth certificate. "Note how Darlene's daughter is named Jane Dow."

"Jane Dow?" I replied. "It sounds an awful lot like Jane Doe. Like she's in the morgue and no one knows who the hell she is."

Crystal nodded. "Or in the legal context where a woman's true identity is not known or being withheld. Which is apropos, Cor, because I've spent the past ten minutes ferreting out her real name."

I was sentient enough to recognize Crystal's rising excitement. "What did you find?"

"First, I plugged Jane Cripps into the Illinois DMV, thinking Olive Cripps would have changed her granddaughter's surname to Cripps," Crystal said. "But Olive didn't; I found nothing on Jane Cripps."

"So then what?"

"So then I ran Jane Dow and, thank God for us, DMV records include previous names and aliases, you know, like maiden names alongside their current name. It comes in handy if someone is using a different last name." Crystal X-ed out of the birth certificate and then brought up the DMV database. "Her maiden name led me to her married name; same birth date as Darlene Cripps's daughter. It's a perfect match." Crystal looked my way. "Buckle your seatbelt, Cory, because she doesn't go by Jane," she said. "You and I know her by her middle name."

I leaned in closer to the screen as Crystal clicked open the driver's license.

"Holy shit!" I said.

"Exactly," Crystal replied. "Holy shit."

SIXTY-SEVEN

Olive Cripps was watering the plants on her pint-sized balcony when she spotted the squad cars pulling into her apartment building's parking lot.

At first, Olive thought they'd come for the pack of feral teenagers who lived in the complex, male youngsters who loitered about together, who never seemed to be up to much good. Last spring, they'd mocked the speed at which Olive, cane and all, shuffled toward the entrance to the building. Evidently, she was blocking their way. The teens didn't appreciate the time it was taking the old bag to get through the front door. Wade had taken her shopping that particular morning, dropped her off at the apartment's entrance, parked his SUV in the lot, and was carrying her groceries when he approached the gang from behind and realized what was occurring. Wade set the paper bags down on the grass off the walkway, gently, so as not to crack any eggs or crush the bread, and then grabbed the two biggest teenagers by their hair—one in each hand—and lifted them into the air, spun around like a human Tilt-A-Whirl, and tossed the two ass over teakettle onto the curb. The group went dead silent as Wade explained in extensive detail what he'd do if any one of them ever so much as looked at his grandmother again.

But then Olive noted two of the squad cars, the ones that pulled up to the entryway, were from the Joliet Police Department, while a third squad car, this one from the Frankfort Police Department, hung back along the sidewalk. Unless the pack of teens had dramatically upped the ante, this procession of police cars from different jurisdictions was not here for them.

And that's when she knew.

Olive had never been arrested. She was only familiar with how arrests were made from TV shows. Olive would just as soon avoid her neighbors witnessing her door kicked in, if that's how it was executed, so she placed the trash bin from her kitchen in the doorway to keep the door open. Then she sat down, took off her slippers and slipped into her sneakers as though to appear she was about to take out the trash.

Olive heard the commotion as soon as the elevator doors chimed open. Within seconds a Black man in a brown suit was knocking on her open door. He was a large man, similar in size to her great-grandsons. In the hallway behind him were two uniformed officers, also looking her way.

"Yes?" Olive asked as she approached the door.

"You are Olive Cripps," the man in the brown suit said. "Correct?"

"Yes, sir," Olive answered, respectfully.

"My name is Gene Ford," he replied. "I am a detective with the Joliet Police Department. I am here to transport you to Chicago, where detectives in their police department need to ask you questions regarding a current investigation."

"Does that mean I'm under arrest?"

"Not at present, Ms. Cripps," he said, dryly; efficiently. She suspected the man was quite good at his job.

"What if I say no?" Olive asked, still respectful.

"My understanding," the detective from Joliet stressed, "is that there is enough probable cause for me to have an arrest warrant here within the hour if you decide to go that route."

"Well, then," Olive said. "I'd better go with you." She returned the garbage bin to the kitchen, turned, and held out her wrists as though for examination. "Please be gentle, Detective Ford." The plain clothes officer had followed Olive into her apartment. He stood two feet away, towering over her. "At my age bones become brittle, like saltine crackers."

Ford stared at her a long second. She felt the detective gauging if he had ever in his life picked up a lesser fight-or-flight risk than Olive Cripps. He must have determined she was not a threat. "I will put them on once you're safely buckled in the squad car," he said. "But let's get you a jacket for the ride."

Once Olive was safe and sound in the back seat of the front

most of the Joliet squad cars, a uniformed officer placed the handcuffs on her wrists and informed her she'd be more comfortable if she let her hands rest on her lap. As Olive waited, she glanced back at the squad car from the Frankfort Police Department. A woman in uniform leaned against the side of the vehicle, her arms folded as she witnessed the proceeding. Olive assumed from the woman's self-assured stance and the way the other officers treated her with deference that she was Frankfort's chief of police. And if Frankfort's chief of police had shown up to observe nonagenarian Olive Cripps being taken in for questioning . . . well, that meant this was it.

Detective Ford spoke to the Frankfort officer for another minute as the woman nodded along. They then shook hands and Ford walked over to the car Olive sat in. He slid into the passenger seat and shut the door.

As they pulled away from the apartment's parking lot, Olive said, "I was once chauffeured in the back seat of a sedan—but that was a long time ago."

The detective looked back quizzically. "You've only been chauffeured once?"

"Once that I recall, Detective," Olive said. "It was a most memorable trip."

SIXTY-EIGHT

"Hey, Cory, we may have hit the jackpot," Crystal said as soon as I picked up my iPhone.

"What's up?"

"Olive Cripps's granddaughter has two sons; they're identical twins," she said. "Remember how you mentioned the assailants seemed a little familiar?"

"Yeah—same height and weight."

"Well, these twins are pretty big guys. From the info on their driver's licenses, Cor, they're football-size big."

I thought about that and said, "And if this turns out to be some kind of family feud, these two are in the family."

"Yes, they are," Crystal replied. "I'm texting you their DMV photos as we speak. See if you recognize them."

A second later I heard the notification and brought up Messages. I stared at the two headshots. Neither one smiled for the camera, but neither frowned nor glared. I took a second to enlarge each picture and sighed. "Crystal—they weren't up close in the warehouse and at the playground they were all hooded up. If I'm honest, I can't say for sure. But I can't rule them out, either," I said. "And if they're football-size big, you've got to bring them in."

"It's in play, Cor," Crystal said. "Olive Cripps is being transported to Chicago for questioning and we'll see where that leads. I'm grabbing her granddaughter in about five minutes. We'll get a cheek swab and find out if she's related to the Shortridges."

"To see if she's Lansing's granddaughter?"

"Yes." Crystal explained how DNA from the inside of your cheek is compared against genetic markers from another individual's DNA in order to determine if a biological relationship exists. Then Crystal said, "I've got to run, Cor. But think about packing your stuff—you may be sleeping in your own bed tonight."

SIXTY-NINE

"When can we go in?" Lahlum asked.

"Let's give it another minute."

Crystal and her partner sat in her Honda HR-V in the nearly packed parking lot of Henry Horner Elementary School in Arlington Heights—the place where it all began. Her eyes were glued to the clock on her smartphone. The two detectives were waiting for the passing time between classes to end so the younger students would be in their classrooms and unable to witness what might prove to be a disturbing scene . . . police marching an individual the children may know out to a waiting squad car, her hands in cuffs behind her back. Crystal wished they had time to wait until after school, until all the buses had departed for the day, but the suspects in the Shortridge murder investigation needed to be swept up ASAP.

"It's time," Crystal replied, and opened her driver's door.

Lahlum nodded and spoke two words into his cell phone. "Let's roll."

By the time the detectives reached the entrance to the school vestibule, a CPD squad car had pulled up curbside. Two police officers exited the vehicle and fell in line behind Crystal and Lahlum. The officers had been briefed on how the arrest needed to be made as quickly and quietly as possible, to avoid any undue scene at the elementary school. The hope was to be out of Henry Horner in record time—on the road back to the precinct with the suspect in tow in under three minutes flat, four if any conflict arose.

As the four CPD officers progressed through the foyer, Principal Isaacson stepped out from the administrative area, where her office and several others were nestled. Crystal swore the principal's hair was grayer than it had been on the day Patrick Shortridge's body was found inside the cafeteria wall.

Something like that could age a person in more ways than one.

Isaacson's face tilted in surprise as she spotted the investigators heading her way. "What's going on?" she asked, a look of concern spreading across her face. Then Isaacson spoke louder, "What are you doing here?"

Crystal ignored the principal as Lahlum peeled off from the group. He approached the principal with a palm in the air and a finger to his lips.

Crystal and the uniformed officers turned left through the open doorway, into the administration suite, and stepped past the reception counter as though they owned the place. The woman manning the counter gaped at them; her eyes wide, her jaw dropped. The three came to a halt at a large desk in the rear of the reception area, the place where the elementary school's office administrator sat.

Suzanne Nickless stared up at Crystal.

SEVENTY

Garrick Nickless was working the controls to reverse the electric pallet jack when he caught movement out of the corner of his eye. As a material handler for Compass Logistics, a trucking and distribution company, Garrick's days were spent mostly alone, warehousing an endless stream of inventory with a forklift and pallet jack as his primary companions. He took the plugs from his ears, turned around, and froze; a statue among a mountain range of stacked boxes.

It wasn't the warehouse manager with whom Garrick had minimal interaction, or the warehouse foreman with whom Garrick had day-to-day interactions, scampering his way, that stunned Garrick. No, what stunned Garrick, and knocked him out of his known universe, was the entourage of uniformed officers led by the lady cop he'd planted the GPS tracker on also hustling his way.

Garrick's heart lodged in his throat, his feet glued to the floor as they closed in on him, but he finally did something that didn't make a whole lot of sense.

Garrick turned and ran.

He had no escape plan in mind; never expected to need one—quite frankly, there was no place here for him to run or hide. He imagined more officers would be waiting by his pickup truck, if he somehow smashed his way out to the employee parking lot. Garrick jerked his iPhone from his pocket as he cut around the forklift and sprinted down the neighboring aisle. He tapped his brother's icon as he turned on the speed.

"Hey, Garrick." Wade answered on the first ring.

"Fuck," Garrick said. "They're here."

"Who's here?"

"Cops."

He tried to say more but as Garrick hit the endcap, a blur of motion took out his legs. An officer had raced down the preceding aisle, cut sideways, and tackled him on the fly. The two men rolled on the hard cement as Garrick's cell phone skipped and skittered. Suddenly other cops were on him; his wrists twisted behind his back and cuffed. Garrick was yanked to his feet. Words were spoken at him by a man in plain clothes he took to be the lady cop's partner, but Garrick's mind was elsewhere, on the lady cop.

He wrenched his head sideways and watched as she knelt down, picked up his smartphone, and glanced his way. "Is this your brother?" she asked.

Garrick said nothing. Instead he continued watching as she raised his phone to her ear and said, "Is this Wade Nickless?" Garrick couldn't hear a reply, didn't think his brother would be dumb enough to respond, and then the lady cop said, "Best turn yourself in, Nickless. I've got your family . . . and I'm coming for you." There was a longer pause and then Detective Pratt caught Garrick's eye and said, "He hung up."

Garrick was pissed off. Lawyered up or not, he knew how screwed he was. "Too bad you didn't meet him when you were in Frankfort," he said, his eyes burning, a thousand suns.

Pratt stepped toward him. "Your brother was there, wasn't he?" she said. "In the other room?"

Garrick knew he'd messed up; that he shouldn't have said a goddamned thing. He pinched his lips together and kept quiet.

Detective Pratt then asked in a low voice, "Were you there?"

He looked down at his feet.

"Oh my God, Mark," Garrick heard as she turned her attention to her partner. "They were both there when I visited Olive Cripps." Another beat passed before she said, "They know where Cory is."

SEVENTY-ONE

"Fuck," Wade heard his brother say into the phone. "They're here."

"Who's here?"

"Cops."

Then he heard scuffling noises, a struggle of some kind, then muffled talk, and finally a female voice. "Is this your brother?"

Wade knew it was the bitch-cop and heard her follow up with, "Is this Wade Nickless?" He didn't breathe; he dared not say a word or give her anything to work with. "Best turn yourself in, Nickless," she continued. "I've got your family . . . and I'm coming for you."

Wade hung up his cell phone, switched it off, and threw it on the bed. It took all of his willpower to keep from wrenching the flat-screen TV off its wall mounting and smashing it against the dresser top. Repeatedly. Until the motel room was showered in glass and plastic, lead and silicon. He should have followed his instincts and taken care of Detective Pratt as she sat at the dining room table at his great-grandmother's apartment.

He fucking knew it at the time.

Pratt and her little shit of a brother had ruined everything.

Wade toyed with popping the SIM card out with the end of a paperclip, but realized it'd buy him nothing. The iPhone was off; it no longer sent signals to cell towers, so they couldn't actively track him. However—he cursed silently—she'd note his last known location based on the last signal it sent before he shut it down.

And that last signal would lead her here.

But tracking him would take an hour of dicking around with the tech staff. He still had a chance. Wade glanced down at his watch. It was nearing the time Pratt took his mutts outside for a walk.

It took Wade all of five seconds to pack his bag. He threw the strap over his arm, left his motel room . . . and went to kill the dog-boy.

SEVENTY-TWO

Per my sister's suggestion, I thought about packing my luggage for maybe ten seconds, but didn't follow through. Once Crystal gave me the go-ahead, it'd take me a minute to toss my clothes, both clean and dirty, into my duffel bag and about two seconds more to toss my toothbrush and comb into my ditty bag.

Alice and Rex would be heartbroken. At the Discount Inn and Suites in Elk Grove Village, the two lived the life of Riley—every day a shining new adventure. Wait until they realized they'd be heading back to work, helping out with the obedience classes, or hanging about the house while I was away at school. It sure would be a massive letdown from the red-carpet treatment they'd been receiving this past week. Petted and pampered by a long line of motel guests and visitors, numerous hikes a day; not to mention how they'd been vacuuming up the too-numerous-to-count bits and pieces of junk food and other crumbs that inadvertently dropped off my room's way too tiny coffee table.

All three of us would need to diet once we returned home.

Speaking of hikes, we were heading out for what may well be our final journey about the streets and parks and pathways surrounding the Discount Inn. We were trotting down a vacant first-floor hallway when my cell phone vibrated in my pocket. I jiggled it out and saw it was Crystal. Perhaps there'd be no need for an afternoon stroll after all.

"Hey, Crys," I said.

"Stay in your room, Cory, and keep the doors locked," my sister replied in her no-nonsense voice. She was deadly serious. "Olive Cripps's great-grandsons—those pictures I sent you—they know where you're at."

"What?" The hair on the back of my neck began to rise as we approached the fitness center.

"We can't find Wade Nickless and he knows you're at the motel," Crystal said. "The cops are on the way." Her voice shook. "I'm on the way."

That's when the dogs began to growl.

SEVENTY-THREE

"What?" Crystal heard her brother ask.

"We can't find Wade Nickless and he knows you're at the motel. The cops are on the way," she shouted into her speakerphone. "I'm on the way."

Crystal listened as Alice and Rex snarled in the background. Something was up and she sensed the three of them weren't safe and sound and tucked away in their motel room. Crystal goosed the gas pedal. She'd been flying down the left lane of Route 53 at ninety miles per hour, her siren blaring. The speedometer on her Honda HR-V now pushed a hundred; Elk Grove Village was two exits away, then a mile or two of side streets.

Crystal placed her ETA at five minutes; she prayed it wouldn't be too late.

"Cory!" she screamed as Alice and Rex's warnings amplified in volume, a Greek chorus of snarls and growls. Red alert—there was an active threat. "Run!"

Crystal had blasted out of the warehouse parking lot like a rocket leaving orbit. Detective Lahlum dove into the passenger seat of a nearby squad car that'd come along for Garrick Nickless's arrest. Her partner would work the radio as a uniformed took the wheel and tried to keep pace with Crystal's HR-V. Lahlum would coordinate with the dispatcher to send cars to the Discount Inn. And Crystal prayed those squad cars were already zeroing in on the motel's location.

She'd never forgive herself if anything happened to Cory. He was the only family she had left.

"Oh no," she heard her brother reply. "Oh no."

Followed by gunfire.

"Cory!" she screamed again.

SEVENTY-FOUR

I locked eyes with the businessman through the fitness center window as Crystal informed me the men after me knew where I was staying, as Alice and Rex began to growl, and as the hair on the back of my neck began to rise. He wore no workout attire this time around, no gym shorts or Green Bay Packers T-shirt. Instead, he stood motionless in jeans and a leather jacket. I almost nodded his way out of habit, out of seeing him about the Discount Inn over the past couple of days. This close up, a thin pane of glass between us, I noted he was taller than me. A big man, too; football-size big. And he no longer sported a pair of glasses.

Déjà vu washed over me as I witnessed the man's eyes turn dark and cold . . . and I knew exactly who he was.

Wade Nickless.

"Oh no." The cell phone remained at my ear, yet I spoke more to myself than my sister.

The big man's hand swung from behind his back; his fingers draped about a firearm.

"Oh no," I said again, dropping to the floor. The window where I'd been standing shattered into a million pieces. I lay sideways on the hallway carpeting, frozen in fear, an ice sculpture staring up as a handgun protruded through the open space where glass had once separated us. It was followed by a wrist . . . and then his face.

The man I'd met at the Kenilworth playground, the same man who'd come for me after my obedience class in Wheeling, was here at the Discount Inn and Suites—a death's head grin spreading across his features.

He wanted me to know who he was; he wanted me to know he'd won.

And he wanted me to suffer in the final seconds of my life.

The barrel of his pistol lowered my way.

"Cory!" my sister screamed as the phone dropped from my hand.

Then a blur of black and tan; a look of alarm and pain on the big man's face as eighty pounds of bloodhound hung from his exposed wrist, a vice clamp with fangs. Alice's nails scratched and scraped at the wall below the window frame, her teeth sinking deep. His pistol dropped to the carpeting. I shot a foot out, kicking at it, skipping it down the hallway. Then I scrambled up to my knees.

Blood dripped from Nickless's wrist but the bastard stayed silent, gritting his teeth as he leaned backward, his left hand wrapped over his forearm, dragging Alice up the wall. I read his mind as he reached for her collar; I knew what he had in store—he was going to slice my sweet girl's throat against the busted shards of glass still caught in the window frame.

"Alice!" I screamed, top of my lungs. "Drop!"

She let go, hit the carpet, and spun about as Nickless kicked open the fitness door and stepped into the hallway. But then Rex was on him; his turn at bat. He caught a pant leg and raised holy hell—all sound and fury—but the big man kicked him with his free foot. Rex squealed in pain as he slammed against the opposing wall. A canister appeared in Nickless's bloodstained hand. He aimed it at Rex's head, point blank. My mind screamed *pepper spray* as he doused my springer as though soaking a wasp's nest. Rex squealed a second time, spun about; trying to escape, unable to see, not knowing where to flee. Alice was in the air but took a drenching mid-flight and went down, tumbling forward, a gymnast botching the landing.

The canister spun my way. I raised an arm to block my eyes. Didn't help—they blurred and burned. Worse yet, I'd caught a mouthful of spray. My lungs were on fire, a bellows in reverse. The pups were a tornado alley of activity, coughing and hacking, spinning about blindly. I held my breath, sprang to my feet, and threw a left hook with everything I could muster. I wanted Nickless to pay for what he'd done to Alice and Rex. But it bounced off his ribcage; felt as though I'd punched the side of a log cabin.

Then I got hit by a bus, a marble fist straight to my gut. I doubled over, no longer holding my breath—there was no breath to hold. A hand seized the neck of my shirt and a fistful of flesh; another grasped my belt. Suddenly I was airborne, flying over the hallway carpeting, past the elevator, and landing on the unforgiving tile of the lobby floor, hitting hard, ribs and chin.

Then came chaos from the front desk. I blinked eyes at a blurred face, like trying to focus underwater. Someone peeked above the check-in counter. It was day clerk Pam and she shrieked at us to *stop it*, that she was *calling the cops*. Another distorted figure crouched beside the front desk, had probably been checking in when a gunshot and exploding glass shattered reality.

The figure must have spotted the big man marching into the lobby behind me—I could sense Nickless coming in for the kill—and they bolted for the entryway and outside to safety.

I yanked myself up a side table with one hand and went for a Hail Mary with my other; grabbing the treat jar by its rim, twisting about, and swinging for the fences. Granola bars showered the room as it connected with the figure approaching me. I hoped to get lucky; I hoped to knock the bastard's head off, but the bowl bounced wildly off the big man's shoulder and nosedived, shattering on the lobby floor.

Then I was in flight once more, this time crash-landing onto the front desk. The velocity sent me and the check-in computers sliding and bouncing into Pam as we tumbled to the floor like human bowling pins.

I listened to sirens off in the distance as Pam squirmed out from under my dead weight—everything hurt, I could barely move—and fled into the back room, into the safety of the manager's office.

A second later Wade Nickless hurtled over the countertop and dropped his knees onto my chest, his fingers coiling around my neck.

SEVENTY-FIVE

Crystal raced through the Discount Inn's parking lot as though it were the Daytona 500 and screeched her HR-V to a halt outside the motel's entranceway. She jumped from the driver's seat, darted around the back of the Honda and onto the sidewalk. She held her badge high in her left hand, her Glock 22 angled downward in her right. The sirens were piercing, seeming to come from every direction at once; the squad cars would be here any second.

Crystal spied a handful of guests cowering near their cars, likely ready to duck and cover if need be. Two figures were near the entryway. A middle-aged woman leaned against the stucco exterior, her eyes wide and mouth open, possibly girding her loins to run like hell at the next clamor. A man knelt along the wall beside her, his head tilted, with one eye peeking through the glass of the front door.

Crystal advanced on the crouching man as three squad cars slammed on their brakes, lining the sidewalk about the motel's entranceway. No way would Wade Nickless be walking out this set of doors—not of his own free will, anyway. An ambulance skidded to a halt along the side of the motel, out of the line of fire.

The paramedics were here to help, not get shot.

"What's going on in there?" she asked the kneeling man in her command voice, trying to get the lay of the land, see what she was walking into.

"I think someone got shot," the man said, glancing up at Crystal. "And a big guy's beating the shit out of someone."

Detective Lahlum and four uniformed officers joined her on the walkway, crouching, their guns also drawn. Crystal breathed out—she had a strong idea who was getting the shit beat out of them and hoped she wasn't too late.

Crystal caught her partner's eye, pointed inside, and mouthed instructions. Lahlum gripped his sidearm in both hands and nodded his understanding. Crystal kept low, shoved open the entrance door, her Glock now pointing forward . . . and stepped into the motel's lobby.

SEVENTY-SIX

I lifted my head, but Nickless battered it back down on the tile—pain stacked on pain. I lay there stuck, a butterfly pinned to a board, as the big man's fingers began to tighten and twist about my throat. I watched Wade Nickless's face; I saw the smirk.

He was enjoying himself.

My mouth opened, a reflexive response, but there was no air for me to suck in.

An instant or a million years passed. Still burning from whatever Nickless sprayed at me, my eyes teared up as I watched my life play out in the big man's cold, dead eyes. I heard sirens, getting louder, and I heard Alice and Rex bounce and scuff about the lobby, hacking and wheezing, still a mess from their drenching. I began to drift away, slowly, a raft at sea . . . an out-of-body experience. Above me floated an angel. She held something in her hands. I thought it might be my mother—I prayed it was—but as the angel hovered closer I saw it wasn't an angel or my mother at all.

And it wasn't a harp she clutched in her hands.

It was day clerk Pam, her face a billboard of terror and fright. In her hands she gripped a fire extinguisher. Wade Nickless's focus lay solely on me, as though he were memorizing my demise in order to replay it later, perhaps over a beer, when day clerk Pam smashed the red cylinder down on the top of his head.

The big man shot a left elbow backward, connecting with Pam's abdomen. She crumpled forward. His head twisted sideways and his fist fired upward, poleaxing Pam in the solar plexus. The woman flew backward as though on a pulley. She vanished from sight.

Nickless's right hand never left my throat; I'd had no reprieve. In a flash his left hand returned. Blood now dripped from his hairline, onto my face, but the big guy was enraged, a wild animal . . . and he squeezed ever tighter.

I'd die of asphyxiation if my neck didn't snap first.

But then my angel—my guardian angel—reappeared. This time pain and determination filled Pam's eyes. And this time she held nothing back. A modern-day John Henry, Pam smashed the red cylinder onto the big guy's crown as though driving a steel spike into rock. I heard a sickening crunch through the sounds of police sirens, through the sounds of Alice and Rex's visually impaired quest to find me. Though Nickless's fingers stayed wrapped about my neck, the tension eased and I gasped for air. Blood flowed freely from his hairline now, yet he remained perched atop my chest.

Pam raised the fire extinguisher a third and final time. She brought it down with another stomach-churning crunch. This time the big man fell over on top of me, coloring the floor tiles crimson. I wiggled out from underneath the man's girth, both hands rubbing at my throat, gasping lungful after lungful of sweet, beautiful oxygen.

Sirens split the air, now piercing—the cavalry had arrived.

Actually, my cavalry sat with her back against the wall, her head hung down, shoulders quivering, and a stream of tears dripping onto the floor tiles. She'd dropped the fire extinguisher as she slid to the ground. It lay next to one of her shoes, its base caked in blood. Pam then glanced my way. I wasn't sure I could speak, so we nodded at each other as I continued massaging my neck.

I sat up, scooched around the pooling blood, and checked on Nickless. There were no signs of breathing, no signs of movement, and, though I'm not good at this, I couldn't find a pulse in either Nickless's wrist or neck.

The big man was dead.

I needn't have checked; it was clear for all to see. He got his bell rung . . . permanently. Day clerk Pam knew he was dead without watching me fumble about his body. The poor woman had turtled into herself, knees up, head drooped, back to facing the floor. I tried to speak, to thank her for saving my life, but it hurt and came out a rasp.

I would thank her later.

Profusely.

Help would be here any second now . . . and Pam would need more than anything I could offer on the spot.

I crawled over to the hinged door at the end of the front desk and slipped around into the lobby. A second later Alice and Rex found me, licking at my face as I hugged them back. Rex was limping from where Nickless had kicked at him. I'd rush both of them to the veterinarian as soon as I finished flushing their eyes, and mine, with a Niagara Falls of saline solution.

I heard a noise, glanced up, and there was my sister—my ride-or-die sibling—stepping into the lobby, noting the shards of glass from the busted treat jar strewn about the floor. She spotted me and lowered her weapon. Detective Lahlum was right behind her, watching her back, with several uniforms on his tail. Crystal and her partner had looks of concern etched across their faces.

Wait until the detectives peeked behind the front desk.

SEVENTY-SEVEN

Four Days Later

"I don't want to go back to school," Charlotte said. "Yuck."

"I hear ya," I said. "I go back tomorrow and, unlike you, I've not cracked a textbook since I've been gone."

I'd been exiled to the living room as, after the cuisine we'd been eating of late, Crystal was cooking up something healthy for dinner. I'd done a bit of recon and it looked like some kind of chickpea broccoli noodle thing. Which meant I'd be sneaking back into the kitchen once Crystal ventured upstairs for the evening. But now Charlotte Shortridge and I were jabbering via cell phones. Her family was on their way back from Florida and had pulled into some hotel somewhere in Tennessee. Her parents were unloading the luggage into their room before they went off in search of a restaurant.

"I don't want to go, because everyone will be asking me questions," Charlotte said. "It'll make me sad."

"Can your parents have someone tutor you at home for another week or two?"

"We've talked about that, but I do want to see my friends."

I couldn't imagine a universe where Charlotte wasn't well-liked at school, where she didn't have a million friends. Sure, they'd have questions, but they would also help with healing. "Maybe just dive back in, Char, rip that Band-Aid off all at once," I said, full of clichés. I thought for a second. "You remember what I said about helping me out with some training sessions."

"Yes."

Rex was on the couch, his head on my lap, eyes open, likely wondering what Crystal was up to in the kitchen. Alice sat at my feet, her long ears hanging down, no doubt eavesdropping on my conversation. Both received a clean bill of health during their veterinary visit. Rex's limp had dwindled away over the past couple of days. In fact, a wayward squirrel barely made it out of the backyard this afternoon with my springer hot on his tail.

"I'm serious about that, as long as your parents are OK with your helping me out."

"They're excited about it, Cory. Mom and Dad think the world of you." There was a pause, and then she said, "They didn't tell me what happened; you know, how the bad guys got caught, but I heard them talking last night when they thought I was asleep. It sounded like you got hurt."

"Nah." I lied through my teeth. "Alice and Rex were with me. I'm never in trouble when those two are around."

To be honest, my body looked like an apple that had fallen to the floor and been soccer-kicked around the hardwood by a squadron of toddlers, before being returned to the tray on the countertop for their parents to find. I had a concussion, which got me out of any sort of physical activity—Crystal mowed the lawn last night, tee-hee—and allowed me to be an even bigger couch potato than I'd been at the Discount Inn and Suites. The bruising around my neck, compliments of Wade Nickless, was still there, but my voice had returned—a ton of tea and honey and juice and lozenges, per my sister's advice, as well as a twelve-pack of beer, per mine. Also, I wound up with six stitches on the bottom of my chin from either crash-landing onto the lobby tiles or bouncing off the front desk.

I hate getting stitches; was a total wimp at the doctor's office, but when I look in the mirror, it makes me look kind of badass, like an extra in *Fight Club*.

Maybe I can scare the mailman or some of the neighbors.

Charlotte then said, "It would break my heart if anything happened to you, Cory."

"Hey, it'd break mine, too," I said, my voice quivering a little bit. "But you don't have to worry, Char. I'm fine. I really am. And me and Alice and Rex will be here when you get back." I added, "We can't wait to see you, kiddo."

SEVENTY-EIGHT

"Garrick Nickless broke today."

My head snapped up from a forkful of broccoli. "I thought Cripps was taking the rap?"

Up until now Olive Cripps had been taking full responsibility. She'd confessed to everything. The elderly woman informed Crystal and Detective Lahlum of how she'd planned the killings, and how she'd pressed hard to get her like-minded great-grandson, Wade Nickless, into making the Shortridge boys' deaths become a reality.

As we expected, Darlene Cripps was Lansing Shortridge's daughter and, evidently, after Lansing promised Olive the sun, the moon, and the stars, he had turned on a dime and run for the hills. Not only was Olive heartbroken over that, but his mob-connected father, Lionel, had paid fifteen-year-old Olive a visit with a mob goon in tow and the two of them put the fear of a wrathful God into her. Subsequently, Olive had not been the best of mothers to Darlene, who escaped Olive's apathy and neglect for the not-so-greener pastures of a 1960s San Francisco, where she fell in with the wrong crowd and battled an addiction that ultimately took her life.

Olive told the detectives she'd been planning the end of the Shortridge bloodline since the moment she'd seen her daughter laid out on the morgue room's examination table.

Cripps held fast that she alone was to blame, that she coerced her great-grandson Wade into implementing her scheme, and that neither her granddaughter, Suzanne Nickless, or her other great-grandson, Garrick, had anything to do with the deaths of either Reed or Patrick Shortridge.

"Yes, she took the rap," Crystal replied. "And I buy the bulk of her confession, except for the part where she shields the surviving family members."

"We know that's BS," I said. "No way was that an old lady

with Wade at the playground or in the warehouse." I speared a chunk of pasta. My sister's healthy dish turned out to be surprisingly tasty once I'd lathered it in Tabasco sauce and pepper. "So what did Garrick have to say?"

"That his mother had nothing to do with the murders. He said Suzanne pieced it together when Patrick's disappearance was in the news last summer. She drove to a strip of land they own near Whalon Lake and caught her boys with Patrick's body."

"OK—but Suzanne is the link to Henry Horner Elementary," I said. "She's the one who wasted your time with all those lists of construction workers."

Crystal nodded. "It was ugly at Whalon—screaming and weeping. Suzanne even threatened to call the cops, but she knew if she did her sons' lives were over. She made them tell her everything. And they did. They even mentioned their concern about where to hide Patrick's body so it wouldn't be found." Crystal added, "Garrick was shocked when she contacted them the next day and told them about the school remodel."

I chewed that over. "After the work crews leave for the day, her sons show up ten minutes later. That way they can take their own sweet time getting Patrick into the pipe chase inside the wall," I said. "Suzanne probably stood watch in the hallway."

"That's pretty much what Garrick said." Crystal set down her fork. "He also said Suzanne drove to Joliet after Whalon Lake and had it out with her grandmother. The two had an *unpleasant* discussion, but when it was over, Suzanne's main concern was in keeping her boys out of prison."

"If she was so rattled over Patrick's death, why'd she let them go after Charlotte?"

"Her sons swore to her at Whalon Lake it was over, all of it, and she believed them. She went ballistic when she found out about Charlotte at the playground."

"Evidently, the bloodline didn't only include male heirs."

Crystal nodded a second time. "Suzanne Nickless may not have participated in the murders, but she aided and abetted after the fact. She'll be charged with accessory and conspiracy."

"So why would Garrick testify against his own mother?"

"We've got the three of them dead to rights and the prosecutor's not in the mood for a plea deal. Garrick's attorney thinks his confession might help Suzanne get a lighter sentence," Crystal said. "Maybe she won't die in prison."

I finished my plate of the chickpea broccoli pasta. There was more in the pan but Crystal pointed at her plate, letting me know she'd finished all she was going to eat. I switched our plates around and said, "You ever find out why Suzanne goes by her middle name?"

"Darlene adored her grandmother, *Suzanne* Cripps—hence the middle name. Olive had no idea where *Jane* came from and called her Suzanne from the get-go . . . and it stuck."

Something else had been troubling me. "This vendetta or blood feud against the Shortridges: I'm not sure it meant that much to Wade Nickless." I recalled the big man's smirk as he began squeezing the life out of me. "I think it gave him free rein to be what he was . . . a psychopath."

Crystal shrugged. "You could be right."

"Thank God Pam was there."

My sister nodded a final time.

We'd connected with Pam at Crystal's precinct a couple days after the attack. The three of us were able to slip into an empty conference room for a few minutes. I didn't mince words as I thanked the woman for saving my life. I don't think my gratitude did much good, though. I didn't know Pam, but it was easy to see she was somber and withdrawn.

I'd have given a thousand bucks to see that stern gaze back in her eyes.

Sure, Pam was pleasant enough; she replied to our queries or comments in short sentences and nodded along as my sister explained how Wade Nickless had been a bad man. Crystal stressed how Nickless had murdered two young men, how he then went after their seven-year-old sister, and how he was in the process of finishing me off when she put an end to it.

Crystal didn't say the main part out loud, but her implication was loud and clear—you did the right thing, Pam; try not to lose sleep over it. Bad man or not, the woman had killed a fellow human being. You could see the pain in her eyes. I'd brought along a plant, which Pam was gracious enough to accept, but the handoff was a bit clunky.

Thanks for saving my life, Pam. Here's an orchid. Water it twice a week.

I racked my brain over what else I could do to cheer her up. I doubted a five-star Yelp review about the motel's front desk being willing to go the extra mile would fit the bill.

My iPhone buzzed. I fished it slowly from my pocket, suspecting who it might be.

"Brielle?" Crystal asked.

I nodded and took a deep breath.

"Are you going to tell her?"

"Yeah." I left the kitchen table and stepped deep into the living room so my sister wouldn't hear me mumble and stutter and make a fool of myself. I slipped the crib notes I'd jotted down in my motel room from my back pocket, tapped the green icon, and answered the phone.

Two minutes later I returned to the kitchen.

Crystal stopped putting dirty dishes into the dishwasher and stared my way. "That was quick."

I nodded; my mind was spinning.

"Did she hang up?"

"No," I said. "I didn't get hung up on."

"Then how'd it go?"

"I didn't tell her."

"Cory," Crystal said, and leaned against the sink and crossed her arms.

"No, Crys, I started in with the speech," I said and held up my crib notes as evidence. "I really did, but she stopped me; said she had something to tell me."

Crystal looked confused. "What?"

"She and Adam broke up last night," I replied. "She mentioned the breakup had been building for a while." I tried looking appropriately pensive, possibly a touch blue, but I don't think Crystal bought it. "The poor kid sounded down in the dumps. I hope you don't mind, but I invited her over for some Alice and Rex therapy," I said. The goofballs headed over when they heard me mention their names. "She'll be here in twenty minutes."

"Unbelievable," my sister said and shook her head. "You know you've got to give her time to heal, right?"

"Of course," I replied, still attempting to look suitably mature. "It goes without saying."

Crystal returned to clearing the table. "The luck you've had this past week, Cory," she said. "Unbelievable."

"I know—I feel like I should hop on a plane to Vegas."

SEVENTY-NINE

Past Days

Olive Cripps sat the two boys down on the sofa facing her. The twins had turned nine earlier in the week. After opening presents—both got baseball gloves—they ate a lunch of hot dogs and macaroni and cheese, per their request, with some corn on the cob tossed in, per Olive's request. Then the two blew out candles and tore apart a chocolate cake.

And now the boys sat in the living room, sensing she had something important to tell them.

Olive was watching the boys, keeping them overnight while their parents took a weekend trip. Evidently, the mini-vacation was another stab at rekindling their marriage—Suzanne informed her their therapist had recommended it—but Olive suspected it'd take more than a couple of nights at a resort near Starved Rock State Park to remedy the situation.

Olive loved Suzanne. She loved her unconditionally . . . as far as Suzanne's husband went, well, not so unconditionally.

Her granddaughter's husband was a large man. He'd been muscular and good-looking when the two had first met. The man was a hard worker and he certainly meant well. Unfortunately, he'd never be mistaken for the brightest bulb on the Christmas tree. The man was a dullard; he was a simpleton. And once the conversation worked its way through the weather, once it got beyond how everyone in the family was health-wise, and once it spun on how the Bears and the Cubbies were doing—there was no more small talk left in his quiver. He had no interest in movies or books or history or politics or hobbies or anything else of significance for him to hold court on.

To be around him was to watch paint dry.

Olive kept it to herself, but she wouldn't lose a wink of sleep if the marriage dissolved and the man faded into the mist and the fog and the background.

Suzanne deserved better; and Olive prayed one day her granddaughter would find better.

But Suzanne's husband had provided Olive with these two beautiful great-grandsons that sat before her on the couch. If for no other reason, Olive would be forever in his debt for that.

"What's up, Grandma?" Wade asked, juggling the baseball in one hand.

Olive loved when the twins called her *Grandma*; she'd always loved how Suzanne referred to her as *Mom*. It was a do-over. It warmed her heart. Olive knew they were aware of the family tree. She'd never lied to them about who was who . . . but Suzanne had never known her mother and the boys had never known their grandmother.

No—Olive looked at the boys on the sofa—they'd never known Darlene. Nor had they known the tragedy that had befallen her. The twins had not known who was responsible.

But today that was going to change.